Death of a Postmodernist

"I never imagined it would be so beautiful," Margo whispered to Barry. She discovered one delight after another: the beautifully embroidered Mexican shawls hanging from the ceiling, the way the candles shed soft light on the red peppers on the wall . . . How had Susana known that all of these disparate elements, which held no magic individually, would combine to create such a breathtaking effect?

In one corner, on the jagged bed, lay the artist . . . wrapped in a dark shawl and turned toward the wall. Respecting her evident wish to be regarded as part of her work, no one approached her.

Mickey, however, was as yet unschooled in art gallery behavior. He broke away from Isa and ran to his second mom. "Susa! Susa!" he said, shaking her shoulder.

"Mick, sweetie, leave Susana alone." Coming to lead the child away, Isa leaned over the bed for a moment. Then she scooped up Mickey and straightened, her feet planted in front of the metal bed.

Holding Mickey tightly to her chest, Isa called out, "Is there a doctor here?"

MORE MYSTERIES FROM THE
BERKLEY PUBLISHING GROUP . . .

JENNY McKAY MYSTERIES: This TV reporter finds out where, when, why . . . *and* whodunit. "A more streetwise version of television's Murphy Brown."
—*Booklist*

by Dick Belsky
BROADCAST CLUES   LIVE FROM NEW YORK
THE MOURNING SHOW

CAT CALIBAN MYSTERIES: She was married for thirty-eight years. Raised three kids. Compared to that, tracking down killers is easy . . .

by D.B. Borton
ONE FOR THE MONEY   TWO POINTS FOR MURDER
THREE IS A CROWD

KATE JASPER MYSTERIES: Even in sunny California, there are cold-blooded killers . . . "This series is a treasure!"
—*Carolyn G. Hart*

by Jaqueline Girdner
ADJUSTED TO DEATH   MURDER MOST MELLOW
THE LAST RESORT   FAT-FREE AND FATAL
TEA-TOTALLY DEAD

FREDDIE O'NEAL, P.I., MYSTERIES: You can bet that this appealing Reno P.I. will get her man . . . "A winner."
—*Linda Grant*

by Catherine Dain
LAY IT ON THE LINE   SING A SONG OF DEATH
WALK A CROOKED MILE   LAMENT FOR A DEAD COWBOY

CALEY BURKE, P.I., MYSTERIES: This California private investigator has a brand-new license, a gun in her purse, and a knack for solving even the trickiest cases!

by Bridget McKenna
MURDER BEACH   DEAD AHEAD

CHINA BAYLES MYSTERIES: She left the big city to run an herb shop in Pecan Springs, Texas. But murder can happen anywhere . . . "A wonderful character!"
—*Mostly Murder*

by Susan Wittig Albert
THYME OF DEATH   WITCHES' BANE

LIZ WAREHAM MYSTERIES: In the world of public relations, crime can be a real career-killer . . . "Readers will enjoy feisty Liz!"
—*Publishers Weekly*

by Carol Brennan
HEADHUNT   FULL COMMISSION

DEATH OF A POSTMODERNIST

JANICE STEINBERG

BERKLEY PRIME CRIME, NEW YORK

For Jack Cassidy

DEATH OF A POSTMODERNIST

A Berkley Prime Crime Book / published by arrangement with the author

PRINTING HISTORY
Berkley Prime Crime edition / January 1995

ISBN: 0-425-14546-8

Berkley Prime Crime Books are published by
The Berkley Publishing Group,
200 Madison Avenue, New York, NY 10016.
The name BERKLEY PRIME CRIME and
the BERKLEY PRIME CRIME
design are trademarks belonging to
Berkley Publishing Corporation.

PRINTED IN THE UNITED STATES OF AMERICA

10 9 8 7 6 5 4 3 2 1

Acknowledgments

Many thanks:

to Kathi George, Phyllis Brown, Mary Lou Locke, Janet Kunert, Dan Lewis, Shannon Rodgers, Linda Felder, Teresa Chris, and Karen Ravenel;

to Marilyn Huder of KFMB radio and Wanda Levine, Karen Kish, and Deanna Martin Mackey of KPBS radio; and to a few of the artists whose work and ideas have inspired me—Ann Hamilton, Llory Wilson, Beliz Brother, Karen Finley, and Diane Gage.

Very special thanks to Jack Cassidy.

Prologue / An Opening for Murder

The Capelli Foundation for Postmodern Art was the kind of place where, if you saw a ton of manure dumped in the courtyard, you couldn't be sure whether to assume someone had a grudge against them or to sneak a look around for the plaque bearing the artist's name and the title of the work. It was a place where the emperor could parade naked and surely people would notice, but no one would be so provincial as to act shocked. "Ah, the emperor has no clothes? How interesting." So it isn't as bizarre as it may sound that several hundred people saw the dead body at the Capelli before anyone realized it wasn't art.

1 / Locked Room

Four Days Before the Opening

There is something uniquely melancholy about a gray day in San Diego—the sense of a tropical promise betrayed. "June gloom," everyone calls the notorious spring overcast, although it can start, as now, in April, and often lingers into July.

In the watery light the small litter of paper and unswept bougainvillea petals in the courtyard gave the Capelli Foundation a deserted air . . . as if, thought Margo Simon, hurrying across the courtyard, the graceful blue and white building were not a recent homage to art deco architecture but a decades-old structure fallen into disuse.

The illusion of abandonment continued inside. There was no one at the reception desk and no sign of recent life except for a slight smell of fresh paint coming from the words stenciled on the wall: UNEASY VISIONS, the title of the show opening at the Capelli at the end of the week.

Margo checked the directions she'd been given. Down a corridor, a sharp right from the foyer, she found a door marked by a flashing neon sign: EXIT/NO EXIT. She knocked, got no answer, opened the door.

"Hi! Tom?" she called perfunctorily from the doorway,

although she couldn't have missed seeing someone. Not with all the mirrors.

Fascinated, she walked inside, the door swinging shut behind her. She looked around for a moment, then pushed the Record button on the large broadcast-quality tape recorder she carried over one shoulder.

"This is Margo Simon reporting for KSDR, San Diego Public Radio," she said into the microphone. "Tom Fall's installation at the Capelli Foundation appears to be a perfectly square room, with full-length mirrors and doors alternating along the walls. Everywhere you look, there's either a mirror or a door." She did a quick mental count. "There are four mirrors and four doors on each wall."

She walked around the perimeter of the space, holding down the microphone to record the satisfying tattoo her shoes made on the hardwood floor. The mirrors caught her from sixteen angles, a slender woman with shoulder-length, haphazardly wavy brown hair, wearing a nipped-in tweed jacket from her favorite thrift store and black slacks in a narrow corduroy. From one shoulder hung the tape recorder; from the other, a large embroidered Guatemalan bag, combination briefcase and purse.

"It's a little like a circus funhouse," she said into the mike. "Except the mirrors don't distort at all." It *was,* however, a bit unnerving, she reflected, seeing herself every time she turned around.

Margo stopped the tape recorder and checked her watch. Where *was* Tom Fall? Their interview was scheduled to begin fifteen minutes ago; she'd arrived a few minutes late herself. Better see if the artist was somewhere else in the building. She turned to the nearest door. Funny, the knob didn't turn. She stood, perplexed, jiggling the knob for a moment, then chuckled at her own foolishness. Of course, not all sixteen doors would actually function!

She returned to the door through which she'd entered the room; at least, she thought it was the right door. There were some tools and a ladder in one corner of the room, and hadn't they been in front of her and to her left when she had walked in? In that case, she must have used one of the two inner doors on the opposite wall. Neither door opened, however. Nor did the outer doors on the same wall.

Lucky she was only stuck inside a work of art in a major city, instead of stranded on a desert island where she'd actually need a sense of direction!

Methodically now, she went around the room, trying the rest of the doors. None opened. She pounded on one door, calling, "Hey, is anyone here? I'm locked in!" No one came. Noticing two video cameras mounted on the ceiling, she yelled toward one of them, "Get me out of here!" That produced no response, either.

Talking into her microphone—always an aid to thinking— Margo pictured the layout of the Capelli Foundation. The building, designed by a very hot contemporary architect from Milan, was roughly U-shaped, with the entrance at the base of the U. However, the architect had cut off one arm of the U partway, for an asymmetrical effect. Tom Fall's installation occupied the shorter arm, which meant both of the other two artists in the show were in the other wing of the building, out of earshot. As for the foundation's administrative offices, they were upstairs but above the longer arm of the building only, so it was no use climbing the ladder and pounding on the ceiling. Only the bathrooms were on this side of the U, just off the foyer. Great! She'd have to shout continuously to catch someone on the way to take a pee.

"Okay, no need to panic," she told herself out loud. She didn't think she was prone to claustrophobia, in spite of the sweat trickling down her sides. It was just hot in here, a little stuffy. She took off her jacket, caught her expression in one of the mirrors—disgusted, frustrated. Not scared, she assured herself.

Tom Fall would probably rush in within moments, apologizing for being late but explaining he couldn't possibly wear a watch because that would stifle his artistic freedom. In the meanwhile, she might as well get comfortable. There were several folding chairs against one wall. She unfolded a chair, sat down, and took out the folder of background material she'd collected for her interviews with the artists in the Capelli show. Fall, at twenty-six, was the youngest of the three, but he had already attracted notice from several major art magazines. His work, according to one article, dealt with the themes of "inside vs. outside, perception and time."

Tom Fall liked to create puzzles, another article said. What a shame Barry wasn't here! Margo's husband, a professor at the Torrey Institution of Oceanography, loved applying the scientific method to the problems of everyday life. (This approach was effective in the kitchen, Barry being a gifted chef; but it yielded mixed results with Barry's two children, Margo's stepkids.) Barry would be tickled to be trapped here and have to figure out how to escape.

Not that Barry, or men in general, had the market cornered on analytical thinking! she thought, standing up resolutely and again surveying the room. She thought she had tried every door, but the walls all looked alike. What if she had missed an entire wall in her circuit of the room? Placing her chair in one corner as a marker, she started on the doors one more time. She pushed at and manipulated the sides of the mirrors as well. *Just because we see a door with a knob doesn't mean it's the only way into and out of a room,* she thought, feeling extremely clever. Perception was one of Tom Fall's themes, after all.

Margo was really certain she wasn't claustrophobic. But her chest felt tight, once she had worked her way around the room unsuccessfully. She sat down, pulled her shoulders down to open her chest, and took several deep breaths. It occurred to her that being trapped in a room with sixteen mirrors was an apt and not a comforting metaphor for her current situation at KSDR, where a faultfinding new station manager was making everyone feel as if they were on continual display, especially half-timers like Margo who'd been thrown into competition for a rumored full-time job.

Her chest felt tighter now and her back was damp with sweat. *Artists!* But remembering her first love did not induce feelings of calm.

With Tom Fall now twenty-five minutes late, the probability was increasing that he had forgotten their interview entirely and might not be returning today at all. Still, four days prior to the opening of a new show, *someone* had to be at the Capelli Foundation.

It wasn't that she was freaked out, Margo told herself, removing one of her shoes, a black lace-up that was thankfully heavy; it was simply that she'd exhausted other alternatives. She heard the lie to that in her own frightened voice, crying, "Help! Help!" as she bashed her shoe against the nearest door. "Help!"

Less than thirty seconds later a door opened—on the wall where she thought she had entered—and a young man came in.

"Hi." He flashed her a dazzling smile.

"Oh, no!" She ran, caught the door before it swung shut, and propped it open with her shoe.

"Hey, it's all right. But we can use this, okay?" He exchanged her shoe for a brick that had been in the hallway, and bowed as he returned the shoe to her.

Bending to tie the shoe back on, Margo glanced at her rescuer. He looked the part, a child of the California gods. Tall, with sun-bleached blond hair in a ponytail at the nape of his neck, he was wearing a tight sleeveless T-shirt that showed off plenty of tanned skin and well-developed muscles. A gap separated his front teeth, and his nose looked as if it had been broken, flaws that lent interest to what might have been ordinary movie-star good looks.

"How did you like it?" he said.

"How did I like it?" she repeated the non sequitur. Hadn't he heard her screaming for help a moment ago?

"You're the reporter from the public television station—Margo, right?"

"Public radio."

"I listen all the time. *All Things Considered* is the best news program in the country. I'm Tom Fall." He extended his hand. She shook it automatically. "My installation, what did you think?"

"I got trapped. I've been stuck here for, I don't know, twenty minutes, half an hour. Didn't you know?"

"Oh, yeah." Tom Fall grinned. "I knew you were okay. I was watching." He indicated the video cameras on the ceiling.

Margo turned on her tape recorder. It seemed a more professional gesture than whacking him with the heavy machine.

"You knew I was trapped in here and you just watched me trying to get out? How long were you planning to keep me here?"

"Like I said, I could see you were all right."

"What if I had a heart condition?"

"Hey, I came the second you got upset. I wanted to give you a unique story." He sounded miffed at her lack of appreciation. "See, I figured I could tell you all kinds of crap about how this piece is about borders and boundaries and how I'm trying to give people a taste of what it's like to cross a border and lose control because they don't know the rules. But that's all abstract. I gave you the opportunity to experience the essence of this installation."

He added, "I didn't mean to upset you." The words had a familiar ring, as did his whining tone; Margo heard the same thing regularly from her fifteen-year-old stepdaughter.

"Is that what's going to happen to everyone? They'll come in here and they'll be trapped here until you decide they've had enough?"

He looked dismayed. "It won't be the same. There's going to be a written guide to the show, and people will know there's a trick to getting out. The damn lawyer for the Capelli insisted." Tom Fall sounded as if he hadn't lost that argument graciously.

"What trick to getting out?" Curiosity was replacing outrage as Margo's adrenaline level dropped.

"The one door gets you in, but it doesn't open from the inside. The exit is over here." He walked to a door on one of the other walls. "The trick is, it's on a computer timer. It only opens twice each minute, at random intervals, for eight to twelve seconds at a time. See?" He jiggled the knob for ten or fifteen seconds. Sure enough, the door opened.

The video cameras would alert the foundation security guards in case someone was having real trouble, he added. Margo assumed the guards would respond more quickly than Tom had with her.

He moved the two folding chairs together, and they continued the interview sitting down.

"If you want my influences," he said, "naturally, there's Sartre, since I'm calling this piece *Exit/No Exit*. And the Velásquez painting *Las Meninas*, where you see the subjects in the foreground, as well as the artist at his easel, the king and queen of Spain reflected in a mirror, and at the back of the painting, an open door. I'm influenced by the circus, too."

Self-advertisement, Margo had heard, was essential to making it in the current art scene. Tom seemed to have it mastered.

"I totally distrust labels," he continued, "but one reason the critics say my work is quintessentially postmodern is that I borrow from a wide variety of sources, including popular culture."

"How would you define *postmodernism*?"

"I wouldn't. Like I said, I distrust labels."

Tom wasn't shaping up as her favorite interviewee, but Margo couldn't help but sympathize with his refusal to answer her question. *Postmodernism* was a term she hoped *she* would never be required to define. Pomo, as she had seen it called, seemed to be something art critics knew only when they saw it, rather than a distinct style like cubism or abstract expressionism. Some postmodern artists had returned to figurative painting, after the distortions and abandonment of the figure earlier in the century. Some did narrative art, using written text and/or performance. Some challenged the concept of originality—for instance, a very hot artist who photographed classic photos by people like Ansel Adams—not going to the same spot and recreating the photo, but shooting the Adams print. And the term *postmodern* wasn't just applied to art but to a weird cultural grab bag that ranged from bowling to Pacific Rim cuisine to MTV. Which made Margo's stepkids more pomo than she would ever be.

"Hey, sorry to interrupt." A face poked in the doorway, a woman with tufts of white-blond hair erupting, owl-like, from her head above big round glasses. "Tom, did you borrow my drill?"

"Nope." The answer was simple enough, but there was an edge to Tom's voice.

"You know, maybe you just needed to drill something and you thought it belonged to the foundation? Actually, it's one I brought in from home." The woman pointedly scanned the tools across the room.

"Jesus Christ, I told you no already!" Tom jumped up, as if he were going to forcibly eject the woman from the room. Did he have an extremely short fuse, especially with his opening just a few days away? Or was there something about the blond woman, who looked gleeful at having provoked him?

"If you happen to notice the drill, get it back to me?" the woman said. "I used it this morning, and now I can't figure out where it is."

"A little less marijuana and you'd be surprised how well your brain might function!" he taunted her.

"A little simple consideration for your wife and I wouldn't have seen her running out of here in tears yesterday. She's going to come after you with a meat cleaver one day."

"Fuck you, Jill!" Tom took several steps toward her.

"Don't forget," she sang out, leaving. "If you see a big Black and Decker, it's mine."

"Jill . . . Was that Jill Iverson?" Margo asked, after giving Tom a moment to cool down.

"The infamous performance artist herself."

Margo did a mental double-take. Short, fortyish, and slightly plump, Jill Iverson in person looked nothing like the woman Margo had seen perform several times. Of course, when she was doing performance art, Jill was always "in costume"—nude and her body painted bright blue, or adorned with thirty plastic breasts, or bloody from crawling over broken glass.

"If anyone gets sliced up with a meat cleaver, it'll be her," grumbled Tom. He was quiet for a moment, as if contemplating doing the job himself. Suddenly he burst out laughing. His laughter, higher-pitched than his speaking voice suggested, sounded childlike and mean. "The thing is," he said, "if Jill got killed, she'd claim it was the performance of the century and charge an admission fee."

2 / An Artist and Her Pet

Tom loosened up for the rest of the interview, apparently cheered by envisioning Jill's murder. Margo understood how he felt. Lately she'd found it therapeutic to dream up ways to dispatch her boss. The tension returned to Tom's voice, however—and the chip to his shoulder—when she asked where to find Susana Contreras, whom she was scheduled to interview next.

"The born-again installation artist?" Tom sneered.

"What do you mean?" Margo doubted that Susana, a lesbian, had taken to quoting Scriptures.

"I don't know how much you know about installation art, but if you're setting up a room in a gallery or museum, obviously you're not making anything that can be sold. And that's the point."

Although Margo had concluded the interview, she switched the tape recorder back on, hearing the passion in Tom's voice.

"Installation art, real installation art, isn't just about creating an interesting environment in a gallery," he continued. "It represents a protest against the gallery system and the way it turns art into one more commodity for the rich, like a diamond necklace or a yacht. When I made a commitment to doing installations, for example, it was a moral decision not to participate in the gallery system. Whereas Susana

Contreras just cruised down here from her L.A. mansion to take a little vacation from selling sculptures to fat cats."

His eyes shone with the idealism of a warrior leading a band of crusaders. The idealism and the intolerance, reflected Margo, whose Jewish ancestors had numbered among the infidels. It was true that Susana Contreras did well financially; at thirty-three, she was one of the most successful young artists on the West Coast. But it was hard to see her sculptures as pandering to any status quo. Threatening structures, they bristled with spikes and barbed wire.

"Not that Susana does anything just for the love of it," said Tom. "I'm sure she's calculated just how much the exposure here will send her prices up. Everyone knows about the eyelash stunt, that's got to be good for a couple thou per sculpture. And have you heard about her pet?"

"Her pet?" Did Susana keep on ocelot on a bejeweled leash?

In a gossipy tone Tom related that Susana had "acquired" a homeless woman at a shelter she'd helped establish in Los Angeles. The woman, Dawn, did odd jobs in exchange for food, showers, and occasional shelter, although rumor had it that sleeping under roofs made her agitated. James Carmichael, the director of the Capelli, had raised hell with Susana after finding Dawn bedded down in the courtyard the week before. Dawn trusted no one but Susana, to whom she was ferociously loyal.

"She might or might not be emotionally disturbed," concluded Tom. "It's hard to tell, because she never speaks."

"Do you mean she's mute? She can't talk?"

"Can't or won't, who knows? My money's on paranoid schizophrenia. The point is, I wouldn't startle Dawn or appear to threaten Susana in any way."

• • •

Frida y Yo—"Frida and I"—was the title of Susana Contreras's installation, entered through a green-painted door at the end of the Capelli's longer arm. Margo was aware that many women artists, especially Latinas, claimed a foremother in the late Mexican painter Frida Kahlo. Susana seemed to go beyond identifying with Kahlo artistically, however. It was as if she wanted to *be* Kahlo. Similar in size to the petite painter, several photographs of whom hung in the room, Susana had copied Kahlo's hairstyle, parting her dark brown hair down the middle and combing it tightly behind her ears. And through a rather startling use of makeup, she had recreated the thick eyebrows that formed a distinctive line across Kahlo's forehead.

Try as she might to resemble the dead artist, however, Susana Contreras's face screamed out her own individuality. Margo tried not to stare, but she couldn't make eye contact with Susana without wondering if pulling out all her eyelashes *hurt*.

Susana's trademark feature—documented in numerous art magazines—resulted from a nervous habit, of rubbing her eyes and twisting the lashes, that had started in childhood. For years, Susana had done everything her parents or doctors suggested, sharing their determination to cure her "affliction." When she went away to college, however, a scholarship student from the East L.A. barrio, she discovered feminism and rejected what she saw as her previous efforts to conform to patriarchal standards, either of beauty or of mental health. Margo didn't accept the cynical notion that Susana kept rubbing off her eyelashes to raise her standing in the art world. But it was true she had chosen a profession where eccentricity could be an asset.

"You know, of course, that Frida was seriously injured in a traffic accident when she was eighteen."

"What? Oh, yes." Margo commanded herself to forget the

damned eyelashes and focus on the soft voice speaking with the energy and rapidity of Spanish, although no accent— Susana had been born in the U.S. Standing beside her, Margo realized the artist was only moderately short, perhaps five-three to Margo's five-six. Susana appeared so tiny because she was anorexically thin. Clad in a black jumpsuit and gesturing as she spoke, she was like an exclamation point at the end of a particularly vehement sentence.

"That's why I'm using the spikes," Susana said. "I'm going to place them all around." She jerked an angular arm toward a dozen metal poles, each about seven feet tall, standing in the center of the room. Cactuslike metal barbs stuck out from them. "They represent the piece of metal that impaled Frida. She was riding on a bus in Mexico City—this was in 1925, she was eighteen—and a trolley ran into the bus. A railing from the trolley entered the side of her abdomen and exited through her vagina. Her spine and pelvis were broken and her right leg and foot were crushed. Nothing healed properly. She had over thirty operations during her lifetime and unendurable pain."

Margo shuddered. She had vaguely known about the accident that crippled Kahlo, but she'd never heard the story recounted with such detail . . . or such avidity. Was Susana simply enjoying shocking a reporter, or did something about the tragedy excite her?

"This is Frida's bed," announced the artist, leading Margo across the room to where four of the tall, barbed spikes leaned at skewed angles, the corners of a rude four-poster. Jagged springs poked out of the metal frame. "She did a lot of her painting lying in bed," said Susana, "with the canvas clamped above her."

Margo had noticed two people helping Susana, a young man and woman who were applying a kind of red paste to one wall, white masks protecting their noses and mouths. Approaching the "bed," she saw that Susana had a third assistant—a woman who crouched, half hidden, behind the bedframe. The woman had been doing something to the bed with pliers, but stopped when Susana and Margo approached. She remained motionless, except for swiveling her head toward them, staring in a still way that reminded Margo of a snake.

"Didn't Frida Kahlo have a fantastic creative output and a very full life?" Margo spoke softly, trying not to frighten the woman, who must be the mute homeless Dawn, Susana's "pet." Trying not to be unnerved herself by Dawn's expressionless stare, or by the serious-looking knife in a sheath on her thin, blue-jeaned thigh.

"Frida had great joy in life, which I associate with her love of Mexico." Susana seemed not to notice Dawn's uneasiness, nor did she react when Dawn bolted out of the room. "I'm going to have, hanging from the ceiling, beautiful Mexican shawls like Frida always wore. And fresh flowers—birds-of-paradise, orchids—they'll be changed every two days. There on the wall I'm doing a *retablo*. Frida painted a number of *retablos*, where you thank the virgin for sparing you from misfortune. The rest of the wall's going to be covered with crushed red chili peppers, *muy mexicano*." She pointed to where the young man and woman were working.

"It looks a bit like . . ."

"Blood! If you know Frida's work, it's full of exposed hearts and bleeding wounds. Louise!" Susana interrupted herself.

The artist ran to embrace the woman who had just walked in, almost disappearing in the expanse of the other's orange cloak, as well as in the force of her personality.

Margo knew Louise O'Quinn by sight, as did anyone who read the local newspapers and magazines, where Louise appeared frequently as "one of the movers and shakers at the Capelli Foundation" or "the nationally known art critic and collector who makes her home in San Diego County." Louise O'Quinn was also familiar as the subject of works by several prominent artists, who were drawn to her springing gray hair, strong-boned face, and the broad body she claimed to clothe exclusively in artist-designed garb. In her mid- to late-fifties, Louise made her age appear a full flowering of her power, just as influential men did. The tall youth in jeans at her side seemed an art world version of a junior executive trailing a Fortune 500 CEO.

"Frida Kahlo had a love affair with death." The critic's voice was a shock. Margo had heard of Louise's roots as the heiress to Oklahoma oil money. Still, the imperious head was made for the syllables of Greek drama—Irene Papas in *Medea*—not the high-pitched grate of a waitress at a truck stop.

"Did you come here just to tell me that?" teased Susana, drawing a laugh.

"No, I just got out of a meeting with James. Foundation business. Have you met Ed? This year's assistant, Ed Milewski." Louise nodded toward the young man who stood deferentially behind her.

After a brief round of introductions, Louise directed Ed to "go chat with" the people applying red pepper to the wall, apparently fellow graduate students in art at the University of California-San Diego. The critic then drew Susana aside. "Just for a minute, Margo, you don't mind." They didn't go far, however, and their conversation was too heated for Margo not to overhear.

"I wanted to see the bed," said Louise. "Susi, you can't be serious about planning to lie there during the opening? James said you're not going to cover it with anything."

Margo glanced apprehensively at the bed, with its savage-looking springs.

"I haven't decided," Susana said. "I'll be wearing layers of clothes, you know. The whole Mexican costume with a thick shawl."

"You know I support the way you've used your body in your work," said Louise. "I was the first critic to notice how the sharpness of your sculptures reflects the way you move. But Susi, this is masochistic."

"Because it may hurt a little? Any pain I experience for a few hours can't come close to what Frida experienced her whole life."

Louise grasped the artist's shoulders, forcing Susana to face her. "You know James was dubious about including you in this show, since you've never done an installation before. I went to bat for you and convinced him that you understood the issues involved in installation, that your sculpture had developed along some of the same paths as installation art. But this kind of grandstanding, you can't believe this is meaningful? In the 1990s?"

"Enough!" Clearly refusing to continue the discussion, Susana brought up a mutual friend in Santa Fe.

Louise O'Quinn, no doubt rarely told to shut up, stepped back as if she'd been slapped. Margo was experiencing her own slap . . . of memory: at the mention of the town, on top of spending the afternoon with emotionally volatile artists, just as her first love, her Santa Fe artist, had been.

"Margo, call me if you'd like a critical perspective." Louise was holding out a business card.

"Thanks."

"Ed!" The critic summoned her assistant and swept out, her orange cloak swirling in the lift of air as she opened the door—Loretta Young on her way to a power meeting.

3 / A Spy in the House of Art

Too many people were in the room. The people got inside Dawn's head and she couldn't think. It wouldn't be so bad if they were quiet, but first the people working over at the wall were laughing, and then the woman with the tape recorder kept talking and talking to Susana. The tape recorder made a terrible humming sound, *hummmmm, hummmmm*, it bored right into Dawn's head, *hummmmm*. Her head hurt so much it might explode. She had to get out! Out of the room and into the hall was better, but even through the walls she could feel all the people, pressing on her. Outside was safer.

Uh-oh! Someone was coming. She scrunched herself as small as she could under a big plant next to the parking lot.

Woman. Going out. Funny blond hair. Dawn knew she'd seen the woman before, but except for Susana, most people only registered as Man, Woman, or Child. Or sometimes. People Nice to Her and People Not Nice to Her.

Fat Man going out, a man who had yelled at her. She made herself even smaller by holding her breath.

In her bag, a nice big one with pockets that Susana gave her, were her treasures. A can opener—it was best to open the can yourself and eat things right out of it so no one had a chance to put any poison in it. Toothpaste, comb, soap, toilet paper, a can to pee into—you could pee into the can standing up, standing way back in the doorway of a building for instance, and then just empty the pee out onto some plants.

Man coming in. Woman going out.

More treasures. Her poncho, which they gave her at the shelter. There was a small tear in the poncho that she could fix. Except did anyone know she could sew? Maybe she shouldn't let anyone know. Hard to figure out what things to show people and what to keep secret. Sometimes you showed what you knew and everyone got angry, so that made it better not to.

Folded in the bottom of the bag were her blanket, two pairs of socks, two T-shirts, an old black jumpsuit Susana had given her, gloves, and a knitted hat. She had found a new treasure that morning, a nice big tool marked Black and Decker. It looked useful, but it was too heavy to carry all the time. She hid it in the bushes; she could come back for it when she needed it.

Man coming out. He walked to the parking lot, looking around like he was doing something sneaky. Oh, no, was he looking for her? Dawn held her breath again. But his eyes passed right over where she was hiding. He looked like he was hiding, too, crouching by a big silver fancy car. Then he took out a knife. Ooh! He was cutting the silver car, grunting *unh! unh! unh!* as he jabbed at the car with the knife. He was saying things, muttering, but Dawn could hear—"Bitch! Fucking bitch!" She could feel the pretty silver car hurting as the man kept dragging the knife over its side.

The man stood up and moved away from the car, back toward her. Dawn made herself be very quiet. Moving real slow, not even breathing, she grasped her own knife, held it ready. If the man tried to hurt her, she would hurt him back.

• • •

Margo was just getting back into the interview with Susana, after Louise O'Quinn's departure, when she heard the art critic's voice bawling in the hallway again.

"Ja-ames! Ja-ames!" Louise was shouting, the rapid beat of her high-heeled boots echoing in the hall.

Susana looked up attentively, but the critic passed by. A door was flung open and Louise's boots clomped upstairs to the administrative offices; the stairway to the offices was at the end of the hall, just past Susana's door.

"So you were saying you went to school here, at UCSD?" Margo tried to resume the interview.

"Yes, to graduate school for my master's in visual art."

The boots were descending the stairs, and now Louise was calling, "Susi!" She started speaking before she was even through Susana's door. "What kind of hours are we paying James to work, that he should be out of here at four-thirty in the afternoon? Tell me, Susi, why didn't I resist harder when Bernard Capelli insisted on building this place in the middle of downtown San Diego?"

"Lou," said Susana soothingly, but Louise didn't miss a beat.

"I'm forty minutes away in Rancho Santa Fe," railed Louise. "It has to take Bernard half an hour to get here from Del Mar. And how many serious art patrons live close to downtown, in Mission Hills, for instance? Those people's idea of art is probably a Norman Rockwell above the fireplace or, to give them the enormous benefit of the doubt, a sweet little French impressionist, but nothing more recent or threatening than that. Of course, how many knowledgeable art lovers live in San Diego at all? That was the whole point of my suggestion to build the foundation in La Costa, to make it accessible to the new blood moving into North

County, not to mention attracting people from Los Angeles, some of whom actually understand art. I was supported by at least one third of the board—why didn't I lobby the rest of them harder? But Bernard was making all kinds of noises about downtown revitalization—the brave, struggling little galleries, the artists moving into old warehouses and converting them into studios. Pah! Bernard Capelli didn't made the five million dollars he used to fund this place by being nice to struggling anybody! God! Skid Row! The Gaslamp Quarter, the city calls it, as if it's quaint instead of populated with psychopaths."

She stopped abruptly. As far as Margo could tell, she hadn't paused once for breath. Margo had seen an African musician who played a horn that way, seeming to sustain a single breath for fifteen minutes.

Susana was stroking Louise's hand, like a mother calming a fretting child. "What happened?" she said.

"Some lowlife expressed his opposition to our capitalist system of rewards by vandalizing my car!"

"The Mercedes?"

"I got rid of the Mercedes. I've . . . You have to see it."

The commotion had brought several people into the corridor, all of whom now trooped outside to view Louise's car. Margo swore under her breath. Her half-time job at KSDR never meant half the work, only half the pay, and with this latest interruption, she would never finish the interview with Susana in one session. In fact, at her first sight of Louise's silver Rolls-Royce in the parking lot, Margo was inclined to sympathize with whoever had unleashed a little resentment in the car's direction. That was before she saw the damage.

This was no juvenile vandalism, but a hash of deep, vicious gouges—proclaiming "Die, Bitch!"—across the car's side.

4 / Mrs. Peacock with a Neutron Bomb

Three Days Before the Opening

Alex Silva was twenty-eight years old and pumped up with testosterone. At least that was the reason someone had proposed, after a few beers, to account for the new boss's abrasiveness. Cheers and friendly groans had greeted this sally five months ago, shortly after Alex had taken over as station manager at KSDR. Since then, however, Alex had managed to divide and, if not conquer, at least make everyone so nervous about their futures that jibes about the boss were rarely aired openly anymore. So it was only Margo's private hunch that half the people at the weekly staff meeting wished Alex were dead.

"I've been looking over our Arbitrons," said Alex, waving a radio ratings booklet in the air. "Our cume, which, as you ought to know, is the number of people who just tune us in, isn't bad for a station with a tight promotion budget." He nodded toward the promotion director, who looked as if she'd gone to the head of the class. Even the people who most hated Alex betrayed themselves by that smug look when he choked out a word of praise. "But our Time Spent Listening stinks. That means people are trying us, but we're not giving them enough reason to keep tuned to KSDR."

"We need to take into consideration that most radio listening occurs on the freeway *here in Southern California.*" Dennis Zachary Powell, the news director, stressed the last four words. Dennis had taken off his shoes and forced his legs into a half-lotus on his chair, displaying lime-green socks. Dennis's overt complaint about Alex was that the Boston native, hired from National Public Radio in Washington, D.C., couldn't possibly understand San Diego. It was no secret, however, that Dennis was furious over not getting the station manager job himself. He had taken to pushing the contrast between himself and the business-suited interloper by exaggerating his usual laid-back style.

"Isn't there a philosophical question as to whether, as public radio, we should be competing for ratings with the commercial stations?" said Ray Fernandez. Ray had been Margo's closest friend at work, B.A.—Before Alex.

Ray and Margo had both started at KSDR as students and were hired for half-time positions after getting their degrees. They had celebrated together when the station manager position opened at the same time as a reporting job. Dennis was sure to get the manager post, they agreed, and everyone would have the chance to move up. That meant both Ray and Margo might be promoted to full-time.

"I'm not talking about doing the radio equivalent of the *Oprah* show, I'm talking about award-winning journalism," Alex snapped at Ray. The fact that Margo felt pleased, even a little, brought home the poisonous atmosphere that had developed at KSDR since Alex had arrived.

The new manager was genuinely increasing the station's professionalism; his comments were astute, if astringent. But the insecurity he spawned was hell. He'd dashed Margo's and Ray's hopes by filling the reporter job with a colleague from D.C., and he was rattling long-time staffers with remarks about deadwood. Jokes about the "NPR whiz kid" had lately given way to a climate of petty competitiveness, especially after Alex had started hinting that another full-time reporting position might be funded. Ray had switched to his formal name, Ramón, as if, thought Margo in a truly small-minded moment, to emphasize that giving him the job would meet Hispanic hiring goals. Jeff, a graduating senior, began dating the reporter from D.C. (once the rumor that she was Alex's lover was laid to rest).

As for Margo, she was feeling keenly aware that all her younger colleagues had been jump-starting their radio careers at the same age she had dropped out of college and gone to make pottery in New Mexico.

"Which are our weakest day-parts?" she threw out, glad she'd studied the ratings terminology, at the same time she hated herself for playing Alex's game.

Arriving at the Capelli Foundation after the staff meeting had dragged on for two hours, Margo felt more than ready to interview someone known for a performance called *Women Who Kill*. Hers wasn't the only frayed temper that afternoon. Stepping inside the Capelli, she heard an enraged voice coming from the direction of Tom Fall's installation. Maybe someone else was trapped inside, having a peak artistic experience. Although in that case, why was the fat, elderly woman at the reception desk reading a steamy romance novel as if nothing were happening?

"Can I help you?" The woman regarded Margo through lavender-tinted eyeglasses.

"Is anything wrong?" Margo inclined her head toward the bellowing voice.

"That's just James." The woman sounded as if she laughed often and heartily. "Our director is known as a *Wunderkind.*

And he really can be a *Wunder*. But sometimes"—her mouth curled slyly—"he's a *Kind*—a small child. Nothing serious—he just yells and throws something or puts his fist through a wall and it's over."

"What's he so upset about?"

"Oh, I try not to listen!" The woman leaned forward, her immense bosom covering the high reception desk. "I believe it has to do with the financial support one of the artists expects from the foundation. It's a shame, isn't it, when art and commerce must mix? It does the business mind a lot of good to be exposed to art, but it never seems to benefit the artist. Most of them are babies when it comes to money. They either get cheated or they end up cheating someone else, not intentionally, you understand, but simply because they don't understand all the rules. It creates bad feeling, all the same. I'm Charlotte Meyers." She extended her hand. "I volunteer at the desk every Wednesday from one to five."

"Margo Simon. From KSDR, the public radio station. I'm here to talk to Jill Iverson."

Charlotte grinned. "*Mrs. Peacock in the Gallery with a Neutron Bomb*. That's what Jill's calling her performance. A takeoff on that mystery game, Clue. Intriguing, isn't it? Funny but also menacing. You could describe Jill the same way. But what do I know? I did my husband Al's books for forty years back in Pittsburgh, and now we're retired here in paradise. Al golfs six days a week and I do this. I find art stimulating. You know where to find Jill?"

Margo nodded and turned toward the long arm of the building.

Sitting back and picking up her bodice-ripper novel, Charlotte called after Margo, "You need a little stimulation at seventy."

• • •

"Hi! Hello! HELLO!" Margo hollered, competing against a racket of construction sounds and blaring rap music in the room Jill Iverson was preparing for her performance on Saturday night.

The artist looked up from cutting two-by-fours with an electric saw. Two men were hammering at a tall structure at the far end of the room.

"Hey, turn that crap off!" Jill bellowed. "Damn," she said to Margo. "I know rap is a significant cultural expression, but I can't stand it."

Margo returned Jill Iverson's grin, as well as her sentiments. The music throbbing from the boom box was the same stuff favored by her teenage stepdaughter, and it sometimes took a major effort to choke back her criticism. She and Barry were having enough trouble with Jenny these days, without sounding like her own parents twenty years ago.

"Turn it off!" Jill yelled again; this time someone obliged. "You mind sitting on the floor?" she said. She arranged a drop cloth, folded her short body onto it, and—after politely getting Margo's okay—lit a cigarette. "You want my philosophy of life?" she said.

"In a sec. Just talk about the weather for a minute and let me get sound levels."

"June gloom, except it's only April. Actually, I like it. I think there's a quality to the light in San Diego when it's foggy that's unlike anywhere else. That enough?"

"Fine, go ahead." Margo was experiencing a major attack of cognitive dissonance, trying to connect the friendly, cooperative woman who shared her middle-aged distaste for rap music with the outrageous performance artist whom several cities had banned.

"A lot of what I do, in my art and in my life," said Jill Iverson, "I do for a reason that's very simple. I'll do anything to get a reaction."

"That's your philosophy?"

"Probably that, rather than something pretentious like, 'All my life I haf vanted to deconstruct ze image of ze feminine.' People say that about my work—that I deconstruct the feminine—and I wouldn't argue. But it's not *my* rationale. I shake things up because it makes life more interesting. When I was a kid, I got in all kinds of trouble because I'd start fires or I did standardized tests by just marking things at random. One time I cut off all my hair." She ran her hand over her blond spikes. "Guess it looked a lot like it does now. Jean Seberg to the contrary, it was not the height of fashion in Baltimore back then." Margo reminded herself that despite Jill's youthful attire—long T-shirt and leggings—and her shock-the-bourgeoisie attitude, the artist was in her forties.

"Wanting to get a reaction," mused Margo. "Is that why you've done performances where you hurt yourself?"

Jill made a face. "I always get asked about those few pieces, and they're not the main thrust of my work. But I realize they hit people someplace very deep, so let me try to explain. I've only hurt myself in a few of my pieces— I'm talking about blood, bruises—and I always do it for a purpose." Cheerful, matter-of-fact, she could have been teaching her students at UCSD, where she was a professor. "I see my body as an instrument. It's one of the tools I use to make art. I never make the decision, 'Oh, I'm going to hurt myself in this piece'—that's not where the impulse comes from. But for instance, I might decide to break a taboo, and some of our strongest taboos have to do with the body. The point is breaking the taboo—any injury is only a by-product. And I go into a kind of trance when I perform, so I don't experience pain the way I would if, say, I tripped and fell down a flight of stairs."

"Are you planning to hurt yourself in this performance?"

A wicked grin. "Hell, I don't know. But look, I'm a relic. I go back to the beginning of performance art, happenings, Alan Kaprow. Let me fill you in. What times those were!"

Jill filled up half a tape with reminiscences, tossing in frequent good-humored gossip about the art world luminaries she knew. As she got to the current state of performance and of her own work, however, her mood darkened.

"I always used to feel my work occupied a certain context," she said, lighting a fresh cigarette and inhaling deeply. "It wasn't just livening things up for me personally, I saw it as part of a changing world-mind. But more and more lately, it's like I'm working in a vacuum. Oh, there are a few hundred, even a few thousand art world types who'll notice my work. And they're the worst. It's just a curiosity for them, not anything that gets inside them. I'd rather get the kind of reaction Jesse Helms has to Mapplethorpe's photos, there's some passion there. Those photographs probably give the man a hard-on! That's real! Even my life-art experiments. I used to do them out of . . . I guess I'd say joy. Now, I don't know. I think they come from feeling nothing has any meaning."

Crash! Margo jumped at the sharp sound.

"Did it work?" Once again animated, Jill jumped up and ran across the room.

"Perfectly." One of her assistants held up two halves of a neatly cut carrot. Margo realized the large structure they'd been working on was a guillotine.

Jill clapped her hands. "Do it again, Bruno, will you?"

She took half of the carrot and extended it. Her assistant pulled a rope to lift the heavy blade eight or nine feet to the top, then let go. Jill didn't flinch as the blade whacked off the carrot, coming within inches of her hand.

"Try it on this!"

Jill's cigarette had less than two inches left. The blade crashed down. Jill whooped as the cigarette was sliced in half.

"How are you going to use it in the performance?" asked Margo, once the jokes about marketing the device as a kitchen aid had died down.

"That's what the board of the Capelli is dying to know. They'd love a little controversy, but puh-lease, no severed fingers. But I never discuss the details of a performance in advance. I never know exactly what I'm going to do, myself. As I said, I go into a trance when I do a piece. A lot is improvised. See, the main person I want to get a reaction from is me."

Although Jill sounded bright and chipper, Margo shivered. Watching Jill hold her cigarette under the blade of the guillotine, Margo had gotten the same adrenaline rush as when one of the kids was about to take a bad fall; when she could see it coming but could do nothing to prevent it.

5 / Artists at Play

Margo was winding up the interview with Jill around six o'clock when Tom Fall came running in—a surprisingly merry Tom Fall, carrying two six-packs and exclaiming, "Quitting time!" He put a tape in the boom box and, to Margo's astonishment, started doing a loose-limbed, exuberant dance to an old Temptations song.

Tom had been followed into the room by a man and a woman, who passed the beers around. Jill introduced them as "Peter Vance, he's helping put up the show" and "Vicki, Tom's incredibly gorgeous wife, who's far too good for him." The description brought a look of acute misery onto the young woman's face. Vicki Fall *was* lovely, her big brown eyes set in a delicately complected face framed by long, coppery hair.

"Come on, Vicki, let's boogie!" Jill grabbed the somewhat reluctant young woman's hand. "Margo, you, too!"

Margo rarely had to be asked twice to dance. An avid dance student as a girl, she currently attended a weekly improvisation class where she'd grown accustomed to "reading" the way people moved as a reflection of their inner selves. Vicki, for instance, looked ill at ease in the free-form, partnerless melee and kept trying to dance next to her husband. Tom, however, jumped and spun with such abandon that he never stayed in one place for long. "Can you believe it!" said Jill, weaving up beside Margo. "The guy's got the heart of a fascist and the body of a wood sprite."

Jill herself alternated between dancing—in a loose, arm-flailing style that Margo associated with parties of an earlier decade, where the drug of choice wouldn't have been beer—and providing a running commentary on the others: "Peter has been helping Tom, who never lets him forget he's an unsuccessful forty-year-old artist who has to work part-time at the Capelli, putting up younger artists' shows. . . . With that fabulous hair, Vicki looks like she stepped out of a Botticelli. And then dieted herself into the 1990s, sacrificing her spirit in the process. You should see the way Tom treats her, and the way she takes it!"

Someone must have summoned the troops from the rest of the building. Susana Contreras was dancing stiffly, with no apparent sense of rhythm, but she looked as if she was having fun all the same, assuming poses in which her angular body resembled her sculptures. Even James Carmichael had come downstairs from the administrative offices to join the party. Margo had seen James in photographs, but this was her first close look at the man who was putting San Diego on the map for cutting-edge art.

Boy wonder was a label the director of the Capelli Foundation had acquired in his twenties, when he had curated some important shows at small but influential New York galleries and was credited with discovering several brilliant new artists. At forty-something, James still affected a youthful image: he had a bristly urchin haircut and, having shed his suit jacket, revealed a sleeveless fuchsia T-shirt underneath. Seen up close, however, James Carmichael looked less an *enfant terrible* than simply terrible, his body bloated as if from various excesses, his face flushed as he pumped his arms and legs frenetically. Jill, dancing over to Margo, whispered that James was behind in his child support payments; his ex-wife had left several scathing messages on the office answering machine, according to gossip heard from James's secretary.

With the opening only three days away, everyone must have needed to let off steam. There were occasional comings and goings—someone made another beer run, Jill went to get a Talking Heads tape from her truck—but most of them danced practically nonstop for the next hour. It took a tape ending to make them finally collapse, laughing, sweaty, and at least temporarily convivial. Even Jill and Tom joked with each other. When someone suggested ordering pizza, there was a chorus of agreement.

Jill put a jazz tape in the boom box, people took more beers, and they spread drop cloths on the floor. The conversation that started up had a bantering, after-hours tone but was about a subject the artists seemed to have given serious thought—the influence and potential of television. Susana remarked that she hated the way women were portrayed. Jill said she knew she ought to object to that, but she adored old sitcoms. Did any future exist for art, said Peter Vance, once the Persian Gulf War had provided the ultimate postmodern image—reporters in gas masks who might at any moment be annihilated on live TV? James articulately advocated making video art available via cable stations.

Tom Fall didn't speak at first. Margo had the impression he might be a bit intimidated by the older, better established artists, not to mention James Carmichael. In a lull in the discussion, however, Tom announced that he only watched television to monitor mass culture. Vicki, who had just started a fresh beer, laughed so hard that a big splash of beer sloshed out of the bottle onto the drop cloth.

"He always says that he watches the telly as research, but

he really does it 'cause he likes it!" she said between giggles. She had chugged her first beer earlier—a shy woman who'd needed Dutch courage to get up and dance—and she had continued to outpace everyone else. Blotting up the spill, she said, "I always want to watch 'Murder, She Wrote' on Sundays and he insists on 'America's Funniest Home Videos.' If he were just studying pop culture, it wouldn't matter what show was on, would it?"

"Vicki!" Tom cut through her cheery drunken haze. She clapped a hand to her mouth and ran out of the room, nearly colliding with the man delivering the pizza.

"True love," said Susana a few minutes later, "is such ecstasy." She had picked a mushroom off her pizza and nibbled half of it during the time most people had polished off half a slice.

"Ecstasy?" picked up Jill. "Now, there's a fabulous drug. Did you know that before it became illegal, you could get Ecstasy through psychiatrists? Really, I saw this flyer, 'Come get Ecstasy.' You just had to go to this shrink's office. Turned out he'd give you Ecstasy, but you had to take it in a group, with people you didn't know. I wasn't sure about that. Then these people who'd already done it came into the office. They were blissed out and they loved everyone. So I tried it after all."

Margo was aware, peripherally, that Vicki had come back, going over to Tom and placing a hand on his arm. He shook her off. Vicki persisted, however. Whatever she said made Tom jump up and run with her out of the room.

"How was it?" Susana asked Jill. She had finished the mushroom and was now giving a piece of pepperoni the same nibbling treatment.

Peter broke in, addressing Margo, "You might notice that Jill does not share the current antidrug hysteria. As a matter of fact, she considers it a public service to try everything, so she can turn her friends on to the best stuff."

"I was blissed out," said Jill. "I loved everyone. And it's not true I'm not antidrug, Peter. I'm not all that fond of alcohol."

Tom reappeared in the doorway and called to Susana to come talk to him. They spoke quietly for a moment.

"You bastard!" Susana screamed and took off at a run.

James Carmichael sprang to his feet, his overweight body moving surprisingly quickly. "What the hell is going on?"

"Hey, it's not a big deal," said Tom. "Dawn just got into my installation, which she never should have done in the first place. She had no business being there. Once she was there, she couldn't get out."

James strode out of the room and down the hall, forcing Tom to trot beside him, continuing to try to explain.

"The timer wasn't on," Tom whined. "She could have gotten out if she'd just tried all the doors. And you should see what she did to a couple of them! Susana had better pay for the damage."

"What about Dawn?" said Jill as the rest of the party scurried behind them.

"Vicki heard her pounding on the door and it's open now. Dawn's a little freaked, that's all."

Margo felt a twinge of sickness, recalling her own introduction to Tom's installation. How much worse for psychologically fragile Dawn?

"She's just freaked out," Tom repeated. By then, however, they could see for themselves.

Dawn was cowering in a corner of Tom's installation, hiding her face in Susana's lap and whimpering like a hurt animal.

"Damn you, Tom," said Susana. "Come here. I want you to

see this." Susana gently reached for Dawn's hand and held it up. The knuckles were bloody.

"Christ, Tom!" yelled James. "Why isn't this place locked up when you're not here?"

"It's just that Dawn sneaks around. Look what she did! Susana's going to have to pay to replace those!" Two of Tom's doors were scored with gouges Dawn must have made with her knife, trying to get out.

"She was terrorized," said Susana. "As far as I'm concerned, Tom, you're responsible. You should have locked the entrance door."

"Shit, Susana, you're the one who has a mentally retarded transient hanging around here."

"Tom!" James roared. His face was bright red. Margo began to wish she'd taken a course in CPR.

Dawn started shaking violently.

"James, please," Susana said. "Look, she's already scared enough. Everyone get out of here, okay?"

Tom waited until he was in the hall to mutter, "Did you see the way those doors looked, the knife marks? I bet Dawn was the one who vandalized Louise O'Quinn's car."

6 / Mothers and Son

The Day Before the Opening

A small child was one of the last things Margo would have expected to see in Susana Contreras's installation when she returned late Friday morning to complete their interview. But the boy appeared at home there, and Susana was kneeling happily beside him, helping him make a design with crushed red peppers on a drop cloth. Several of her assistants were exhibiting signs of urgency, but Susana played easily with the boy, as if she had delegated her day-before-the-opening anxiety as well as various last-minute tasks.

"Hi, Margo, meet Mickey," Susana introduced the child. "Mick, say hello to Margo."

"Hi," mumbled the child, absorbed in his design.

"God, he's just like me!" Susana beamed. "Once he starts doing art, nothing else exists."

"How old is he?" asked Margo, in place of the real question piquing her curiosity: What was the relationship between Susana and Mickey? Susana had come out as a lesbian over ten years ago, and while that didn't rule out motherhood, still there was no physical resemblance between the olive-skinned Chicana artist and the blond child.

"He's three," said Susana, then called out, "Isa! Keep an eye on him, will you? I've got an interview."

"Sure," said one of the women assisting her.

Margo looked up . . . and saw Mickey's mother, their kinship unmistakable in the two heads of fine, curly golden hair.

"Miguelito, my love." Isa strode over barefoot, unhesitating in spite of the construction materials scattered over the floor. Of medium height and sturdily built, she seemed to carry her weight equally over both sides of her body. Her legs, in purple tights under a filmy print skirt, made Margo think of stalks rooted in the ground.

"Margo Simon, Isa Reid," introduced Susana.

Isa shook hands, then said, "Christ, Susana, I didn't know you were letting him play with those peppers. Do you know what that's going to do to his allergies?"

"Clean out his sinuses?" From the edge to Susana's voice, Margo figured preopening jitters were affecting her after all. And she was taking them out on the person she felt closest to, obviously her lover.

Fortunately, Susana was pleasant and cooperative when she sat down to resume the interview. Margo got through the remainder of her questions in half an hour.

Margo was packing up her gear when Vicki Fall came by. Vicki dropped into a squat beside the little boy, who had stuck with his pepper art in spite of Isa's obvious efforts to distract him. Several toys lay abandoned nearby, apparently found inferior to the lovely, sneezy peppers.

"What a darling!" Vicki turned to Isa. "Is he yours?"

"Ours," declared Susana rather fiercely.

"Um, you mean from a previous marriage?" Vicki glanced nervously at Susana, but addressed Isa again.

"His daddy was a goddamn turkey baster," Susana said.

"What she means is, I was artificially inseminated," Isa explained. "God, Susana, you do get pissy right before an opening." The remark was teasing, affectionate, but Susana didn't smile.

Vicki looked about to burst into tears. Twisting a lock of her hair, she murmured, "Um, Tom knows a good, um, cheap Mexican restaurant in Barrio Logan. A bunch of us are going. Would you like to come?"

"Sounds good." Isa retrieved a pair of Birkenstock sandals from a pile of clothes in the corner and slipped her feet into them. "Susana, do you know where Mickey's sweater is?"

"Why don't you leave him here with me?"

"Aren't you going to come?" coaxed Isa. "You'll be here all day. It'll do you good to get out for an hour."

"I'm not hungry. And you know Mickey's not crazy about restaurants. You can relax more without him." Susana didn't sound, however, as if she was really trying to spare her partner the burden of child care.

"I'd like to be with Mickey," said Isa. "And you."

Margo hadn't given any thought to Isa's age. Now it struck her that Isa was several years older than Susana. And, like many women with younger lovers, she was insecure.

"Besides," Isa added, "you've got to eat something."

"You always say that and no, I don't, Mom." Susana seemed to regret her bad temper instantly, however, because her voice softened as she said, "Bring us back something, Isa, thanks." But Isa had already, stiff-backed with hurt, gone out the door.

Margo quickly said goodbye to Susana and followed. The lunch invitation had included her, and she loved good, cheap Mexican food.

"God, I knew this lunch thing was a mistake," wailed Vicki.

Margo was beginning to agree, as she, Vicki, and Isa waited for the other lunch-goers in the Capelli parking lot. Vicki was babbling and Isa looked grim.

"Peter and Tom are going to carp at each other the whole time," Vicki said. "And you can count on Jill to talk about something disgusting, like intimate, and I mean intimate, details about her ex-boyfriends' physical attributes. Carola Yang is coming, too—James Carmichael's secretary. Carola always looks at me like she's just found a bug in her bathtub and she's deciding whether it's more trouble to squash the bug and have to clean up the mess, or to rescue it and carry it outside. You know how it is, don't you, Isa?" she appealed. "Carola may work as a secretary, but she *isn't* a secretary, she's an artist. I work in the shoe department at Nordstrom, and as far as Carola's concerned, I *am* a shoe saleswoman."

"Dammit, I'm not Alice B. Toklas," snapped Isa.

"Who?"

"Vicki, don't you read? Alice B. Toklas was Gertrude Stein's lover. She had to entertain the wives of geniuses while Gertrude hung out with the geniuses. What I'm saying is, don't assume you and I are exactly alike just because we're both artists' 'wives.' "

Tears welled in Vicki's eyes; the woman, thought Margo with a mix of pity and irritation, was a waterworks. Isa looked as if she might apologize, but then the rest of the group arrived and rubbed salt into Isa's recent wounds.

"Hey, Isa, can we take Susana's Voyager?" Tom ran an admiring hand over the new van, a giant leap up from what most artists could afford.

Bitterly Isa said, "I'm not allowed. I wanted to take the train down from L.A. last night because my car is missing on a couple cylinders, but Susana won't let me drive the van."

"Don't you and Susana pool your expenses?" asked Jill as they piled into Tom's aged VW bus. "I thought she made enough for you to have a working car."

"We keep our finances separate. The law isn't exactly set up to give a lesbian couple community property."

"And Susana doesn't like to share?" probed Jill.

"She does all the house payments. But then, the house is in her name."

"So she could kick you out any time? Take in Dawn and put you on the street? I suppose she'd fight for custody of Mickey, too. You're the sacred birth mother, sure, but which of you can really provide for him?"

"Jill!" protested Vicki.

They rode in near silence the rest of the way to the restaurant, except for Carola Yang asking if anyone had seen her snowball. Carola's snowballs, Margo had learned, looked at first glance like the glass paperweights that you shake and white "snowflakes" drift over an Alpine house. But Carola made them with gritty urban scenes inside. She had missed one several days ago and had inquired about it so insistently that no one even answered her when she asked about it this time.

Once seated at the restaurant with tortilla chips, salsa, and beer, however, the group became talkative. Margo received permission to turn on her tape recorder and sat back to listen.

Tom Fall had been reading about the surrealist André Breton, and he was taken by Breton's statement—he pulled a slip of paper from his pocket and read aloud: " 'The simplest surrealist act consists of dashing down into the street, pistol in hand, and firing blindly, as fast as you can pull the trigger, into the crowd.' "

"That's horrible!" began Vicki, but faded into silence when Jill broke in.

"The point is," said Jill, "that's such a stupidly male formulation. The idea of harming other people for one thing, not to mention doing it with the ultimate phallic symbol, a gun."

"You don't think women carry guns?" said Peter.

"Women don't use guns the way men do," said Jill. "Women don't see them as extensions of their bodies."

"Bullshit!" said Tom. "I bet a third of the women who come to the Capelli pack pistols in their Gucci bags."

"Not because it makes them feel sexually potent," Jill countered. "It's because the Capelli's in a neighborhood where they're concerned about their safety. Look at Dawn. Of all of us, she's the one who's really at home downtown, and she carries a knife."

Isa entered the conversation then, muttering, "Let's not use Dawn as an example of rational behavior."

The waiter came and put down plates of enchiladas, chile rellenos, tostadas, and burritos.

"I know that snowball was on my desk Tuesday afternoon," said Carola.

"Christ, do we have to hear about that again?" moaned Peter.

"It was my best one, with the big rat in one corner. A gallery in L.A. was interested in it."

"Back to Dawn," said Jill. "I wouldn't say she's rational. But she's streetwise."

"What's the story on Dawn, anyway?" Peter asked Isa. "Is she really mute or does she talk to you and Susana?"

"Not to me, which is fine. Dawn has a bad aura. I'm sorry for her, I'm sure she's had a terrible life, but I don't want her in my space. Or Mickey's. I'd rather she wasn't in Susana's, either."

"You sound jealous," said Jill.

"No. I'm just uncomfortable with Susana's reasons for having Dawn in her life."

"For instance?" said Tom.

Isa dug in her purse for a pencil and a piece of note paper. In short, angry strokes she sketched a rough portrait. "Who's this?"

The drawing was clearly of Susana.

"And now?" With the eraser, Isa pared the thickly made up eyebrows. Instead of hair parted severely down the middle and pulled back, she gave the portrait messy bangs and hair falling on either side of her face.

"My God, they could be sisters," said Tom. "I wouldn't have thought Susana was so vain!"

He laughed maliciously. Isa looked distressed, as if she'd let her sense of hurt toward Susana push her into performing a small act of betrayal.

"So Dawn looks like Susana," said Jill. "Wouldn't any of us feel an affinity toward, or at least curiosity about, someone who looks like us? Someone with such a different life?"

"Right, maybe Susana sees having Dawn around as a life-art work," said Peter. "Like the piece where the two artists were tied together for a year with a six-foot rope between them."

The subject changed then and there were no more surprises until the end of the meal, when Jill took a sip of coffee and went into convulsions.

7 / Art and Life

Jill fell sideways from her chair onto Peter. He caught her and kept her from crashing onto the floor, but he seemed stunned, as if he had no idea what to do next with the thrashing woman in his arms.

"Oh, God, somebody help!" wailed Vicki. Unable to get to Jill, who was across the table from her, she reached over and righted the coffee cup Jill had dropped.

From the kitchen of the restaurant several waiters and a woman in an apron ran out yelling in Spanish.

Isa took charge. "Let's get her chair out of the way and lower her to the floor," she said, putting her hands under one of Jill's shoulders to help Peter. "Tom and Margo, move the table back, so she can't hurt herself on it. And everybody stand back, give her some space."

Once on the floor Jill continued to jerk and utter small moans. Isa sat beside her and stroked her face, but didn't try to restrain her.

"I'll call 911!" Carola sprinted to the back of the restaurant.

"What about artificial respiration?" Margo knelt alongside Isa. "I think I know how to do it."

"No, she's breathing just fine. Does anyone know if she has epilepsy?"

"Epilepsy! What about the coffee?" said Tom. "She had

some right before this happened."

"Nothing is wrong with my coffee!" cried the woman in the apron, in strongly accented English. She picked up Jill's cup, which still had an inch of coffee in the bottom, but couldn't actually bring herself to drink from it. "Maybe this lady takes drugs," she said, brandishing the cup.

"No fooling," muttered Peter.

Jill gave a louder moan and went limp as a rag doll. On the other side of the table, Vicki sobbed in Tom's arms.

Carola ran back into the room, announcing the paramedics were coming.

Jill's eyelids fluttered. "Wha . . . what happened?" she whispered. She started to lift her head, but sank back down with a sigh.

"Take it easy," said Isa. "It looks like you had some kind of seizure."

"A seizure?" This time Jill made it to a sitting position, Isa and Margo supporting her. "I'm all right, really," she said weakly. "A little drained, but I'm okay."

"The paramedics are on their way," said Margo. "They can check you over."

"I don't need that." Jill stood, a bit wobbly, and grabbed onto a chair. "I'm okay, really. Please, let's go." She stumbled toward the door.

"We've got to pay." Vicki pulled out her wallet.

"No pay, no pay," said one of the waiters quickly. "Is all right, no pay."

"Okay, Jill, what are you on?" demanded Tom when they were back in the van. "PCP? Cocaine?"

Jill, curled up on a blanket in the back of the van, didn't answer.

Tom started driving. A small argument ensued. Isa insisted they should take Jill straight to a hospital, but Tom was anxious to get back to work.

"I've always wanted to do that." Jill's voice was strong and triumphant, with none of the frailty of a moment before. "Art-life, just what we were talking about. I always wondered what it would be like to have a fit in a public place."

"Damn you, Jill, you mean you faked that?" Tom, driving, half turned.

"Tom, for chrissakes, watch the road!" Peter lunged forward and grabbed the wheel of the van.

"I was curious how much I'd have to let go of ego," said Jill.

"Jill, I can't believe you!" said Vicki. "You sound like a scientist reporting on an experiment. Don't you realize you put us through hell? And what about the poor people in that restaurant, scared they might have poisoned you?"

"I didn't know everyone would get so upset," Jill said consideringly. "Of course, that's one reason I did it, to create an unexpected situation and see what happens. Why do it, if I knew how it would turn out in advance?"

They arrived back at the Capelli, and most of the lunch party went back inside. Margo, however, sat in her car for a moment, taking notes on what had happened. She had considerately switched off her tape recorder during Jill's fit, and now she was kicking herself.

Parked beside Tom, she heard Isa's voice coming from the other side of the VW bus.

"Jill, tell me the truth," said Isa. "Did you really fake that attack or did you just not want us to take you to the hospital?"

"I faked it. Ex-scout's honor."

"I don't care if you were on something," said Isa. "But I want to know. If you were conscious the whole time, then tell me what happened."

Jill did. "You were terrific, Isa," she said.

Margo heard the sound of a slap.

"I'm sorry for you, Jill," said Isa. "You have no heart."

"What do you think, Jenny?" Margo turned—in her calf-length black skirt, mustard jacket, and red beret—toward the girl lounging on the bed, whose heart-shaped face was dwarfed by the radio headphones over her ears. "Does this look right to wear to an art opening?"

Jenny gave her a long look, and Margo mentally prepared herself for the blistering criticism likely to come these days from her stepdaughter. In addition to the typical rigors of being fifteen, Jenny was having a rough time accepting the recent remarriage of her mother, with whom she lived most of the time. Margo sympathized, but she missed the sunny child who had adjusted so easily (too easily?) when Margo had started seeing Barry six years ago. From the living room, she heard Barry and eleven-year-old David yelling over a basketball game on television. David had fussed when Margo first entered his life, but now he was as unflappable as his father. Who knew what his adolescence would bring?

"Lemme see that one. The black." Jenny lifted one headphone from her ear and indicated a toque among Margo's hat collection hanging on hooks on the wall.

Margo put it on.

"Now, that's cool."

It was amazing how good Jenny's praise could make her feel. Margo knew the goal was not to take the girl's mercurial behavior personally, and theoretically that applied to sweet tempers as well as foul. Nevertheless, she was delighted when Jenny came over to her (earphones off completely) and said, "Know what you need with the hat? A French knot or something."

"That'd be lovely." Margo took off the hat and ran her hands through the unruly brown waves that fell to her shoulders. Often she just tied the whole mess out of her way at the nape of her neck. "Could you do it?"

"All right. Don't look in the mirror, okay? Not till I'm done. What kind of art are you going to see?"

Margo discussed her impressions of the three artists, in response to the girl's astute questions. Susana Contreras's installation could be a sensual feast of color and texture, or it might be overwhelming, the poles too spiky and the walls too bloody. Margo had already had a vivid experience of Tom Fall's work; she wondered how it would feel to enter the room in the midst of a champagne-sparkling art opening crowd. As for Jill Iverson, the artist herself didn't seem to know what she would do with her guillotine.

"You can look now," said Jenny shyly.

"Oh, Jen, it's fantastic!" Margo hugged her. Jenny had created an upswept hairstyle that made Margo look unusually sophisticated. What pleased Margo even more was the warmth between them, once a common occurrence and now a rare gift.

Jenny beamed as she angled the hat on Margo's head and helped her choose a pair of earrings. Before Margo and Barry left for the Capelli opening, Jenny insisted on taking their photograph.

When Margo looked at the photo a week later, she barely recognized herself, whether because of the unaccustomed hairstyle or because so much had happened since then.

8 / Art and Death

A three-piece combo was playing Latin jazz, and the rhythm infected the bodies of the crowd in the courtyard of the Capelli Foundation. Heads might be discussing the latest French film or trends in the bond market, but hips wiggled and shoulders twitched, as if the bodies had a sly Brazilian life of their own.

While Barry sambaed to the buffet table, Margo stood at one side of the courtyard and held up her microphone to capture the ambience of music and chatter. The mass of people in front of her bobbed like tightly packed driftwood, men and women alike fashionably attired in black. Even those whose casual garb identified them as artists wore black slacks and jackets.

"Hi, Margo. Nice hat." Vicki Fall looked like a model in a slim, off-the-shoulder black dress. But wasn't she freezing? The April night was hardly balmy.

"Have you seen Tom's installation?" Vicki asked anxiously.

"Not yet."

It turned out the computer program had a few glitches, and Peter Vance was supposed to be working things manually during the opening, but Peter hadn't shown up. So Tom had to stay inside and do it himself, instead of being out meeting people the way he'd planned. Not that he believed in "sucking up to rich art collectors," it was just that some important critics were here, as well as other artists. Anyway, Vicki hoped everything was working in the installation, but since Tom couldn't be outside, he had asked her to talk to people, but she really, really hated that, she never knew what to say.

As Vicki chattered, it became obvious why she wasn't feeling any chill. She had gotten an early start on the wine.

"I'd better go, there are people I'm supposed to see," Vicki mumbled, slinking miserably away.

How could Vicki let herself be pushed around like that? Margo asked herself, annoyed, and then thought of her own first love, the impossible artist in Santa Fe. She hadn't let him push her around, but neither had her behavior been any model of psychological maturity. She spotted Barry—garbed in his favorite Hawaiian shirt under his sport jacket—returning from the buffet table and felt a rush of thankfulness that she'd done so much better the second time.

While she and Barry feasted on crab puffs, stuffed mushrooms, strawberries dipped in chocolate, and Chardonnay, Margo picked out several familiar faces. James Carmichael, chubby body swathed in a beautifully tailored tuxedo, was clearly on duty as director of the Capelli, circulating from group to group of well-dressed art lovers. Charlotte Meyers, the septuagenarian volunteer, waved as she passed by on the arm of a short, rather dapper man, no doubt the retired husband who golfed. A trumpet of color announced the arrival of Louise O'Quinn. No slave to fashion, Louise stood out from all the uniform black in a deep burgundy suit with an emerald green shawl draped over one shoulder.

And wasn't that Bernard Capelli? Stooped and sixtyish, the benefactor of the Capelli Foundation wore an ill-fitting tuxedo and looked slightly out of place at the glittery art opening. If Margo hadn't recognized Capelli, she might have assumed he was one of the better-dressed of the down-town transients, who'd wandered into the courtyard for some free eats.

She went over with her microphone extended. "Mr. Capelli, could I have a minute?"

"Of course."

"What do you think of the show?"

"Both installations are thrilling. Disturbing. And I'm sure Jill Iverson's performance in half an hour will afflict the comfortable as well. That's the purpose of the show, of course, to disturb. I believe that's the purpose of the best art."

In spite of the bantering, cocktail party atmosphere around them, Capelli sounded completely in earnest. Margo responded as seriously: "Isn't it enough just to create beauty?"

"If, by beauty, you mean the merely decorative, then no, that's never enough." With a deft swoop he placed his arm around her. Margo squirmed for a moment, but Bernard Capelli was stronger than he looked; and all he was doing was fondling her shoulder in a very public, very safe set-ting . . . while he gave her interview material that might help her get a promotion. Capelli went on: "Beauty—real, wild, raw beauty—is inherently disturbing. I'm sure you know the line from Keats: 'Beauty is truth, truth beauty.' Art has an obligation to tell the truth, and the truth is beautiful, although not in the clichéd way many people define beauty. Think of Picasso's painting, *Les Demoiselles d'Avignon,* where the women are distorted and frightening and full of mystery. That's real beauty." He gave her arm a friendly parting squeeze.

●　　●　　●

"Who were you interviewing?" asked Barry. They had braved the crush to get inside and were standing in line for Tom Fall's installation, to which only twenty people were being admitted at a time.

"Bernard Capelli. He quoted Keats."

The line began to move forward toward the EXIT/NO EXIT neon sign. Margo felt a rush of nervous warmth through her body. She reached for Barry's hand.

She'd expected to be blasé about entering Tom's installation at the opening, being in a group of people and even knowing the exit door. Tom had added several embellishments, however—purple lighting and loud circus music that carried a dark undertone, not the fun of the big top but the weirdness of the freak show. Margo wasn't the only one discomfited by the room, she noticed. People had joked and laughed when they first went in and saw themselves reflected in the mirrors. After a few minutes they began trying the doors; Margo turned on her tape recorder to catch the sound of jiggling doorknobs.

One person, at any rate, found Tom's art totally delightful. Mickey, Isa Reid's—and Susana's—son, was running up to the mirrors and making faces.

"This is our third time in here." Isa sighed. "Mick thinks this is the best art opening he's ever been to."

"Open door! Open door! Lift me up, Isa!" he clamored.

Isa drew her son against her, her shoulders sagging. "We haven't even gotten to Susana's piece yet. She'll be pissed, but she doesn't know how hard it is to drag a kid around an opening. I'm the mommy who always does that job. Plus, I've had to placate Susana's dealer. She's not exactly thrilled that Susana did an installation—no commission for her, of course. I think she came down from L.A. tonight mainly to protect her investment and make sure Susana never does this again."

"Open door!" demanded Mickey.

"I'll take him," Margo offered.

"Bless you."

Margo hoisted up the child, a squirming, sweet armful—a stage she'd missed with Barry's kids—and held him so he could reach the doorknobs.

"Isa got mad at . . ." The name Mickey said sounded like Ryan. "He was s'posed to babysit me this afternoon, but he went away."

"What did you do this afternoon, Mickey?" She steered him toward the right door.

"Went swimming at the hotel. I know how to swim."

"I bet you swim like a fish."

"Hey! Look what I did!" He had opened the door, to a round of applause.

"Thanks, I needed a break," said Isa as she and Margo strolled together into the foyer, Barry joining them. "Mick, let's go see Susana's art now."

"I want to open the door again! Open door! Open door!"

"How about a piggyback ride?" Barry crouched and Mickey hopped on his back.

"You must have kids of your own," remarked Isa.

"A girl and a boy," said Barry. "It took years, but I finally learned how to distract them. Except that now they're way too old for that to work, fifteen and eleven."

"My older son, Orion, is sixteen," Isa said. "That's right, Orion, like the constellation. I had him back in my commune days. Believe me, that was one of the straighter names at the time. He got his driver's license last month. I thought I'd passed every test of motherhood—the broken bones, the F in history, the kid screaming he hates you. But nothing prepares you for having a kid who can drive. Hey, Mick," she said, lifting him from Barry's back as they got to the doors of

Susana's installation. "This is Susa's art. Come see."

Dimly lit by several dozen candles placed throughout the room, *Frida y Yo* was both a shrine, perfumed with fresh flowers, and an obstacle course, where one constantly had to dodge the tall, cactuslike spikes that appeared at random throughout the room. "I never imagined it would be so beautiful," Margo whispered to Barry; the installation was a place in which it seemed necessary to speak softly. Margo discovered one delight after another: the beautifully embroidered Mexican shawls hanging from the ceiling, the way the candles shed soft light on the red peppers on the wall, the small painting Susana had done on one wall—a *retablo*, she'd called it, to thank the Virgin for sparing one from misfortune. How had Susana known that all of these disparate elements, which held no magic individually, would combine to create such a breathtaking effect?

In one corner, on the jagged bed, lay the artist . . . although she seemed less "Susana Contreras," a specific person, than a sculptural form, wrapped in a dark shawl and turned toward the wall. Respecting her evident wish to be regarded as part of her work, no one approached her.

Mickey, however, was as yet unschooled in art gallery behavior. He broke away from Isa and ran to his second mom. "Susa! Susa!" he said, shaking her shoulder.

"Mick, sweetie, leave Susana alone." Coming to lead the child away, Isa leaned over the bed for a moment. Then she scooped up Mickey and straightened, her feet planted in front of the metal bed.

Holding Mickey tightly to her chest, Isa called out, "Is there a doctor here?"

9 / The Crime Scene

"A doctor?" repeated Isa, her voice thin.

A woman in a black miniskirt and stiletto heels strode over briskly, followed by a conservatively dressed young man and, reluctantly, an older man with a clipped gray beard whom Margo found oddly familiar. The rest of the forty or so people in the installation pressed after them—no longer browsing art aficionados, but witnesses at the scene of an accident, murmuring excitedly, "What happened?" . . . "Is she ill?" . . . "Do you think it's drugs?"

A uniformed security guard sprinted to the front. After a quick exchange with the doctors, he asked Isa to move back a few steps and stationed himself in front of the bed.

In deep shadow (there were no candles near the bed), the three doctors bent over Susana and spoke to her. The artist didn't move, and the collective anxiety increased. Someone spilled a drink; Margo felt the cold splash on her ankle as, obeying her first impulse, she pushed through the crowd and put an arm around Isa's shoulder.

"What is it? What did you see?" she asked Isa, following her second impulse—to turn on her tape recorder.

"I'm not sure. The doctors . . ." Isa was trembling violently.

Someone should turn on the lights, Margo thought, but was

grateful no one did, as if whatever was happening required the soft candlelight.

"Is Susa sick?" said Mickey in Isa's arms. He was subdued, clearly knowing with a three-year-old's emotional radar that something was badly wrong in the adult world.

"A little sick." Isa nuzzled her son's blond curls. Her gaze was fixed on the figure on the bed.

The young male doctor whispered to his colleagues. He looked alarmed. The woman doctor joined him on the far side of the bed, and they lifted Susana slightly. Still, Susana didn't respond.

"Please, what's wrong?" Isa took a step forward, but the guard stopped her. "Please!" she repeated. Mickey started to wail.

"I don't really know, my dear, it's not my area of expertise," said the gray-haired doctor, coming over to her. "I'm a psychiatrist."

Margo took a deep breath, fighting an urge to break into hysterical laughter. No wonder the doctor seemed familiar. He looked like Sigmund Freud!

"Oh, God," breathed Isa. "Oh, God, I couldn't find her pulse."

James Carmichael arrived, with another security guard in tow. He patted Isa's arm, then conferred with the doctors, too quietly for Margo to hear, and the young doctor left with one of the guards.

The director of the Capelli Foundation faced the crowd.

"We have a bit of a problem here." James spoke calmly, but his face was beaded with sweat. "The doctors have requested that everyone leave the room. Thank you all very much." The woman doctor whispered something to him. He frowned, then made a second announcement. "We would like to ask you to stay here at the foundation for a short while.

There's another installation to see and plenty of refreshments, so please do enjoy yourselves. We appreciate your cooperation."

"What's going on?" Margo tried approaching James, but the security guard, professionally but very firmly, guided her toward the door.

"Margo, find Orion and send him to me?" Isa called after her. "He's probably the only teenage kid here. He's got long brown hair, and he's wearing a Cure T-shirt."

From the street came the sound of sirens.

Huddled on the floor of the Capelli Foundation's ultra-modern—no doubt postmodern—women's bathroom, Margo leaned her head against the cool Italian tile lining the stall and waited for her stomach to quit doing loop-de-loops. Questions flew, panicky chittering birds, through her mind. Susana Contreras was dead, of that she was certain. Isa hadn't found a pulse, and the doctors hadn't even attempted artificial respiration or CPR. Had she died of a drug overdose, as several people had speculated? Or, continuing along the line of more or less natural causes, had anorexic Susana suffered a heart attack? In that case, why did everyone have to remain at the Capelli, like characters in an old detective movie? And why, when Margo was leaving the installation, did she see two uniformed police officers entering the building? (Margo had marched toward the officers, microphone in hand, but that was when her stomach lurched and she'd had to race to the ladies' room. Did Diane Sawyer ever experience moments like that?)

Slowly Margo got up from the bathroom floor. All she really knew, she cautioned her overactive imagination, was that Susana was dead. Surely the police would be called in the case of any death occurring under such strange circumstances—Susana lying there as Frida Kahlo, dozens of people passing by. Even a heart attack couldn't be proved without an autopsy. Margo splashed cold water on her face, then cupped her hands and drank some—San Diego city water, it tasted like chemical tea. Did Susana die before the opening began? Or could it have happened during the event, with people right there in the room? And if she hadn't died naturally, who had killed her? What did the doctors see when they examined her? Strangulation marks on her neck? A knife wound? Where was Dawn?

Under the perky hat, Margo's coiffure still looked perfect, which struck her as somehow obscene. In half a minute she ripped out all the bobby pins, strewing them on the floor. She jammed the hat back on and went out . . . into pandemonium.

At least three hundred people were packed into the Capelli's courtyard, the police having closed Tom Fall's installation as well as Susana's; both hallways were cordoned off with yellow plastic tape. The only part of the foundation remaining open was the foyer, for access to the bathrooms and telephone. "That's right, hon, we're going to be late," a woman was saying into the phone when Margo went by. "I want you to get Lindy and Hal ready for bed. Yes, we'll pay you time and a half."

Margo eyed the line for the phone and considered calling KSDR to report Susana's death. But Saturday nights at the radio station were devoted to jazz, with no news breaks for anything less than an earthquake or nuclear war. And she felt a sudden, nearly primal desire to see Barry. Wildly she began scanning the crowd for Barry's thick, sandy hair and stocky, ridiculously comforting body. Wonderful man, he was waiting for her right outside the door.

Holding her tight, Barry said that James Carmichael had come out and made an announcement, merely that Susana was ill and people were asked not to leave. "She isn't just ill, is she?" he said into her ear. Margo shook her head. She wanted to discuss everything with him, but not in the raucous crowd, where, in addition to comments about Susana, there was a clamor of people indignant at being detained. An iron gate, guarded by a police officer, had been drawn across the entrance to the courtyard; it was a real-life version of Tom Fall's *Exit/No Exit*, the aesthetic virtues of which were clearly unappreciated. Adding to the commotion, the band was still playing and the bar had started dispensing free drinks, turning loud, nervous, excited people into louder nervous, excited people.

"What's a Cure T-shirt?" Margo yelled to Barry over the din.

"Got me. No, wait, the Cure's a rock group. Jenny listens to them. Why?"

She explained her mission, and she and Barry split up to hunt for Orion Reid. As she looked for Isa's son, Margo kept her tape recorder going. It seemed impossible to learn anything of substance. *Everyone* who had gone into Susana's installation had, in retrospect, sensed something was wrong. "I said to Bob, 'Look, Bob,' I said, 'how can she lie so still?' Didn't I, Bob?" said a woman in furs. A man with a nimbus of white hair related seeing Susana's aura turn black. Another man said he had ventured to one side of Susana's installation and slipped in a big puddle of water.

"Please, you must tell me how Susana is." A small, firm hand, sparkling with rings, grasped Margo's arm. The woman was exquisitely dressed in a tight black suit, with a tiny black-and-white hat perched on a pageboy that was an improbable, expensive-looking shade of red.

"I'm sorry, I don't really know," said Margo as she'd done several times already. She didn't fancy being the one to start the bad news flying through this drunk, jittery crowd.

"You don't understand, *ma chérie*." The voice was Boston Brahmin, the French *r* flawless. "I'm a close friend of Susana's and Isa's. Barbara Scholl, Susana's art dealer. What happened to her? Why are the police here?"

Margo had heard of the Scholl Gallery, one of the hottest venues in L.A.'s very hot art scene. So this was the dealer Isa had to appease, who would lose money if Susana continued to do installation art. Petite and blue-eyed, Barbara Scholl looked younger than Margo would have expected, not much more than thirty. No, closer to forty, she amended her observation, as the art dealer pressed nearer and Margo got the impression of cosmetics that must cost the earth. Margo told her a partial truth, that the doctors felt Susana was quite ill. Then she thought to enlist Barbara's help.

"Do you know Isa's older son, Orion?"

Barbara Scholl giggled; it was a rude, unsophisticated sound coming from that perfectly made up face. "No one but Isa would name a child Orion, *bien entendu*," she said, still chuckling. Margo explained that she was looking for the young man, and Barbara said of course, if she saw Orion she would send him inside to Isa. "But you haven't told me how Susana is," she pressed, taking Margo's arm again.

"Sorry." Margo pulled away. She had just seen the policeman at the gate admitting two men in slacks and sport jackets, who carried a variety of cases and camera equipment. They couldn't be media people; there were several reporters gathered noisily in the street, but the barred gate was keeping them out as well as detaining everyone else within.

"Margo Simon, KSDR," she said, trotting beside the two men, who were shouldering their way toward the building's entrance. "Are you police officers? Has a crime been committed?"

They passed her without answering. A man with a well-tended three-day beard voiced her own assumption. "Plainclothes. Bet they're homicide dicks. Hey, is this art imitating death or death imitating art?" he quipped into her microphone.

"Clever the way Susana set it up," put in a leather-clad woman, leaning forward to get close to the mike and let the man eye some cleavage. "This'll get her into every art magazine in the country. God, what it's going to do for her prices! When is this going to be on television?"

It never mattered that Margo didn't carry a camera, people always asked. "Radio," she said. "KSDR. Tomorrow morning."

Shortly after eight o'clock—to Margo's amazement, not more than forty-five minutes after the discovery of Susana's death—James Carmichael and Bernard Capelli came out of the building with one of the homicide detectives and two uniformed police officers. It was Capelli, looking even more disheveled than before, who stepped up to the microphone used by the band.

"I'm deeply, deeply saddened to have to tell you we have had a death here," Capelli said. Margo had moved in close to catch him with her own mike; she saw tears in his eyes.

"Was it Susana Contreras?" someone called out.

Capelli looked confused. The detective took over. "Sorry, identity can't be divulged pending notification of next of kin."

Surely Isa had been "notified." But Isa, Margo realized, had no legal rights regarding the woman she loved, with whom she had shared her life. And apparently none of Susana's family had made the relatively short trip from Los Angeles for the opening. What did they think of their lesbian daughter/sister? Margo hoped, for Isa's and Mickey's sakes, that Susana had left a will.

"Was it murder?" she asked.

"I can't answer that," said the detective. "We'd like some of you to remain and talk to us tonight. If you were here at any time this afternoon, prior to the opening, or if you noticed anything unusual in Ms. Contreras's . . . in her—"

"Installation," supplied James, with a slight sneer.

The detective barely glanced at James. "As I said, if you were here earlier today or you were in the installation at the time someone realized there was a problem, we'd like to talk to you tonight. Please line up and give your name to the officers here. For the rest of you, there will be several officers at the gate. If you'll just give them your names, you're free to leave. You'll be contacted within a few days."

Damn, it was going to be a long night. After Margo got away from the Capelli Foundation, she still had to go to KSDR and put together something about Susana's death for the Sunday morning news. Even as an eighteen-year-old college freshman, her body had protested when she had pulled all-nighters. Twenty years later no amount of caffeine was going to compensate for the lack of sleep. She thought of sneaking out; how would the cops at the gate ever know she had been in the installation at the relevant time? But if she stayed to answer questions, she could ask some as well.

She was standing near the door when a woman dressed as Madame de Pompadour emerged from the corridor to Susana's installation. The woman bunched up her full skirt and ducked a high white wig under the plastic tape at the entrance to the corridor.

"What's going on?" asked Jill Iverson, tripping into the courtyard on little high heels. "Why isn't anyone coming to my performance?"

Above cheeks decorated with beauty marks, the pupils of Jill's eyes were pinpoints.

10 / A Coup

Water dripped down the walls, slow tears squeezed from under the eyelids of the ceiling. The water formed a puddle around the perimeter of the room—a deep red puddle, because the walls were covered with something red. The water crept inward over the floor. The essential thing was not to get wet, perhaps because the water was toxic and contact with even one drop caused instant death? The water was closing in, however, leaving a smaller and smaller dry space at the center of the room. Was it better to risk running through it on tiptoe, kicking off her shoes the second she got across? Or to yell for rescuers to lay planks to the door? Now everything was shaking, and the water splashed bright red, rising.

"Margo! Margo!" Barry continued to jog her shoulder.

She opened her eyes, then squeezed them closed against the cruel light. "What time is it?"

"Eight," his voice boomed horribly. Only three hours since she had finally gone to bed. She pulled the covers over her head. "I hate to do this," said Barry, rubbing her back, "but Alex has called. Twice. Here, I brought you some coffee. French roast."

"Alex?" This had to be chapter two of her nightmare. "What does he want? My head hurts."

"He wants you to come in to the station."

"Now?" She had planned a fuller story on Susana than she'd had time to do at three A.M., but later—after a reasonable amount of sleep. "Do I smell coffee?"

"Here." Barry gave her a cup and let her take a few sips, then handed her the cordless telephone.

What a coup that Margo had interviewed Susana extensively the week before she was killed! Alex crowed over the phone. Could she get to the station in half an hour? It wasn't a question but a demand.

Standing in the shower, Margo tried to feel like a reporter with a coup. Maybe the problem was the military metaphor. It could be that coups were limited to men, a sex-linked condition like color blindness. What did *she* have, then? A massive headache. Aspirin and coffee ought to help that. Food, too—had Barry said something about bagels?

As steam from the shower worked its blessed way into her sinuses, she reviewed in her mind what had happened after Jill emerged from the Capelli, a stoned blond mole who had burrowed into an exterminators' convention. Whatever drug Jill was under the influence of, it hadn't made her belligerent or violent. She did ask what the hell was going on when three police officers surrounded her, but she appeared dazed and didn't protest when one of the officers led her back inside.

Margo assumed that, apart from predictable questions about her use of controlled substances, Jill was then subjected to the same routine she and Barry had been: a one-on-one interview with a homicide detective in one of the Capelli's second-floor offices. In Margo's case this took place in a plush conference room dominated by a large painting she'd been told was a Jennifer Bartlett during a tour she'd received a few days before. A very expensive painting, thanks to the handsome acquisition fund Bernard Capelli had established for the foundation's permanent collection. Margo had no time to admire the art, however, before the interrogation began.

When did she arrive at the opening? With whom? When did she enter the building? When did she go into Susana's installation? What happened then?

The detective questioning her was a man of about thirty, whose body looked like a battleground between doughnuts and jogging—muscled verging on beefy. So far the jogging was winning, but Margo wouldn't bet on his luck holding out for another ten years. The rebellious tone of her own thoughts startled her. Was the encounter with Authority bringing out remnants of an adolescent self, hauled to the vice-principal's office for passing notes in study hall? As the detective asked about events earlier in the week, however—and especially, when he showed great interest in obtaining her unedited interview tapes—she understood that it was more than just youthful memories that made her chary of cooperating fully. She was holding back because it seemed dangerously easy to misconstrue small incidents or comments, little episodes consistent with the stress of preparing for the opening and with the highly strung natures that were accepted among artists. But how would an outsider interpret Susana's anger at Tom the night Dawn had been locked in? The domestic tension between Susana and Isa? Margo could almost hear the detective thinking *Lezzies!* as he quizzed her about Susana's and Isa's relationship. Those were the kind of questions Alex was likely to ask.

Alex! At the thought of the station manager, Margo forced herself to turn off the shower and grab a towel. Why had *Alex* called, anyway? she wondered, sufficiently awake at last to register the departure from KSDR's chain of command. If a higher-up were going to get involved in one of her stories, it ought to be Dennis Zachary Powell, the news director, not Alex. Maybe Dennis would be at the studio when she arrived.

Half a cup of coffee was sitting on the bathroom windowsill. Lukewarm but still bounteous in caffeine. She drained the coffee, then forced her contact lenses into her eyes (more bloodshot than brown this morning) and gave her hair sixty seconds with the dryer. Starting to pull on jeans, she thought better of it—no telling whom she might have to interview— and instead chose an olive green knit jersey and matching skirt. She took another two minutes to smear concealer on the circles under her eyes and apply blusher to her sallow cheeks, deeply grateful for the Body Shop and all of its products.

Eating a cinnamon-raisin bagel in the kitchen, she skimmed the story about Susana's death in the morning paper. It was sketchier than her radio piece; the reporter must have had a hell of a deadline. When it came to facts, however, the police had told the journalists at the gate of the Capelli precisely what they'd revealed to her, once they had finished questioning her: Susana had died of "unnatural causes." No one was saying what those causes might be.

"Isn't that your third cup?" said Barry, seeing her reach for the coffeepot again.

"Is it?" She had a feeling she was going to need it.

"Who dunnit?" Alex sounded as happy as a kid who'd gotten a pony for Christmas.

Margo recoiled from his enthusiasm, thinking of Susana lying dead and Isa torn between wanting to give vent to her grief and trying not to terrify her son in her arms. At the same time she was keenly aware that this was the most interest Alex had ever shown in one of her stories, and that the Sunday morning powwow didn't include Dennis Zachary Powell.

"I don't know." The same answer she'd given the detective the night before.

"Any guesses?"

At least with Alex, Margo was willing to speculate. He couldn't turn her musings against innocent people.

"There's Dawn." She described the mute homeless woman. "She seems to be mentally disturbed and she carries a knife—although I don't know if that's how Susana was killed, the police wouldn't say," she added quickly. "At any rate, it's conceivable Dawn was alone with Susana late yesterday afternoon."

"What about last night? Was this Dawn at the opening?" Alex was disgustingly bright-eyed and bushy-tailed. He looked a bit like a fox, with his sharp nose. A happy, crafty fox.

"At the opening? No. But she wouldn't have been. That kind of event would terrify her."

"So one thing to do is look for her. You've got good contacts among the local homeless population, don't you?"

No thanks to you, Margo grumbled mentally. She used to do a weekly report on the homeless, keeping in touch with a variety of organizations, as well as individuals who were more or less regulars in the transient community. Alex had insisted she cut back unless something really juicy happened, like a charity pocketing donations . . . or a murderer lurking in the community's midst. As if it weren't important to follow the daily struggles of people who had fallen out of the bottom of the economy.

"What about the girlfriend?" pursued Alex. "Does she inherit?"

Margo cringed—"the girlfriend?"—but answered, "I was there when Isa found Susana. Believe me, she was in shock. Besides . . ." Alex's questions were forming a definite pattern. "That's what the police will be doing. Looking for Dawn, seeing who gets Susana's money."

"Yeah, but people may not tell them everything. They're more likely to tell you. Not just because you're not the police, but you've already established a relationship with them. You can just say you want comments about Contreras's death as part of your original story."

"Alex, we don't investigate murders." Crime reporting was hardly a staple of public radio, for a number of reasons. A low-budget public station could never hope to hold its own against the big commercial TV and radio stations and newspapers; KSDR didn't even monitor the police radio band. Furthermore, the KSDR audience didn't listen out of an interest in crime. Both nationally and at the local level, public radio excelled in in-depth features, the kind of stories that gave the headlines complexity, history, and especially humanity. That was what had drawn Margo to KSDR in the first place.

"I'm not asking you to track down the murderer." Alex spoke in a cajoling tone Margo had never heard before; it made her uneasy. "I'm still thinking in terms of your doing a story about Contreras and her work, the same thing you were doing before she died. I'm just proposing a slight shift in focus, to asking what about her might have led to her being killed. As I said, people are going to tell you things they won't tell the police or other reporters. They've probably already told you their opinions of Contreras—"

"Susana. Her name is Susana."

"I'll take you off any other assignments while you work on this. And you should keep track of your hours. If you put in a lot of overtime, I think we can pull something out of the consultant fund or at least give you comp time. This is the kind of story we can sell to NPR. So, you mentioned this homeless woman, what's her name, Dawn? Look for her. And you'll want to talk to Susana's girlfriend. I bet she stayed in town last night. Do you know where to find her?"

Margo balked. She had never seen herself as the kind of journalist who'd stick her microphone in a newly bereaved lover's face and ask how she felt . . . or a journalist who would be pleased that she knew, as the result of a casual chat, where the lover was staying.

"Of course, if you can't do it, I guess I could assign Claire," said Alex. "There's a news conference scheduled for the Capelli Foundation at noon. You could brief Claire and I'm sure she could make it." Claire De Jong was the bright, blond, infuriatingly talented twenty-five-year-old Alex had hired from NPR to fill the full-time reporting job Margo had desired.

"Isa's staying at the Tropico on Shelter Island," Margo said.

"She's not available," said the woman who answered the telephone in Isa's room.

"Is this Barbara Scholl?" asked Margo. She'd recognized Barbara's Boston inflections.

"Ye-es?"

"Margo Simon. We met last night. I was with Isa in Susana's installation. I"—she took a deep breath and let out the lie—"wanted to see how she was doing, if there was anything I could do to help."

"Who's that?" came from somewhere in the hotel room.

"Shhh, not so loud," Barbara whispered. "A friend of your mother's, *chéri*." The other voice was too old for Mickey; the errant Orion must have returned to the bosom of his family. "Thanks for your concern," Barbara told Margo. "But Isa is sleeping. *La pauvre petite* was up all night. She finally let me give her something at five this morning."

"Did the police tell you anything about how Susana died?"

"Not a thing. I'm sure after the ordeal they put us through last night, it will turn out to be something hereditary. A bad heart, something like that." Barbara clearly hadn't picked up a newspaper this morning. "I told Isa she should sue. The police were treating her like a murderer."

"Did Isa at least have a chance to see Susana yesterday afternoon?"

"I didn't ask. The police had already asked her so much."

"How about you? Were you able to get over to the Capelli before the opening, just to say hello?"

"In the afternoon? I wish I had. As it is, I hadn't seen Susana for the past three weeks. But I arrived, uh, right before the opening started. Uh, that is, I arrived an hour or two earlier, but the drive from L.A always exhausts me. *Bien entendu*, I had to take four aspirin and lie down for an hour just to feel human again. I must go now. We're still waiting for our breakfast. Room service here is atrocious. I'll tell Isa you called. Your name again? Margo, yes."

What *had* Barbara Scholl been doing that afternoon? Margo would bet the poised art dealer rarely said "uh" twice in one week, much less in one minute, unless there were some clever way to express it in French.

Margo had both Tom Fall's and Jill Iverson's home phone numbers. She had to leave a message on Jill's machine. Tom, however, answered the phone and was willing to be interviewed. In fact, he sounded as if he had plenty to say.

11 / The Crime Beat

Margo would have expected Tom and Vicki Fall to live in the North Park or Golden Hill neighborhoods of San Diego, with their cheap rents and ethnic diversity. To her surprise, Tom gave her an address in La Mesa, a well-off suburb bordering the eastern city limits. La Mesa had a few mildly downtrodden sectors, where peeling stucco houses perched too close to the noisy Interstate 8 freeway. But Tom's directions took her up winding streets that boasted large, well-kept homes, none alike, most of La Mesa having been developed before the scourge of tract housing.

A profusion of daisies bloomed beside the walk of the Falls' sprawling, ranch-style house. More of the flowers filled a ceramic vase on the table in the kitchen, to which Tom led her through a well-furnished living room.

"Who's the gardener?" said Margo appreciatively.

"Vicki. This is her folks' place." Tom grimaced as if he were apologizing for his middle-class surroundings. He looked at home, nevertheless, sitting at the bright Formica table, crisp white curtains framing the window behind him. His longish blond hair was damp, as if he had just showered, and his T-shirt and jeans smelled of some lemony detergent. He reached for the pot warming on a Mr. Coffee and poured cups for Margo and himself, using matching mugs from a wooden rack on the wall. Margo had wondered what kept the Falls together, besides the unhealthy if compelling dance of bully and victim. Seeing Tom in the suburban house, she surmised that part of Vicki's appeal was her domesticity, a quality Tom surely wouldn't admit wanting for himself.

"Is Vicki here?" she asked.

"She should be back in a few minutes. She couldn't handle the idea of having you over without serving breakfast." Another grimace indicated what he thought of his wife's sense of social niceties. "Hope you like doughnuts."

Margo smiled weakly. After ten years in San Diego, she had become a good Californian, genuinely preferring whole-grain bread, grilled fish, basmati rice, salads, fruit, and vegetable stews. Not that she didn't experience regular cravings for Häagen-Dazs Vanilla Swiss Almond, and she adored sourdough bread. But the thought of greasy doughnuts made her stomach turn.

"Is it okay to tape?" She placed the tape recorder on the table.

"Sure, record away. If you're going to be interested in anything Tom Fall has to say, now that Susana Contreras has staged the art event of the decade."

"You don't actually think Susana staged her death?"

He shrugged. "Let's just say I think Susana had definite suicidal impulses and it would be natural for her to play them out in her work."

"Wait a second. Did she ever talk to you about killing herself?"

"She didn't have to talk about it. The entire body of her work is anti-life. All those barbs and sharp edges in her sculpture. That's why it sells so well, because this is essentially a death-loving culture. Besides, all you had to do was look at Susana. I don't know the official theory on anorexia, but it strikes me that someone who doesn't take any nourishment may be someone with a profound distaste for life."

Tom Fall seemed a dubious source of psychological insight; still, could he have hit on some nugget of truth? Susana, defending her plan to lie on the spiky "bed" in her installation, had said that any pain she might suffer was minor, compared to Frida Kahlo's suffering. How far might she have taken her attempt to identify with an artist whose work, as Susana had said herself, was full of bleeding wounds?

Nevertheless, "The police say she died of unnatural causes," said Margo.

"Sure. Pills." He paused. "Could you turn off the tape recorder? Thanks. I don't want anyone suing me. Like I said, I bet it was pills or some kind of drug. Jill could've gotten anything for her."

"Did Susana act like she was on drugs Saturday afternoon? Did she act strangely in any way?"

"I didn't see her Saturday." Tom made an odd stroking movement. A furry head poked up past the edge of the table, a white cat that had settled in his lap. "I went into the Capelli around eleven to take care of a few final details. Figured I'd be there an hour and then spend the afternoon surfing. Everyone has a way to psych themselves up for an opening and that happens to be mine. But I discovered a major programming problem, and I literally didn't leave the computer until the police showed up that night."

"Where is the computer?" Margo realized she'd never seen it.

"There's a control booth just past the installation. Here, I'll show you." He found a piece of paper and drew her a diagram, assured freehand strokes attesting to years of traditional art training.

There was the sound of the garage door going up and a car entering. Tom stood, spilling the cat onto the floor, and opened the door between the kitchen and the garage. "Vick, you promised not to let Blanca in again!" he called.

"Oh, gosh. Sorry," came from the garage. "But I didn't let her in, I'm sure I didn't."

Tom winked. Margo was sure he'd admitted the cat himself. Nasty games he played with his wife's mind.

"Sorry, I'll get her out." Vicki came in carrying two plastic grocery sacks. "Blanca!" she called. "Here, kitty!" But the cat, evidently in league with Tom, had disappeared. "Sorry," Vicki apologized to Margo this time. "Gee, I hope you're not allergic to cats. Oh, you're not? Good. Are muffins okay? Blueberry and bran?"

"Great!" said Margo; if she'd been Blanca the cat, she would have purred with happiness at not having to eat doughnuts. "How about you, Vicki?" she asked as Vicki put out muffins, butter, and jam. "Did you see Susana on Saturday afternoon?"

"Think of how the space is set up," Tom answered for his wife. "Susana's door is on this side, toward the rear of the building." He added it to the diagram he'd made. "Look, you never have to pass it to go into or out of my installation. You ought to ask Jill, she was right down the hall. Hey, Vick, let me do that and you tell Margo what we did yesterday." Vicki had been unpacking the groceries. Tom gave her his chair and took over the task. As a show for company, it was wasted. Margo didn't believe for two seconds that Tom regularly did his share of household chores.

"We got to the Capelli at eleven and started working on Tom's computer problem," said Vicki, picking at a muffin. "I don't know anything about computers, but Tom stayed in the control booth, and he'd make an adjustment to the program, then I'd test the door. And I did little things to help, like calling Peter to ask him to come in that night—of course he didn't, even though he said he would. I went out around three, to shop for something to wear at the opening. I came back at five with my dress and some Chinese takeout. Then, before I knew it, it was six and the opening was starting."

"So just in case you were wondering if there are any witnesses to prove Tom Fall didn't sneak down the hall and off Susana between three and five P.M.," said Tom, "the answer is no."

"Tom!" Vicki gasped.

He laughed and went on, "The problem is, why would I do it? I was no fan of Susana's, but aesthetic judgment isn't generally a motive for murder. Maybe it should be. Thing is, I'd do in a lot of people before I got to her. I'd start with the watercolor painters who set up their pathetic little seascapes in Mission Bay Park on Sundays and then the idiots who buy them and brag that they've got a masterpiece. Next I'd get the grade school art teachers who reward mediocrity and stifle genuine creativity. Then there are a few critics—"

"I think the show is just jinxed." Vicki glanced at Tom anxiously. "Think of what happened to Louise's car, and Dawn getting stuck in Tom's installation, and that horrid trick Jill played at the restaurant on Friday."

"I figure that might have given Susana the idea, what Jill did," put in Tom. "Like I said, the person who most wanted Susana dead was Susana."

The Falls walked Margo outside. They appeared to be arguing as she drove away. Good! Maybe Vicki was standing up for herself for a change.

Susana Contreras—whose name could now be released, her family having been informed—had died late Saturday afternoon as the result of a trauma, announced Lieutenant Donald Obayashi. The lieutenant stood in the same place as when he had come out with the Capelli officials the night before; and he looked as if he was wearing the same clothes. The courtyard bore signs of a late night as well: scattered paper plates and broken plastic wineglasses that a hasty cleanup had missed.

"What kind of trauma, Donny?" asked a reporter.

"We'd rather not say at this time, Norm."

Although the drama of Susana's death had drawn a number of reporters, like Margo, who weren't crime beat regulars, it was easy to spot those who were. They'd chatted and laughed with the police officials before the news conference started. And they seemed to be the only ones being called on.

"Is there any—" Margo yelled, waving her hand. Although she was standing at the front, in order to record Obayashi, he pointed to a woman from one of the television stations.

"Donny, I understand she was found lying on a sort of bed, as part of an art exhibit. Could she have been killed during the art opening?"

"We don't think that's possible, Joyce," he said, then added, "We do have a request to make. We hope you can help us put out the word that we're looking for someone." He displayed a sketch of Dawn and briefly described who the homeless woman was. Copies of the sketch would be available, he said.

"Is this lady a suspect?"

"No, Steve, we just want to talk to her."

The lieutenant stood aside to allow a pale but impeccably dressed James Carmichael to express the deep shock and sorrow he felt personally and on behalf of the Capelli Foundation. James announced that the foundation would be closed to the public for the coming week.

"Can we go in and look at the room where this artist was killed?" someone called out.

James deferred to the lieutenant. "You can't go inside the room," said Obayashi. "But you can take photographs from the hall. That's it, folks."

There was a rush of reporters and camera crews toward the door of the Capelli. Margo wanted another look at Susana's installation, but she hung back—Lieutenant Obayashi had remained outside.

"Donny!" she said, approaching him. Could you sue your parents for sticking you with a name that stopped being cute when you were fifteen?

"News conference is over, miss."

"Hey, Donny, she's okay." Margo looked over and saw . . . Could it be Kevin Marsh, minus the Lord Byron locks he'd worn when they had taken classes together at San Diego State? "Donny, this is Margo Simon," said Kevin. "You still with KSDR, babe?"

Kevin's affinity for Byron had been more than tonsorial. He had written poetry and edited a literary magazine. An "older student" like herself, he'd gone back to school after working in coffeehouses and trying his hand at technical writing for several years. He'd decided journalism was a better way to support the muse. After graduation, he had taken a job with a small Arizona newspaper. "Nothing happens in Yuma," he'd said. "There's got to be time for poetry." So how did he get to be pals with a San Diego homicide cop?

"Pleased to meet you, Margo," said the lieutenant. "What can I do for you?"

"Is there any chance Susana's trauma could be self-inflicted?"

Donny Obayashi shook his head. "We're regarding this as a homicide."

"I'm curious about the way she was lying on the bed."
For a moment the picture appeared vividly in Margo's mind:
Susana turned on her side, face toward the wall. "Was she
killed there, or could she have been killed somewhere else
and then placed on the bed?"

"This a good friend of yours, Kevin?" said Obayashi.

Kevin nodded. Maybe Obayashi wrote poetry on the side?

"Then why don't you tell her what you know? This guy,"
Obayashi said to Margo, "has better sources than I do."

Everything looked much the same as before in Susana's
installation. But the bed was gone and the wooden floor,
where it had stood, bore a dark stain.

"Blood?" Margo gulped.

"Sure is." Kevin ought to know. It turned out he'd been a
crime reporter on one of the county's larger area newspapers
for a year. Still staring at the blood stain, Kevin said, "Want
some lunch? I know a Japanese place near here."

Margo harbored no illusions that Kevin would give her
any information gleaned as the result of months of devel-
oping relationships with people in the police department.
Sharing didn't come with the territory. Furthermore, Kevin,
for all his poetic posturing, had always had a competitive,
manipulative streak. That was one reason, although his wit
had brightened their classes together, she hadn't kept in touch
after graduation. (Another reason was Kevin's persistence,
that had yielded to neither calm requests nor rage, in calling
every woman "babe.") Still, she'd had nothing but a bagel
and a muffin all morning. If she didn't eat a real meal soon,
she was going to start gnawing on her tape recorder.

"What about your poetry?" she asked when they had sat
down in the restaurant and ordered—the sushi platter for
Kevin, shrimp tempura for her.

"I still write it. Grittier than before, but that's good."

"Tempura shrimp. Is crime reporting the way you're paying your dues before you get to edit the book review section?"

"Can you believe it, babe?" he said. "I've found my spot, as that old shaman, Don Juan, used to say. I dig writing about crime. It's real, it's immediate. I got into it in Yuma. The paper I was on was small and general assignment reporters did damn near everything. Turned out I had a talent for it. Every poet needs a second calling. Wallace Stevens had the insurance company. William Carlos Williams was a doctor and wrote poems between patients. Me, I've got rape, arson, assault, murder. Want some yellowtail, babe?" he said when their meals arrived.

"No, thanks." Margo had to be in the right frame of mind for sushi, and this wasn't it.

"So," concluded Kevin, "they were looking for another crime reporter here, and I figured it was time to come back home. What are you doing covering a murder? It's not exactly public radio's cup of tea." He lifted his teacup in appreciation of his own pun.

She explained about the story she was doing on the Capelli artists.

"Sounds like you spent a lot of time with Susana Contreras just before she died." Kevin spoke casually, but he had a predatory look.

"Um," she said, finishing a mouthful of tempuraed zucchini. Equally casually, "I guess you've found out some things that Obayashi wasn't willing to disclose officially."

"A few. Of course, nothing for publication or broadcast until the cops give the go-ahead."

Over green tea ice cream, Margo traded her impressions of Susana and the people surrounding her for what Kevin had learned from his network: Susana had not been lying on the bed when, in the prose of Kevin's informant, "she suffered the trauma that resulted in her death."

"In other words," he translated the police jargon, "someone moved her to the bed afterward."

"Why?"

"Think about it, babe. She's lying on the floor with blood all around her and someone looks in, say someone checking to see if she's ready before the opening. Right away, the cops are called, everything's sealed off before the crowd gets in. The way it happened, the killer had more time to get away. Plus, it created confusion as to exactly when and how Susana was killed. And look at all the people who went into that room. There've got to be fingerprints on top of fingerprints on top of fingerprints." He paused, as if tasting the repetition for a future poem. "It turns the police investigation into a nightmare. Instead of just having to talk to ten or twenty people who were hanging out before the opening—the artists, caterers, what have you—they've got to question two or three hundred people who went into that exhibit."

"But if they're sure she was killed before the opening, why question people who got there later?"

"What if there's a piece of evidence that someone moved? Or say the killer was at the opening and acted weird? You know the saying about the murderer returning to the scene of the crime."

"Do you know how she was killed?"

"Only in the weird terminology the cops use." Kevin sighed, fluttering long, silky eyelashes, the kind reserved for men in an unjust world. "Do you know they don't say 'postmortem,' they call it 'the morgue scene'? I used that in a poem—'the morgue scene.' "

"What did they say about Susana?"

"A sharp object entered her left side and went straight to her heart. She died almost instantly."

"A knife?" Margo pictured the blade Dawn carried. No wonder the police were asking every television station and newspaper to carry her picture.

"All they're saying is 'a sharp object.' "

Kevin was clearly holding back. But Margo hadn't answered all of his questions, either. For instance, she had claimed not to know how to reach Isa. That was where she went next.

The Hotel Tropico was the kind of place Margo could imagine Susana and Isa staying, or maybe it was just a place she liked herself. Resembling a Mexican hotel more than one north of the border, the Tropico consisted of half a dozen two-story stucco buildings, clean but slightly blowsy. The buildings were plopped around a swimming pool, amid lush, haphazardly tended greenery. The receptionist had mentioned Isa's room number when Margo called earlier. It was a second-floor room, and Margo walked up the stairs and knocked. No answer.

"Isa? Barbara?" she called.

The drapes were drawn, so she couldn't look inside.

Downstairs, one of the poolside lounge chairs beckoned her. Ah! She would just sit for five minutes, then go to KSDR and do her story. In spite of the rather brisk, overcast afternoon, four children were playing in the shallow end (a glance, none of them was Mickey) and an older boy was doing his best to swim laps around them. Margo thought of herself as a touchy sleeper; for instance, she never even attempted to doze on airplanes. But she must have dropped off, because when she jerked upright, she was surprised to find herself a thirty-eight-year-old woman lying on a chaise at the Tropico. In her mind, she had been riding a roller coaster, and no older than the teenage boy who had dripped water on her, waking her up.

"Gee, I'm sorry," the boy said. He flinched as she looked at him—self-conscious about his body in baggy, surfer-style swim trunks? He was nicely proportioned if a little scrawny, a problem a few years would solve. He grabbed a T-shirt from the chair next to her and pulled it over his head. The T-shirt bore the words *The Cure*.

"No problem," said Margo. "You like the Cure?"

"Yeah."

"My stepdaughter does, too. Her birthday's coming up. Where could I get her a shirt like that?"

"Dunno. I got mine in L.A."

"You're from L.A.? Oh! You must be Orion. Your mom said you were staying here. In fact, I came to see her. Are you going up now?"

"Uh . . ."

"I was nervous about knocking, I thought she might be sleeping, but if I could go in with you . . ."

What a jerk she was for taking advantage of a kid! She'd give hell to anyone who did that to Jenny or David. Isa must have felt the same way.

"What the fuck are you up to?" said Orion's mother, running barefoot down the stairs. She planted herself between Margo and her son.

"I came over to see if you were all right."

"Mo-om," said Orion, glancing nervously to see if anyone was looking.

"The hell you did," said Isa. "I suppose that's why you're carrying a tape recorder, just to see if I'm all right. You called this morning and didn't remind Barbara you're a reporter, and now you're trying to get information from a teenager. You've got your nerve."

Orion grabbed for Isa's hand. "It's okay, Mom. I didn't tell her anything. Please, let's go."

"If you want to talk to me, you ask me," said Isa. "Don't try to pump my friends. And goddammit, you stay away from my kids."

Isa hurried Orion up the stairs. Standing at the top of the stairway, looking frightened, was Barbara Scholl.

Margo doubted that Barbara's original hotel had been the faded Tropico; probably she'd only come there to assist Isa. Still, it couldn't hurt to try to solve a small mystery: Why had Barbara acted so flustered on the phone that morning, when she'd talked about what time she'd arrived in San Diego?

Margo went into the lobby. The desk clerk, a gum-chewing young woman probably not much older than Orion, didn't look as if discretion ranked high on her list of customer services. Still, this felt like a job for which journalism school was not Margo's best resource. Instead, hiding her tape recorder in her big Guatemalan bag, she called on another aspect of her education: high school drama club.

"I'm looking for a friend of mine," she told the clerk. "She's staying at a hotel on Shelter Island, but would you believe I forgot which one? Barbara Scholl, is she registered here?"

"Yeah, she's here. She a friend of yours?" The desk clerk frowned.

Margo, taking the cue, frowned back and sighed. "Actually, my cousin."

"Oh." The woman snickered.

"You'd think Barb could come out to see me," Margo continued the fiction. "But no, I had to hire a babysitter for the kids and drive in from El Cajon." She was having so much fun lying, she stopped herself before she got tangled up in a whopper. "I bet she's giving you grief, too. She got here yesterday, didn't she, around four, four-thirty?" Barbara had said she'd arrived an hour or two before the opening.

"I wish," said the clerk. "Then my shift would have been over. She checked in at one-fifteen, see?" The clerk called up a computer screen. "And then it was room service this and room service that, you'd think this was the fucking Hilton. Look what she ordered." Everything was neatly listed on the screen. "A bottle of champagne and a six-pack of Coca-Cola. Except none of the champagne we had on hand was good enough for her, so Alberto had to run out and get something French. I guess our Coke met her standards.

"Well, I guess you want to see her even if she is a pain," said the desk clerk as Margo turned to leave. "Don't you want to know what room she's in?"

"Oh, of course." Lucky she hadn't tried a more elaborate lie.

"D-108."

"Is that near A-211?" Isa's and Susana's room number. Barbara had probably chosen the Tropico because her client was staying there.

"No. In fact, your cousin specifically asked not to be near building A. Her room is at the other end of the courtyard."

Curiouser and curiouser, as Alice in Wonderland would have said. Barbara *had* lied about when she'd arrived in town. And why stay in the same hotel as Susana but request a room as far away as possible? Margo had no time to think about it, however. Like the White Rabbit, she was late.

Margo had called Frank and Laura Van Dyne earlier in the day, and they'd promised to wait until five o'clock for her, but no longer. At four-fifty-eight, when she reached their house, they were already in their van. Margo jumped out of her car and joined them.

"Thanks for waiting. I hope I didn't screw you up."

Frank grunted and started the van.

"Don't mind him," said Laura. "He just liked the way the soup smelled tonight, and he can't wait to get back home and have some himself. Hey, you look beautiful but a little tired," she added, with genuine concern. Laura seemed to have enough caring for the entire world, certainly for the eighty or so homeless people in Balboa Park that she and Frank fed nightly.

"I am. Tired, that is. How are you doing?"

"Same old same old," said Frank, in better humor now that the van was moving down the freeway.

Since Margo had first met the sixtyish couple two years ago, she had tried to accompany them on their nightly rounds once a month, and not just for their connections among the park's homeless. She sought out Frank and Laura for inspiration. They were the most truly religious people she'd ever met. They saw their mobile soup kitchen as a natural expression of their Quaker beliefs, of which they spoke simply and only when she probed. They preferred to discuss bargains they had found on vegetables or day-old bread—"good whole wheat bread, better for the bowels"—or tell stories they'd heard from their homeless friends.

"Are you still getting flak from the downtown shelter?" Margo asked as they exited the freeway onto Sixth Avenue, toward the park.

"No, that stopped after some of their people came out with us last month." Laura had tried a new hair color, an interesting shade of brown with violet highlights. "They worry because people like us, amateurs, don't offer the full range of services to the homeless that they do. The problem is, and they admit it, there just aren't enough of those services to go around."

Frank turned the van into the park, saying, "Another thing is a lot of the homeless here just will not go to the facilities downtown. They could see we reach people they're not getting to. The folks in the park have a real community among themselves, and they don't want to leave it. They don't want to have to deal with any of the bureaucracy at the shelters, either. I expect that's why you think the lady you're looking for might be here."

Not to mention the fact that—away from the popular zoo, theaters, and museums—the fourteen-hundred-acre park in the center of the city offered a multitude of places to hide.

Frank stopped near the shuffleboard court. With night falling, the Sunday afternoon park-goers—families with kids, people who used the shuffleboard court to do tai chi—had trickled away, leaving the area to its permanent inhabitants. Margo recognized several regulars among the dozen or so people who approached the van from the trees. She joined Frank and Laura in chatting with the group, which included only two women, typical of the park's homeless population. While the Van Dynes passed around big Styrofoam cups of soup, plastic spoons, and sandwiches, Margo got out the drawing of Dawn and showed it around.

"What do you want with her?" Lee, a Vietnam vet, was something of a leader of the loose tribe that congregated in this part of the park. The question wasn't combative. Lee, who was articulate and smart when sober, made Margo think of an insurance purchaser reading the fine print, the middle-class family man another history might have made him.

"She's in trouble. I want to talk to her, I think I can help her."

"Police?"

"They're looking for her."

He gave Margo a measuring look. "Okay. I'll put the word out about her, and if someone sees her I'll tell Frank and Laura."

She had similar conversations at the Van Dynes' three other stops. Her hopes went up in the Pepper Grove, at the southeast end of the park, where there were more women than usual, half a dozen in a group of eighteen or twenty people. The women were protected, confided Laura, by one of their own—Holly, a delicate name for a woman who was six feet tall and must weigh two hundred pounds. Word had it Holly was ex-Navy, and even the biggest men stayed out of range of her fists when she got mad.

No one Margo asked, however, claimed to have seen Dawn.

They might well be telling the truth, said Frank as he drove back to the freeway. Since Dawn had been well fed by Susana, she could probably hide for several days before hunger forced her to surface.

"We'll keep you posted if we hear anything," Laura said. "Want to try the soup? We've got extra. Turkey noodle. The supermarket down the street donated the turkey, and it's delicious, if I do say so myself."

"Thanks, I'll take a cup home with me."

"Take one for Barry, too. With our compliments."

Dawn heard a rustling in the bushes, somewhere off to the right, and flattened herself against the ground. The ground was cold, but that wasn't why she was shivering. Two things kept coming back to her, the way she'd seen Susana last and the way the man attacked the big silver car. It was like the two memories were blending together and the man was thrusting the knife at Susana, saying, "Bitch! Bitch!" the same way he'd hurt the car.

The rustling got closer and she grabbed for her knife. But it was only the big woman who'd found her this morning and promised to help. Holly. Dawn was beginning to recognize Holly, like she used to know Susana when everyone else was just a blur.

Holly handed Dawn a cup of turkey soup and half a sandwich. "I'm not hungry tonight," the big woman said. "Really, you eat it. Us women have got to stick together."

12 / Purple Haze

How many of the green pills had she taken, anyway? And why weren't they putting her to sleep? Blearily Jill tried to read the lighted numbers of the digital clock on the dresser. Boy, those pills weren't knocking her out the way they were supposed to, but they sure made things soft around the edges. An interesting effect. Hell no, wait a second. She groped across the night table for her glasses, knocked them to the floor. Reached over the side of the bed—damn, she'd better find the glasses now or she'd step on them in the morning. Maybe it was morning already. But once she found her glasses, she saw it was only two A.M. Too early to get up and . . . and what? That was a problem: She had no will to do anything, an affliction for which there must be a long, guttural German name. Well, no way was she going to spend the rest of the night lying sleepless in bed.

She pulled on sweats over her T-shirt and panties and rinsed her face. The night was chilly, but she'd been sweating. Her hair was matted to her head. She ruffled it into spikes, went into the kitchen and poured herself a glass of apple juice, then headed for the living room. She turned on the TV. Sat in her favorite chair. Rolled a joint, lit it, and took a long, satisfying toke. That was more like it. Stick to the drug you know best. Drugs, she amended, watching the picture flickering on the black-and-white set. Nothing like telly to turn your brain to happy jelly. An Edward G. Robinson flick was on, *The Amazing Dr. Clitterhouse*. Wait a sec, she must have heard that wrong. No, it really was the title. How did that ever get by the censors? "The Amazing Dr. Clitoris," she said out loud. Definitely a name for a future performance. That turned her to Drug Number Three. She sent her hand on a languid dive into her panties. From the time she was little, pleasuring herself had been one of the best ways to blot out everything else, first her mother's drinking and later her own thoughts.

But tonight nothing kept her from thinking. She watched Edward G. on the tube and saw the same thing she'd been seeing while she lay awake for hours: Susana at the Capelli on Saturday afternoon.

Stick to the drug you know best. Jill ought to embroider that on a sampler, the kind her great-aunt used to make. If she went to a craft store, would they help her get one started? The afternoon before any performance, she always sent her helpers away, looked over the final setup of the space, and then got stoned. It was a ritual, a way to soften her intellect so she could dive through it to the visceral core from which she pulled her art. She had tried new stuff on Saturday and maybe she should have tested it first, but it was supposed to be from one of the best growers in Mendocino County.

She always liked to do the grass about two hours before a show, so the most intense, immediate effect would wear off by the time she was actually performing. She would be at the perfect level of stonedness then to feel loose and courageous, but totally in control. Just that stoned, she'd had the guts to walk on a catwalk in high heels at a gallery in Denver; and in New York, to nick her own fingers with razor blades. A joint before one of her earliest performances had helped her find the nerve and rage and sorrow to talk about her mother's alcoholism, breaking the family secret. "No more lies" was her motto after that, and Jill had leaped toward truth like wax-winged Daedalus, with that little boost she got from the grass.

The stuff was just starting to hit on Saturday when Susana came into her room. Jill was sure she remembered the beginning of the conversation. Susana had heard about Jill's fake seizure in the restaurant the day before, and it made her think about Dawn being trapped in Tom's installation. She had told Dawn never to go into Tom's room alone, but maybe, she said, looking directly at Jill, someone had coaxed Dawn inside?

"Sure, I did it," Jill admitted easily. When an art-life piece was in progress, revealing her role in it would contaminate the experience. Later, it didn't matter. "I wanted to find out if she could yell if she needed to."

"Goddamn you!" Susana grabbed Jill's shoulders and screamed into her face. "Did you think about how it was going to affect Dawn? She's not all there mentally, and she doesn't have the ability to take care of herself the way the rest of us do. You had no right to fuck around with somebody so helpless!"

Jill took a moment to review her feelings, looking for any remorse. She found none. Nor was she angry at Susana for yelling at her. She could have twisted out of Susana's grasp; although shorter, she had the advantage in weight. But the confrontation was interesting. Jill assumed a psychiatrist would consider her lack of feeling problematic, even pathological. However, she truly believed that experience was worth whatever discomfort it took to achieve it, and that the experiences she created for others were ultimately liberating, no matter how furious people got at the time.

Getting lost in her thoughts must have speeded up the action of the dope, because her recollection of things after that was really fuzzy. She and Susana had both yelled, maybe they had even pushed each other? Whatever happened, it was gone now. Just let it come, she always told herself when a memory eluded her. But there was only one more image, and it was the one she couldn't stop seeing: Susana standing in the doorway of Jill's room. The look on her face was terrible.

After waiting for half a dozen rings, Margo heard a receiver being picked up. Then it sounded as if the entire phone was dropped and the receiver snatched up again.

"Hello?" came a muzzy-sounding voice.

"Jill? Are you okay?"

"God, what time is it?"

"Ten. I'm sorry if I woke you. It's Margo Simon."

"Um, oh, right, the radio person," croaked Jill. "Dances like a fiend. Shit, I'm really . . . I fell asleep in the chair."

"I just wanted to ask a few follow-up questions from our talk last week."

"Um, no. I can't. I was blown away by what happened to Susana, I can't talk to anybody."

"I could come by this afternoon, just for a few minutes. Jill?"

She'd hung up. Margo slammed down her own receiver. She generally did stories where people were eager to talk to her—they saw being interviewed as an opportunity to tell the world about their youth program or the play they were producing or their opinion of U.S. immigration policy. If Alex had given Claire De Jong the assignment, as he'd threatened, would the savvy young reporter have tricks to get Jill to spill her guts?

Margo had better luck with her next two calls. Louise O'Quinn agreed to see her at eleven. And Carola Yang was sure that her boss, James Carmichael, could give Margo at least fifteen minutes late Wednesday afternoon. James's secretary sounded aggrieved.

"Things must be crazy for you," said Margo sympathetically.

Carola had clearly been itching for someone to complain to.

"I have to cancel all James's appointments for today and tomorrow and call the media to make sure they know we're closed this week," she said resentfully. "Thirty different calls! As if I didn't work all day Saturday getting ready for the opening, not that this job pays overtime. And I had to come in before eight this morning and would you believe it, organize breakfast! James and Bernard are meeting all day with Esther Praske and three of her people, they're figuring out what spin to put on this thing." Praske Associates was one of San Diego's top public relations firms.

"You can't just get a dozen doughnuts for them, either," Carola continued. "It's got to be croissants and scones. And I was making the coffee and Esther said, 'Don't you have any decaf, dear?' Decaf at seven-thirty in the morning! I had to make two different pots. Esther's got three-inch red fingernails, never has to touch a computer keyboard herself, I guess. Personally, I don't think we need any PR help. The phone's ringing off the hook today, everyone wants to know how to get here and when we're going to open again." Margo was hearing ringing in the background; Carola must be ignoring the other lines. "I say as long as nobody here actually did the deed, Susana's murder is the hottest publicity the Capelli will ever get."

"Do you have any idea who did it?"

"Dawn, who else? Unless it was a street person from outside. The side door was unlocked—it's where you go upstairs, at the end of the hallway past Susana's door. Someone would be getting major shit for leaving the door open if anyone knew who was responsible. Not me, at any rate. I was out in front the whole time."

"You said you worked on Saturday. What did you do?"

Carola's sniff was audible over the phone. "If it was menial, I did it. Met the caterers and musicians and showed them where to set up. At least the guitarist was cute. Made sure we had press packets ready for the art critics attending. Picked up trash around the building. I've got the real glamour job here."

"What about Susana? Did you see her?"

"Not me. One of the caterers wandered down that way, around four or four-thirty. His supervisor bawled him out— they were told just to go inside for the bathrooms and to stay away from the art, just in case anyone had any illusions this wasn't an elitist institution. Who knows what would happen if a Filipino food service worker got a look at high culture? Anyway, you'd think if Susana was being murdered at the time, he would have said something about it.

"Well, look, I'd better get moving on these phone calls," said Carola. "Lawrence Presley will show up at eleven-thirty if I don't head him off at the pass. That's the one good thing about all this. James is canceling the meeting with Presley, so I don't have to spend the entire morning trying to get together financial records for them to review. I haven't broken it to James, but whenever I have to do anything financial, I usually save it and ask this one volunteer to help me when she comes in. James seemed happy about that, too—calling off the meeting with Lawrence Presley, I mean. I asked if I should reschedule it and he said yeah, make it for the next millennium on Jupiter. Well, bye-bye."

Margo hung up the phone and turned toward Ray Fernandez, with whom she shared a cramped office.

"Lawrence Presley, what do you know about him?" she asked Ray. *Someone* had mentioned Presley's name during her interviews at the Capelli—who?

"As well-known as Elvis in certain local circles," said Ray. "And debatably more alive. His firm, Ormond, Gelb, Presley, and Hyatt, does the accounting for most of the top businesses in town. Don't tell me Presley killed Susana Contreras?" There was an edge to Ray's voice, and he exaggerated the perfect trilling *r* in *Contreras* that Margo, for all her years of Spanish, would never master.

"Hey, what's the problem?" she asked.

"No problem. I think any time a major Chicana artist dies, you should get the story and Alex should supervise it personally. Did you know he told Dennis to keep hands off?"

No wonder, when Margo had said hello to Dennis in the hall earlier, the news director had shot her a resentful look, just as Ray was doing now. Margo needed to have a talk with Ray, but it would have to wait. If she didn't leave now, she'd be late for her interview with Louise O'Quinn.

13 / An Arbiter of Taste

When the occasional Hollywood star buys a San Diego County hideaway, it's often a little place in Rancho Santa Fe. Located some twenty-five miles north of downtown San Diego, and just inland enough to still get an ocean breeze—but avoid the beach riffraff—Rancho Santa Fe's wooded hills contain some of the priciest real estate in the nation. The minimum lot size is two acres and about one-fifth of the residents stable their horses at home.

Louise O'Quinn had sixteen acres, she informed Margo, who was trying to control the gape that had taken over her face as soon as she'd approached the entrance to Louise's estate, a stone gate embedded with tiles, reminiscent of the Spanish architectural genius, Gaudí. After she had identified herself—via a speaker concealed in a similarly Gaudí-like post—the gate swung open and she nursed her six-year-old Toyota down a curving road (intimidated, the car started missing on one cylinder). At last she arrived at a monumental structure standing on a rise.

If Louise had had a motto emblazoned on her gate, it should have been: "If you've got it, flaunt it." As large as a mid-sized library, the art critic's house was classical in its clean, symmetrical arches and proportions, yet boldly contemporary in the way the cream-colored concrete served as a grid for color and line. Two strips of ocher brick girdled the lower part of the building, and a thick horizontal of jade green went around the top, outlining the arch above the green door. Playing with elements of classical style, Louise's architect had placed column-shaped verticals of rose concrete bisecting the horizontals. These were topped by ocher plates suggesting capitals.

Incongruous against this *Architectural Digest* background, Louise herself looked as if she'd just stepped off the ranch. She was wearing a gray sweater, faded jeans, and boots. Riding boots, observed Margo enviously. She had adored riding when she'd lived in New Mexico, but had rarely done it since moving to San Diego. The for-hire mounts at local stables couldn't compare with the horses her friends had cared for lovingly.

"I planned to get my exercise before you came." Louise, walking to greet her, completed the ranch hand look by hobbling slightly, like Walter Brennan. "But it's been one phone call after another. *Artforum* wants me to write Susana's obit, the *New York Times* needed a quote by ten-fifteen, and my husband—the film producer George Wiksel—called from Rome. And of course there were a few of the predictable media vultures digging to see if I knew whether Susana had any enemies.

"I don't suppose you ride?" added Louise.

Margo felt a softening in her limbs akin to sexual desire. Trotting along a trail was not the least bit conducive to recording a radio interview, but oh! the chance to be on a good horse again.

Louise clinched it. "We can stop along the way," she said, "and talk into your tape machine."

Margo followed her through the living room, receiving a brief impression of an eclectic mix of furniture and paintings. In the guest room to which Louise escorted her, Margo took off her good slacks, silk blouse, jacket, and pumps, and donned the jeans, sweatshirt, and boots Louise had given her. The jeans were loose, but the boots fit, which was all that really counted. Two paintings hung in the guest room. One was a triptych in which two of the panels depicted a family picnic and the third a machine gun. The other canvas showed a business-suited man in a contorted position. Sure enough—Margo checked the signature—it was one of Robert Longo's *Men in the Cities* paintings. It must have cost more than most people's entire houses, and Louise hid it away in the guest room! Then again, where better to impress the hell out of guests?

As they walked toward the stable, Louise's hobble became more pronounced. "Fifth lumbar," she explained. "My doctor says I shouldn't ride when it's acting up. But my doctor's from Manhattan. He may be the most brilliant orthopedist in Southern California, but what does he know about horses?"

Louise's equally brilliant landscape architect hadn't tried to fight Southern California's dry climate by planting grass or flowers, she continued her monologue; rather, he had left the native chaparral as the raw, vital setting for her sculpture garden, which was spread throughout her property. (Margo noticed that despite the mention of her husband, Louise consistently referred to "*my* sculpture garden," "*my* property.") Louise drew Margo's attention to a George Segal, a life-size couple turned away from one another under an oak tree. Nearby was a sculpture by Susana. "A student work," Louise said. "Susana had such astounding ability even then."

Then Margo was introduced to the bay horse Rauschenberg—Louise, not favoring any single period in art history, rode Botticelli—and Margo gave in to the bliss of feeling the strong, intelligent animal beneath her. They proceeded at an easy walk down a trail along the edge of Louise's land. Instead of the hazy Southern California sunlight, Margo imagined for a moment that she was riding under the purple dusk of the mountains; how caressing that light had been.

"Robert Irwin," Louise called out.

"What?" Pulled from her daydream.

"The screen in the treetops over there. It's a Robert Irwin." Louise twisted to point at it, then clutched at her lower back. "Goddamn it to hell!"

"Can I do anything?"

"Are you any good at massage?" Louise pulled up in a clearing and half-fell off her horse, in obvious pain.

"I can give it a try."

Even leaning forward against her horse, groaning while Margo rubbed her knotted muscles, Louise exuded an air of command.

"Thanks, that's much better," she said, turning to face Margo after five minutes of massage. "Since we're taking a break, why don't you turn on your tape recorder and I'll talk about Susana." Louise wore no makeup, and, whether from her back pain or from grief, her face looked as gray as her hair. Even her eyes were pale, a washed-out blue.

Margo took sound levels and invited Louise to begin.

"I discovered Susana," declared Louise O'Quinn. "I lecture at UCSD and every year I choose the most promising graduate art student to be . . . the job title is my assistant, but in essence I'm choosing a protégé, someone in whose career I take an interest and whom I do my best to guide and promote. Naturally, I'm in a position to help a young artist considerably, through my contacts with galleries and collectors, the major journals, things like that. Some years—and off the record, this was one—it's difficult to choose because no student really shows that combination of vision and talent that tells you this one could be a major artist. But

Susana! Susana was simply a revelation. Even at twenty-one or twenty-two, she knew her media and was claiming her themes with the kind of authority most artists work years to achieve. Of all the artists I've helped, she was the shining star."

Louise's Oklahoma twang stretched thin for a moment, then resumed. "We were very close friends as well. I become close to all my assistants—as I said, it's not just an employer-employee relationship, we're mentor and protégé. But Susana and I had a special bond. She and I were both, in our own ways, art world outsiders, westerners not just by birth but by temperament. And of course, she was with me for two years instead of the usual one."

"What do you mean?"

"Usually I choose a second-year grad student to be my assistant, after I've observed them all during the first year. So a young artist is with me for one year only. But I couldn't fail to recognize Susana's genius instantly. The first day I saw her work, I had no choice but to dismiss the student who had started with me that fall and give Susana the job. I've helped her career ever since. I pulled some strings that led to her first New York show, shortly after she completed her MFA. A great success! It was even at my urging that she was included in the current Capelli show. She had spoken to me about wanting to try an installation piece, and I convinced James to take a chance, even though she had never done installation art before. Oh, God." Louise placed her palms over her face and slowly drew them up to grasp her hair. A dramatic gesture, by a woman suited for drama.

"What did you think of Susana's installation?" asked Margo, when Louise had recovered her composure.

"More sensual than her sculpture, but it had the same integrity of purpose." Crisply, the professional critic replaced the bereaved mentor and friend. "Susana brilliantly appropriated Kahlo's images. As if she became almost more Kahlo than Kahlo herself."

"Was that good?"

"My back feels better, let's ride." Louise turned toward her horse.

"In a minute." Smiling, Margo placed a hand on Louise's arm. The art critic had been trying to manipulate the interview from the beginning. Was that because she had something to hide? Or was she simply accustomed to controlling everything around her—her art collection, her employees, her horses, her sound bites?

"Didn't you say, when you visited Susana last week, that Frida Kahlo was in love with death?" said Margo.

"I might have. I happen to believe that about Kahlo. And I've never been noted for keeping my opinions to myself." A wry smile made Margo smile back; Louise might be manipulative as hell, but she manipulated through a certain charm as well as through power.

"Was it good, if Susana became more Kahlo than Kahlo herself?" Margo asked.

"Artistically? What Susana did was marvelous. On a personal level, I was disturbed by the direction she was taking, not just in this piece but in her life. Keeping that homeless woman around—what was her name, Dawn? Susana didn't do that to be kind—kindness wasn't part of her psychological repertoire. I suspect she was fascinated with Dawn because Dawn was someone whose needs and ways of coping were reduced to the purely physical. Whereas Susana dealt in abstract symbols and ideas. You know the concept of the shadow? Dark parts of ourselves that we deny, but that sometimes appear in dreams or in people to whom we react strongly? Dawn was a part of Susana's shadow that she shouldn't have had around. I doubt that any of us is meant to know our dark side completely."

Louise swung onto her horse and urged it into a fast trot. Margo's mount needed only the lightest touch to follow. She would ache later, but this was glorious.

"My, you do know how to ride!" exclaimed Louise, slowing after ten minutes to a walk. Had she figured the fast pace would leave Margo lying bruised beside the trail? Maybe kindness had no place in Louise's repertoire, either.

"Here's Susana's other piece," she said, pointing out a harsh wire framework. Ferns grew within the frame, however, threading softly through the wire and providing an enchanting contrast with the sharpness of the sculpture.

"Did it start that way? With the ferns?"

"No. Susana loved the idea of the piece's changing over time like this. We spent a wonderful afternoon selecting the right site for it."

"Did you see Susana on Saturday?"

Louise O'Quinn had an expressive face. At the moment it was saying, "Media vultures," the term she'd used for the reporters who had asked her about Susana's murder.

"If I understand the disgusting thing you're getting at," the art critic said, "the last time I saw Susana Contreras was at the Capelli Foundation, the same day you and I met. Last Tuesday, wasn't it? On Saturday, I was with my assistant, Ed Milewski, downtown. We visited two galleries and did some shopping at Horton Plaza. Satisfied? I can't understand why anyone would waste their time or mine asking questions like this, when they should be looking for that crazy woman, Dawn."

"Dawn had problems, but it's hard to imagine her hurting Susana." Margo doubted she'd make the "A" list for

Louise's next party, anyway. "What about someone who hated Susana?"

"Do you think it's only hatred that leads to murder?"

The challenge in the critic's tone so engaged Margo that she was tempted to leap into the philosophical debate. But she persisted, "I'm wondering if someone had it in for Susana. Say, the student you fired when you gave Susana the job as your assistant. Has that person been successful?"

"As an artist, no. But she wasn't cut out for art. She had a certain talent, but not the kind of ambition you need, and definitely not the vision. At any rate, she's one person who'd never have begrudged Susana her success."

"Is she still in the area?"

"I shouldn't have mentioned it. If you must know, it was a woman named Isa Reid. You may have met her. She's Susana's lover."

14 / Downward Social Mobility

"I didn't know Isa was an artist," said Margo as she and Louise headed back to the stable.

"She's not." Louise dismounted gingerly, but gave no other sign that the ride had exacerbated her back pain. "Isa was always something of a flower child—into art a little, into herbs a little, into yoga. She teaches yoga now. The point is, one thing that held her back as an artist was that she's not competitive. She lacks the proverbial fire in the belly. So even though she was unhappy to lose the job with me, that wouldn't have turned her against Susana."

Margo had known a lot of noncompetitive people when she'd lived in New Mexico. At least she'd known people who claimed to be noncompetitive . . . and although there might be a few saints and gurus who had banished all those nasty competitive urges, she had never met one.

"I have to talk to my stableman for a minute," said Louise. "Can you find your way back to the house?"

"Yes. Thanks." Margo started to walk away, but turned back, saying, "Oh, just one other . . ." She stopped as she saw Louise clutching at her back. "Are you all right?"

"I'm-fine-what-do-you-want," Louise got out, as if through clenched teeth.

"I'm supposed to go to Jill Iverson's from here and I've lost the address. I wondered if you had it?"

"Ask Ed. The office, side of the house." Louise seemed to be in agony, but she clearly didn't want Margo's help.

Ed, Louise's assistant, was holding a submarine sandwich in one hand while he wrote Jill's address with the other. Seeing the mustard drip onto his desk, Margo realized she was ravenous. She smelled ritzy enough for one of the posh Rancho Santa Fe eateries, having spritzed on the Eau de Joy she'd found in Louise's guest bathroom, but she'd had her fill of the rich for one day. She drove out of Rancho Santa Fe into Encinitas, the more modest neighboring community where Jill lived. (Even the street names became more prosaic, Mimulus and Avenida del Cielo giving way to Encinitas Boulevard.)

Not far from Jill's, she stopped at a taco stand and ordered a burrito. "Make it two," she said, on what turned out to be a fortunate impulse.

Although Encinitas had its share of soulless new developments—identical stucco houses marching up manicured hillsides—Jill lived in a small wooden bungalow on a street of older houses. The main door was open, and Margo heard a television through the screen door.

"Jill?" she called, ringing the bell and knocking. "Jill?"

A gray cat padded toward her.

"Jill!" The door was unlocked and she went inside. The cat fled.

Margo found Jill Iverson sprawled in a chair in the living room, amid scattered clothes, magazines, and two full ashtrays. A bottle of pills stood on the table next to her, and the place was redolent with the sweet odor of marijuana.

"Jill! Wake up!" She shook Jill's arm roughly. She couldn't handle finding another dead artist, two days after Susana.

"What . . . ?" Jill's eyes opened to a squint. She reached toward the table, fingers searching. Recognizing the movement, Margo handed Jill her glasses from the floor. Jill put on the glasses and pushed herself up to her full five feet. "Go 'way."

"I just want to talk to you for a few minutes. I brought some lunch."

"No. M'lawyer says . . . Lunch?"

"Vegetarian burritos."

"I like carne asada better. But all right. I've got a violent case of the munchies. Did you get salsa?"

"Extra hot and also gringo strength. Why don't I make some coffee?"

Searching for the coffeemaker among the dirty dishes, used tea bags, cigarette butts, and opened cookie boxes in the kitchen, Margo nonetheless sensed an underlying order to the little house, as if Jill were an essentially tidy person who had let things go for a few days. Into every life a little chaos must fall. She got the coffee going and returned to the living room.

"My lawyer says not to talk to the media," said Jill. She had already polished off half her burrito.

Margo switched off the television. "How come you have a lawyer?"

"Strictly off the record and only because you're feeding me, the police have been coming around asking lots of questions. They see a dope-smoking hippie and it's Charles Manson time. I'm in real trouble if they find out one of my performances was *Household Hints from Squeaky Fromme*. Squeaky was one of Manson's women, remember?" Something in Jill's laugh reminded Margo of their interview the week before—not when the artist was gaily recounting her wild youth, but when she had talked about despair.

"Is that what you were on, on Saturday night? Marijuana?"

"That's the kind of question the lawyer says not to answer. He costs too much not to follow his advice. Are you going to eat that whole burrito?"

Margo cut off a chunk oozing with guacamole and handed it over, although she was tempted to bargain with it—two bites for each answer Jill gave her?

"I suppose you saw Susana Saturday afternoon," she said.

"Saturday's a closed book. I promised Lyman. Lyman's my lawyer, although he says he really lives for art. He's one of those literary types who went to law school to make money, and now he hangs out around people like me so he can feel authentic. Did you know it was a lawyer who nailed Chris Burden to the Volkswagen for his crucifixion piece? No shit. No one else would do it. The lawyer just picked up the hammer and Chris became Christ. Anyway, Lyman tells me he's followed my work for years. Not that he's giving me a cut rate for all the thrills I've provided. I may have to fuck him to get that. Does it help if you're fucking your lawyer? Maybe you have to fuck a cop. I'll go see if the coffee's ready."

"Come on, off the record," Margo called after her. "You aren't really expecting to be charged with something?" Jill might have had the opportunity to murder Susana, the two of them down the hall from each other at the Capelli on Saturday before the opening. But for what conceivable motive?

"Margo, do you take sugar in your coffee? 'Fraid the milk's gone sour."

"No. Black, thanks."

After one more unsuccessful try to penetrate Jill's adroit defenses—Lyman had coached his client well—Margo gave up and let herself linger in friendly silence with the artist, relishing the coffee and the ocean breeze through the door; feeling her limbs deliciously tired from riding that morning, as well.

"I don't seem to be able to tell you anything," said Jill companionably. "So why don't you tell me something? How are they taking all this at the Capelli?"

"They've declared a PR emergency and canceled an appointment with Lawrence Presley." Margo suddenly remembered, if not what she'd heard about Presley the week before, at least who had given her the information, amid a stream of art world gossip. "Jill, what did you say about Lawrence Presley when we talked last week?"

"I was saying how brilliant it was of Bernard to put Presley on the Capelli Foundation board. A few months ago some of the board members were agitating to hire a financial director, someone to be on staff full-time. James argued, quite rightly, that too many suits destroy the art. He felt so strongly about it, he said that if the board insisted, he'd resign. It was pretty tense, but then Bernard suggested that, instead of hiring someone, they should put Presley on the board. Board members never do much besides raise money and show up at parties, but it appeased the conservative contingent. More coffee?"

"No, thanks, I've got to get downtown. Hey." She put a hand on Jill's shoulder as she left. "Take care of yourself." It was funny the way Jill brought out in her the same feelings as the kids when they were acting reckless—the urge to protect her and the helplessness of knowing complete protection was impossible.

Driving down the San Diego Freeway toward downtown, Margo considered the implications of what Jill had said. James Carmichael had resisted hiring a financial officer, even putting his own job on the line, and this morning he had happily canceled a meeting with the accountant who had joined the board as a compromise. Okay, but what could that have to do with Susana's death? Susana would hardly have concerned herself with the foundation's balance sheets.

And why wouldn't James have been relieved to put off a meeting with Lawrence Presley? she continued to argue with herself. Margo didn't relish her own annual sessions with her tax woman. Accountants were like dentists, necessary but painful, except you didn't get a free toothbrush afterward.

"My favorite radio reporter!" declared Kay Lorenzo, her arms open wide.

Hugging Kay, Margo was amazed, as always, at the social worker's birdlike rib cage and at how much energy and savvy resided in the deceptively fragile body. A force in local politics, Kay had founded the G Street Women's Center, a daytime refuge for homeless women housed in a sparkling white downtown storefront. Margo had done several stories on the center . . . which was never enough for Kay, who called her at least once a month to pitch new ideas. But Kay did it with such warmth and genuine concern for the women at the center that Margo didn't object.

She hadn't seen Dawn, said Kay, and she speculated that if Dawn felt threatened, she might have tried to make it back to Los Angeles, to the shelter where she had met Susana originally. If she *had* remained in San Diego, she would most likely avoid any of the official shelters, fearing she'd be turned in to the police. Someone might have noticed her on the street, however. Kay offered to let Margo ask questions among the thirty or so women gathered at the center this afternoon.

Several women in the lounge and the children's play area claimed to recognize the drawing of Dawn. But each one, having gained Margo's attention, launched into her own story. Margo vowed to do another piece on the center soon, as she cut short the tales of Gail's belongings stolen on the way from Ohio, the job Roseanne was sure to get soon since she had plenty of waitressing experience, the man who'd abandoned Nancy after she got pregnant—but look, isn't the baby beautiful?

In the laundry room, Margo received an unexpected piece of information from Christina, a sour-looking black woman who was swathed in a blanket so she could wash everything at once.

"She's the one the cops been lookin' for, ain't she?" said Christina, perusing the sketch. " 'Cause of that murder at the artsy place down the street? See, I knows 'bout that 'cause I reads the paper. Some of them women dunno the first thing 'bout what's goin' on. But me, I's info'med. Keeps my eyes open, too. Seen some'in' funny at that art place las' week." She paused.

"What did you see?" Margo prompted. Inexplicably the sound of mariachi music came into her mind.

Christina walked to the other end of the small laundry room, humming to herself. Margo suddenly knew why she had thought of Mexico—remembering a hotel in Ensenada where the desk clerk had waited five minutes until she and Barry, naive Anglos, finally understood he wanted a "tip."

"You're sure you saw something at the art foundation?" she called over the thrum of the clothes dryer. "The blue and white building?"

Christina strolled back to her. "Said so. Din I?"

Margo pressed a ten dollar bill into Christina's hand. The same amount in Mexico had gotten them a romantic room with an ocean view. Christina looked at the bill and frowned. Taking back the ten, Margo gave her a twenty instead. Did KSDR reimburse for this kind of thing?

"Thanks," said Christina gravely, stuffing the money into the top of her blanket. "See, I been walkin' down the alley behind the buildin', by the parkin' lot, y'know? I seen a man squattin' down like he hiding, next to a big car, one of them Mersaydees or some'in'. He was scratchin' the bejesus outa that car wit' a knife, like carvin' up somebody's face, y'know? Somebody he really hates."

"Was the man a street person?"

From the thin, unhappy face came a whoop of laughter. "Course not! Street people got betta things to do than that. You mess with rich people's cars like that, so you can get inside and see if they's got money or some'in' to sell. This musta been somebody from that art place."

"What did he look like?"

"Some white guy, not real young, not real old. Dressed, not fancy but nice. Clean clothes, y'know, and they fit. I ain't seen 'im up close 'cause when I seen what he doin' I get outa there real fast. They blamin' things on people like me all the time. But man!" Christina laughed so hard she had to clutch the blanket around her to keep it from slipping. "Why would we do a dumb thang like that?"

15 / Ask Dr. Science

She had gotten fair value for her twenty dollars, thought Margo, walking the three blocks from the women's center to the downtown library. Christina's story jibed with what had happened to Louise O'Quinn's car. The story also raised some disturbing questions. If the person who had vandalized the car had come from inside the Capelli, as Christina said, then he must have known the Rolls belonged to Louise. That meant he had slashed her car not as some random antisocial act but as something personal and very frightening. At best, it might be an extremely twisted art-life performance. (Jill? But Christina said she'd seen a man.) At worst, it indicated a capacity for violent rage—" . . . like he carving up somebody's face," Christina had said. "Somebody he really hated." If the man hated Louise so much, could the hatred have extended to Susana, as Louise's favorite protégé?

Entering the library, Margo tensed in response to the atmosphere there, a mutual distrust that prevailed between the overstressed librarians and the homeless people who used the library as a haven where they could sit all day if they appeared awake. Chronically short of funds, with its decaying building long slated for replacement, the library was a grim place where people avoided one another's eyes . . . and everyone avoided the bathrooms, in the wake of a stabbing. It was a place where Dawn might hope to fade into the stained green walls.

Margo scanned the collection of young students, intent readers in business suits, and ragged street people on the library's ground floor ... and returned in her mind to the Capelli the previous Tuesday, when the knot of people had gone out to view Louise's car. Which of the men there might have had it in for Louise; might have been secretly gloating at the sight of the gashed Rolls-Royce? Tom Fall? Peter Vance?

She pictured the fresh young face of Ed Milewski, Louise's current assistant ... in whom, Louise had confided to Margo, she saw none of the talent she had spotted in Susana.

Louise had described her relationship with her assistants as that of mentor and protégé. But Margo would bet Ed had to jump through hoops to earn his employer's patronage. What if Louise had given him a dressing-down on the way to the Capelli that afternoon? If she'd bluntly told him her less-than-avid opinion of his abilities? Ed had probably had to wait while Louise conducted her business in the foundation; he would have had time to vent his fury on her car. Still, what a tremendous risk; whether Louise thought he was the next Picasso or merely a minor talent, just having worked for her would give a boost to Ed's career.

Moving her search for Dawn to the second floor of the library, Margo considered the other men who had been on the scene. Any of them might resent Louise's prodigious influence in the art world, but Margo knew of none for whom the animus was more personal.

One more man must have been at the Capelli that afternoon, she realized; although he had apparently left before Louise discovered the vandalism. Was that because he had inflicted it? Louise's purpose in visiting the Capelli, she'd said, was to meet with James Carmichael on foundation business. That brought Margo back to the question of James and the Capelli's finances. What if Louise had questioned him about his fiscal management, had even confronted him with suspicion of mismanagement? The elderly volunteer, Charlotte, had said sometimes James was a tantrum-throwing child who put his fist through walls . . . or who might have slashed the hell out of Louise's car and written "Die, Bitch!" on the side?

Climbing the stairs to the third, final floor—where again, she failed to locate Dawn—Margo became increasingly aware of the effects of her horseback ride that morning. She longed to go home and soak in a hot bath. Only by promising herself a double dose of bath oil later (and a large glass of brandy on the side of the tub) could she force herself to enter the library's California Room, with its files on local luminaries and institutions. She found the two files she wanted and, muscles yelping, took a seat next to a woman in a three-piece suit who had half a dozen folders on real estate companies spread in front of her.

Among a stack of articles on exhibitions and glittery events, the only financial information in the Capelli Foundation file consisted of announcements of various grants and acquisitions, each accompanied by a happy quote ostensibly from Bernard and/or James (and undoubtedly written by the foundation's PR firm).

More interesting was the thick file devoted to James Carmichael. James had been hired as the Capelli's director five years ago, before the foundation building had even been designed, and his hiring amounted to a statement about the progressive kind of art institution Bernard Capelli envisioned. In various interviews and profiles, James emerged as a self-made man culturally, a pharmacist's son whose relentlessly middle-class background in a Cleveland suburb gave no clue to his future as a leader of New York's dynamic Soho art scene. Asked by one reporter how he could abandon Soho for relatively sleepy San Diego, James had talked about new challenges, Bernard Capelli's commitment to cutting-edge art, and the good environment for his family. Evidently his family, at least his wife, had seen things differently. Photographs initially showed James in New York with his wife, Sophie, and their two children; and then James newly arrived in San Diego with same. Later, James posed alone in his posh downtown penthouse, his growing collection of contemporary art filling the space wife and kids had once occupied. He had recently made one magazine's list of "Most Eligible San Diego Bachelors," apparently qualified not only by his prestigious job but because—in what he referred to as his "postmarriage" phase—he'd taken to driving a Maserati and wearing custom-tailored suits, purchased on semiannual jaunts to Milan.

"Sounds like Mr. Right to me," muttered Margo.

"A little tubby, don't you think? Beer bellies are such a turnoff." The woman next to her glanced over from her real estate files. "But the Harbor Esplanade," she said, brightening at James's address. "The three-bedroom condos there were going for eight hundred thou. What do you say the penthouse cost a million five?"

"In other words," Margo summed up for Barry, tears trickling down her cheeks, "James Carmichael lives as if he's in the cast of *Dallas*, but his resources sound more like *The Cosby Show*—well-off professional, but nowhere near as wealthy as the circles he moves in. Jesus, onion soup takes a lot of onions!" She put the knife down for a moment and dabbed at her eyes.

"Maybe," said Barry, chopping next to her, "he spotted some hot new artists early, bought their work cheap, and made a killing when they were discovered. It didn't hurt, of course, that he was the one who discovered them."

"Maybe the art is all gifts from grateful artists."

"Maybe the Maserati comes from a grateful car dealer."

"Maybe he made a fortune in real estate," said Margo, thinking of the woman at the library next to her.

"Maybe his ex-wife was a Rockefeller."

"He has a booth at the swap meet on weekends and cleans up selling bootleg designer jeans."

"Elvis memorabilia. Especially those velvet pictures of the king."

"It's wonderful to talk to you at last!" Margo gave him a hug. She had come home the night before to find Barry had taken the kids to the movies before returning them to their mom. Tonight, as they cooked together, she had finally had a chance to recap the past two days . . . and to deflect some of the awfulness with humor. No wonder cops were notorious for making morbid jokes; Margo now understood how they must need it.

"Even if James is doctoring the books, is there any connection with Susana's death?" Barry dumped the onions into the kettle to sauté.

"Exactly." She stretched, her body still warm from the bath she'd just taken, and sat at the big wooden table. The kitchen was one of the old house's best features, a spacious room where parties inevitably began, friends leaning against the refrigerator discussing politics or pitching in to chop ingredients for one of Barry's gourmet inventions or Margo's famous salads. The liveliest discussions always started in the kitchen and were carefully transported to the dining room.

"There's plenty of guilt to go around," she said. "But does any of it have to do with Susana? James may be guilty of embezzling, but if he were going to commit murder, why not kill Bernard Capelli or Louise? Or, for maximum efficiency, go after the accountant. Barbara Scholl, Susana's art dealer, told me she arrived in San Diego at four or five that afternoon; really she got into town at one. But is she guilty of stabbing Susana or just of hiding out at the Tropico screwing someone else's husband? Not that that isn't a heinous crime."

"There's another possibility." Barry lowered the heat under the onions. "The art dealer didn't have to be screwing someone's husband. What if she was having an affair with Isa? You said she asked for a room away from where Isa and Susana were staying. Could she have wanted to be near Isa without Susana knowing, so they could meet on the sly?"

"Of course! I wonder which of them drinks champagne and which likes Coke. Or, what if Barbara wasn't seeing Isa, but Susana?"

"Either way, it looks bad for Isa. If Susana was having the affair, Isa might have killed her out of jealousy. And if Isa was the one seeing Barbara Scholl, maybe Susana found out and threatened to leave her."

"No."

"Just because you like her . . ."

"Isa couldn't have been putting on an act on Saturday. I had my arm around her when the doctors were examining Susana, I could feel the way she was shaking. That was real. Besides, I can't see Isa sticking a knife in Susana."

Barry fell silent and—strong as his culinary opinions were—he only mumbled when Margo asked what fresh herbs she should pick from the pots on the patio. Abstractedly he stirred in sugar to caramelize the onions, poured in broth, and added a splash of wine. He didn't look up until, having chopped the herbs (parsley and marjoram), Margo tossed them into the soup pot.

Having opened a bottle of California zinfandel for the soup, he poured them two glasses and spoke finally. "What if it wasn't a knife?"

"The police said a sharp object."

"Right. Think about that room," he challenged, as if coaxing his students toward a complex theory of tidal movements.

Sipping her wine, Margo visualized the magical room Susana had created, taking in the bloodred walls, the fragrant flowers, the rich textures . . .

"Oh, my God. The bedposts and the poles," she said, picturing them vividly—with the sharp metal spines sticking out of them.

"Bingo." A good scientist, Barry had refrained from forming his own hypothesis until he had assembled all the facts in his mind. And a fanatic cook, he waited until the soup was simmering before he put the lid on the pot, sat at the table with her, and explained.

"Here's what I think happened," he said. "Someone came to see Susana that afternoon and they got into an argument. A serious argument, they got physical. The person hit Susana or pushed her and she fell against one of the poles. She hit it just wrong and died. Technically, was that even murder? It probably depends on several things. Was it a real fight, with Susana pushing as hard as she was being pushed, or did the other person just attack her? How close was she to the pole? Close enough that someone could have pushed her into one of the spines deliberately, or was it just bad luck that she fell the way she did?"

"But if it was essentially an accident, why didn't the person run and get help? It must have been too late," Margo answered her own question. "The police said Susana died almost instantly. And as you said, the person might have pushed her into the pole deliberately. At least they'd be terrified that's what the police would think. They must have panicked. Okay, but if they panicked, how could they stay and do all those things to cover up the fact that Susana was dead? Wouldn't the natural reaction be to get out of there as fast as possible?"

"Who knows what's natural, when you've just killed someone? I think someone would go into survival mode. But what does survival mode mean, for a given individual? Know what intrigues me even more than their staying to cover up Susana's death?"

"What?"

"The fact that they succeeded. What they did required fairly complex planning, and it had to be done under incredible stress. Think about it. Someone gives Susana a push in anger and all of a sudden she's dead. What are they going to do? They think of moving her to the bed. She planned to lie there during the opening, right? How many people knew that?"

"Everyone around the Capelli was talking about it."

"So they decide to move her." Barry mimed the action. "But it isn't that simple. The first impulse is just grab her and do it fast. But this is someone who stops and realizes they're going to have to put something on the floor to catch the blood."

"A drop cloth. There were drop cloths all around."

"So they get a drop cloth and put it on the floor." He threw down a dish towel and draped another over his shoulders. "They probably put another drop cloth over their own clothes. They move Susana to the bed—she was small, wasn't she, so most adults would be strong enough to carry her?"

"Tiny."

"They arrange her on the bed so the wound's hidden underneath her and turn her to face the wall. Then they cover her with the shawl and clean up."

"The puddle of water. Someone mentioned finding a puddle of water on the floor the night of the opening. Susana kept big bottles of mineral water on hand—the murderer must have used it to wash."

Barry's eyes gleamed, the scientist unraveling the puzzle. "If they had screwed up, the first person who walked into Susana's installation would have known something was wrong. Or they could have left traces so the police could identify them right off the bat. But neither of those things happened. That tells us either this person is extremely calculating by nature or they were extremely lucky, because they didn't make any of the obvious mistakes."

"That has to eliminate Dawn. She'd see Susana was dead and she'd split. Isa, too. Well, maybe Isa would have the nerve to try covering up Susana's death, say she was scared that even if she didn't go to prison she'd lose her kids. But she'd mess up the details. She'd get blood all over or leave fingerprints—the murderer must have worn the plastic gloves Susana's helpers were using. Another thing, even if Isa faked her reaction when Susana's body was discovered, how could she have acted normal at the opening before then?"

"Margo, how do you know what's normal for Isa? How do you know what's normal for any of these people?"

She poured another glass of wine, frowned. "The scientific method is relentless."

He gave her a hug. "Hey, this is only a theory. The point is, if it did happen this way, the murderer didn't have to be some coldblooded person who intended to kill Susana and plotted the whole thing out. All it took was someone angry enough to get into a serious argument with her and out-of-control enough to push her."

Staring into her wine, Margo remembered standing with her own arm raised, so out-of-control that she was about to fling a pot at a man she had once loved. She felt an uncomfortable flash of understanding for Susana's murderer.

She had been so young, she reflected, as she went through the motions of assembling a salad. She was only nineteen, a sophomore at the University of Wisconsin, when she'd met Rick Dunham, a fellow student in her ceramics class. She was drawn at first to the way the handsome blind man worked the clay and the originality of the things he made—not the lumpy, utilitarian bowls she and the other students labored to produce, but lyrical, abstract forms. She had wondered how those creative hands would feel on her body and soon she'd found out; that memory still brought a smile.

It was natural, in the questioning, questing spirit of the time, to drop out of college and move with Rick to Santa Fe. In the same spirit, if she and Rick seemed to clash too often, or too bitterly, Margo contrasted it with the deadly domesticity of her parents' generation . . . and attributed it to artistic sensibility.

Rick *was* an artist, there was no doubt about that. In the old house they rented in Santa Fe, they set up a pottery studio, he focusing on one-of-a-kind ceramic art and she making simple household items—bowls, cups, teapots—to sell in the craft shops in town. It was hard to remember, the fact of how things had turned out staining everything that came before, but she knew that at first they were happy. Their business did reasonably well, they enjoyed the work, they helped each other. When sales lagged, Margo picked up extra money at part-time jobs, mostly waitressing. Friends of theirs owned horses and they discovered, city children both of them, that they loved to ride.

Margo still didn't know if the clashes between them became worse or if she simply changed, so that what she'd once seen as grand passion finally seemed nothing but ordinary incompatibility. Rick had an affair. She had an affair. One day she stopped herself as she was about to heave a pot across the room; stopped just in time to throw some things into the car, get on the highway, and preserve some sense of her own decency, although that was badly tattered. She, who'd never dreamed she could take advantage of her lover's blindness, had aimed to hit him.

For years Margo wouldn't touch clay—Rick had been the one with the real talent. She used her odd jobs background to make a living in the city she chose by default: San Diego, because the friend she'd expected to find in San Francisco had settled there instead. While working at a bookstore, she'd started doing book reviews on the San Diego public radio station. She became so fascinated by radio—and so disillusioned by the job prospects without a degree—that she went back to college, majoring in broadcast journalism at San Diego State. Finally she was able to do ceramics again, just for fun, whether because she had found her own calling at last or because she'd met Barry at around the same time.

Margo figured Rick knew about her marriage, just as she'd heard of his marriage and child, via a mutual friend. She knew he had stayed in Santa Fe and sold his work widely. It was ten years already. For a long time she had wished him well in her heart. Occasionally she felt an urge to call and tell him so.

As if in response to her thoughts, the phone rang. She started to let the answering machine pick it up, but then heard, over the speaker, "Margo, this is Isa Reid." She snatched up the receiver.

"I want to talk to you," said Isa. "Will you come to L.A.? First thing tomorrow?"

"Sure."

"There's plenty of room, you can stay here. Wait a second, okay?" Isa returned after a moment. "Just more police at the door. Every few hours they think of a new reason to harass me. Here's how you get here." She rapidly gave directions, pausing twice to yell at her "visitors," "In a minute! Look, Margo, I can't talk any more now but please!" Her voice sounded ragged. "Come as early tomorrow as you can."

16 / Dawn in Hiding

Blue car, seven hundred twenty. Red car.

Sitting on the hillside on her folded poncho, because the ground was damp, Dawn counted the cars going by on the freeway below. But only the blue cars.

Blue car, seven hundred twenty-one. Yellow car. Brown car. Red car. Blue car blue car, seven hundred twenty-two, seven hundred twenty-three. It was exciting when they came one right after another like that!

The freeway went right through the middle of the park. The road was so close she could see some of the people in the cars. But none of them ever stopped. And no one even looked up at the hill to where she was hidden, protected by the bushes and the trees.

Blue car, seven hundred twenty-four. Inside that one a lady was putting her lipstick on while she drove. Susana always wore lipstick, bright red. At the thought of Susana, the thought of bright red, Dawn felt an explosion of red inside her, like the kind of fireworks that shoot out in every direction. She held herself very still, blotted the color out of her mind, made herself focus on the cars again.

The blue cars were the most interesting to count because you weren't always sure if a car was blue or green, it could be an in-between color and you had to decide real fast before the car got out of sight.

Better to be staying outdoors like this than to be inside the art museum. Better to get soup and sandwiches from Holly, and whatever else the big woman picked up. Holly—as real to Dawn now as Susana had been—was out this morning, scavenging. Holly found a lot of good things in the park that people just left behind. All kinds of food and clothes, especially jackets and sweaters. The first day Dawn was here, on Sunday, Holly even found a stuffed rabbit that she gave to Dawn. Dawn kept it in her special bag. She'd wanted to give Holly something, and she found the glass ball in her bag, where if you shook it, white flecks danced around. The ball would be nicer without the rat inside, but Holly acted like she liked the gift.

Blue car, seven hundred twenty-five.

Dawn heard something in the bushes. Just a squirrel. She touched her knife anyway, sheathed around the leg of the black jumpsuit Susana had given her. The jumpsuit was getting grimy, but she couldn't wear her jeans anymore, not with the sticky stain on them.

17 / The Lover

Margo detested the two-and-a-half-hour drive to Los Angeles. Past the Camp Pendleton Marine Base—a fifteen-mile stretch at the north end of San Diego County, where the freeway runs through undeveloped coastal foothills—Interstate 5 becomes progressively more congested and the industrial areas beside it grayer and grimmer, approaching L.A.

At least she had plenty to distract her mind from the drive this morning . . . starting with the phone conversation she'd had with Lieutenant Donny Obayashi just before she left San Diego.

Was Susana killed by her own artwork? she had asked the lieutenant, floating Barry's theory.

"What TV station did you say you work for?" Obayashi said sharply.

"Not television, radio. KSDR, the public station."

"You're the one who interviewed the three artists last week, aren't you? Did one of them tell you that was what happened?"

"No. But I spent several hours in Susana's installation, and I noticed how sharp those metal spines were. Is that how she died?"

After a little verbal tangoing, they'd struck a deal. The lieutenant confirmed that Susana had died by falling—with some force—against one of the metal bedposts; and that a bloodstained blanket was found stuffed under the bed. Margo, on her side, agreed to give Obayashi her raw tapes from the week before. The interviews concerned only the artists' work, she reassured herself. There was nothing that could harm the innocent.

Barry had scored a near bull's-eye with the scene he'd laid out the night before, reflected Margo, driving through Orange County. (A few of the fragrant orange groves had still remained, when Margo first moved to California. Now, she passed nothing but mammoth mirror-sided corporate edifices.) Susana must have finished her preparations and donned her "Frida" costume, probably late Saturday afternoon. Then someone came to see her, Susana and the visitor argued, and Susana was pushed into the bedpost, fatally. The visitor then made it appear as if Susana were lying on the bed, ready for the opening to begin. Even the candles had been lit! Had Susana done that before the visitor arrived, or was it another detail her visitor—her killer—had seen to, coolly circling the room and lighting twenty or more candles after transferring Susana's lifeless body to the bed?

Nearly impossible to comprehend anyone proceeding so methodically, having just committed a murder. As to the first part of the scenario, however, Margo could imagine any one of several people arguing with Susana and even getting into a shoving match with her. Of those who had definitely been at the Capelli that Saturday afternoon, Tom Fall had had a bitter tiff with Susana just a few days before, over Dawn's being trapped in his installation. Jill might have provoked Susana "just to get a reaction"—and Jill had retained a lawyer. Certainly Dawn, if she felt threatened, could have struck out, her survival instinct overriding her loyalty to Susana—though surely Dawn lacked the cunning to cover up the death.

Other people must have had access to the building as well, people who might have entered—and slipped out unnoticed—through the side door next to Susana's installation. James Carmichael, possible financial misdealings aside, was prone to fits of violent anger. And Margo assumed that Bernard Capelli's "dirty old man" act at the opening, fondling her arm, was less a tribute to her own fabulous seductiveness than a display of Capelli's standard behavior toward women. What if he'd made a move on Susana, she pushed him away, and Bernard pushed back? All it required, Barry had said, was someone angry enough to get in a fight with Susana and out-of-control enough, just for a moment, to push her.

Where, she wondered as she took the interchange onto the Hollywood Freeway, had Isa spent Saturday afternoon? Had she helped Susana with the last-minute details of her exhibit? Perhaps dressed her in the Frida Kahlo costume? (And then killed her?)

And *why* had Isa virtually begged Margo to come see her? The last time the two of them had spoken face to face, Isa had read her the riot act for questioning Orion.

Why the change of heart?

It was the first thing Margo asked, when she and Isa sat in the garden behind Isa's (legally, at the moment, Susana's) house and Isa poured cups of herb tea.

"The cops think like the *National Enquirer*—'Lesbian Love Nest Fatal to Famous Artist.' Ooh la la!" Bitterness and exhaustion colored Isa's words. "They figure I'm totally immoral and perverted to start with because I'm a dyke. And now I'm a dyke who benefits financially from another dyke's death." So Susana *had* made a will. "So of course that means I offed her."

The *Enquirer* had in fact tried to reach Isa, relentlessly, as had several other publications; she had unplugged all the phones. Dark cars, she assumed driven by police officers, followed her everywhere. Every few hours they'd find a new excuse to come to the house and ask more questions. And that wasn't the only problem.

Isa's voice became tight, as if the words were almost too painful to speak. "Orion's father—although that's hardly the word for him—has taken a sudden interest in the kid. Funny thing, he ditched me the first time I had morning sickness. He loved the idea his precious sperm turned out to be potent, but holding my hand while I threw up was way too middle class. And by the time nurturing got to be sexy for men, he'd cut his hair, changed his name from Bullfrog back to Dan, got married, and bought a house in the suburbs. He never provided a penny of child support, never even sent Orion a Christmas card. Yesterday I heard from a lawyer. The asshole's filing for custody, saying I'm an unfit mother."

Isa reached for the teapot, but her hands were shaking.

"Here, let me." Margo refilled their cups, noting the delicacy of the earthenware teapot, of a piece with the beauty of the setting. Susana's money had no doubt bought the large Spanish-style house located in the hills of Silverlake, an older area (with a large gay and lesbian population) at the east end of Hollywood. Margo felt sure it was Isa's nesting ability, however, that had created the terraced garden perfumed with freesias and the inviting interior she had glimpsed when she arrived: natural wood and soft fabrics in coral, orchid, off-white.

Isa cradled the teacup in both hands as if needing the warmth. Looking at her, pale but with bare feet solidly planted beneath a gauzy lavender skirt, reminded Margo of an old Joni Mitchell tune, "Ladies of the Canyon," a ballad of gentler days when independent women dressed like gypsies, not like corporate raiders. The sun was warm and Margo shed her blazer and wriggled her feet out of her shoes. Isa was one interviewee who wouldn't demand formality . . . if Isa really was an interviewee. She hadn't yet responded to Margo's first question.

"Why did you ask me to come here?" Margo asked again.

Isa looked up. She wore no sunglasses, despite the hazily bright morning. Margo removed her own sunglasses, sensing the importance of directly meeting Isa's gaze.

"To say I trust you would be going too far," said Isa. "But I teach yoga, I'm tuned in to nonverbal language. You came over to me Saturday night and put your arm around me. I know you were doing your job, I saw your tape recorder. But that wasn't the only reason you put your arm around me. I felt your genuine compassion. The body doesn't lie about things like that. I'm being investigated now whether I like it or not. I'd like at least one person looking into Susana's death who has a little compassion for me."

Melodramatic, Margo labeled the speech, trying to maintain her emotional distance from this woman who might be trying to use her; but the same tears that welled in Isa's eyes came briefly into Margo's own. She blinked them away, reached for her sunglasses again.

"If you want me to help you, you need to answer my questions," she said briskly. She had left the tape recorder in her Guatemalan bag, wanting to proceed slowly with Isa; now she placed the machine in the middle of the table. "All of my questions. You may not like some of them."

Isa nodded that she understood.

"Where were you on Saturday afternoon, say until six?"

"Until five-thirty, I hung out with Mickey and Orion at the hotel. We spent a little time in the pool, watched television, took a walk. Then we changed and drove over to the opening."

"Were you together all afternoon? All three of you?"

"I said so." Sharply. "Why wouldn't we be?"

"If you were spending the afternoon in Barbara Scholl's room."

Isa looked truly puzzled. "You mean . . . Oh, God, you do mean, don't you? Because she was staying at the same hotel?" She grinned. "Not my type! In fact, I was amazed to find out she was at the Tropico. I'd have expected Barbara to stay at—what's that posh pink hotel in La Jolla, La Valencia?"

"How did you find out she was staying at your hotel? From Susana?"

"Actually, I didn't know till that night, after Susana died. Barbara stayed up with me for hours. She and Orion and I played hearts until our hands got tired from holding the cards. And early the next morning she came back."

"You and Barbara must be good friends."

"Actually, no. We've known each other for years, of course, because of Susana, but I was amazed how great she was. All that WASP snobbery, and the make-a-buck mentality that comes with being a dealer made me think she was a cold fish. But she was really loving, even toward Orion, and believe me, I never imagined Barbara Scholl as someone who'd have patience with a kid whose idea of a work of art is a poster of Madonna." Isa lifted the teapot. "Oops, we need fresh tea. And how about something to eat?"

While Isa busied herself inside, Margo remained in the garden, keeping the tape running to catch the ambience of birds chirping, the breeze in the foliage, and the rumble of traffic from the street below; she'd need the ambient sound in her story, each time she switched from her narrative to the actuality of Isa speaking. She reviewed the conversation with Isa . . . and became aware of a what's-missing-from-this-picture feeling, as if Isa had been nervous about something but Margo had missed the precise moment of nervousness that would have told her to dig deeper. Maybe Isa had lied—but how skillfully!—in denying a relationship with Barbara Scholl?

Isa returned with a plate of banana bread, cheese, fruit, and homemade pasta salad. All her friends were cooking, she said, country wives at heart when faced with a death.

Margo directed the mike back at Isa. "Tell me about your last memory of Susana. Your last conversation, whatever."

Isa rested her chin in her hand, reflectively. "We had breakfast Saturday morning, in a little café down the street from the hotel. Just Susana and me—Orion and Mickey ate cereal in the hotel room. You want to know everything, like what we ordered? Okay. I had oatmeal. Susana ate half a piece of French toast, drenched with syrup, and lots of coffee." Wryly, "I never could get her to eat right."

"What did you talk about?"

"We didn't talk much. We never did over breakfast, we liked reading the paper. We got both the San Diego paper that day and the *L.A. Times*. One of us would notice some item and mention it, odd things, you know? Like some woman caught two bank robbers by hanging onto the outside of their getaway car for a mile, Susana mentioned that. I saw a 'Dear Abby' I liked, one of those things where the neighbor comes over every afternoon for three hours and the lady doesn't know how to discourage her—Abby always has such wise things to say about those situations."

Margo was aware of a lump in her throat. She and Barry read the morning paper together the same way.

"Susana left for the gallery around ten. And she called me on the phone around three. Let's see, she asked how Mickey was. And we discussed the installation. She said Dawn was helping her finish up." Isa's face contracted in pain. "God, I had such a bad feeling about Dawn from the very beginning."

"Did you and Susana ever talk about that? About Dawn?"

"We had a policy never to interfere in each other's friendships. But, yeah, I actually did ask Susana to stay away from Dawn. I told you about the good vibes I got from you. With Dawn it was the opposite—there was something deeply, deeply sick about her. Susana got furious, of course, and I dropped it." Her voice choked with tears. "Christ, I'd never asked anything like that before. What if I'd just made an ultimatum? Susana might still be alive."

"So you're convinced Dawn killed her?"

"Oh, yes. Like I said, I sensed something very wrong in Dawn. She pulled her knife once, on Orion. Susana and Orion were having some kind of spat. Nothing serious, just the old story of stepparent clashing with stepkid—you're familiar with that one, I suppose. Dawn got the idea that Susana was in danger, and she came at Orion with the knife. Susana managed to stop her. But after that I put my foot down about Dawn being around the kids."

"She came at Orion, but she was *protecting* Susana—"

"Oh, damn!" broke in Isa. "What time is it?"

"Two-thirty."

"I've got to pick up Mickey at nursery school. Want to come? We can talk in the car."

Still barefoot, Isa led the way into the garage, where Susana's new van stood next to its poor relation, a battered brown Dodge. Isa unlocked the van, saying a bit uncomfortably, "The Dodge needs six hundred bucks' worth of repairs, and at the moment I haven't got diddly."

"Don't you inherit from Susana?"

"In a hundred years!" Isa brought the van to a purring start and backed down the driveway. "Her will leaves me almost everything, but I've already gotten word that her family's contesting it. I've even been specifically uninvited to the funeral they're putting on. Can't say I'd relate to a Catholic service, anyway. Some friends and I are going to create our own ritual this weekend."

Margo returned to their earlier conversation. "You said you and Susana didn't interfere in each other's friendships. Does that mean you didn't insist on fidelity?"

"Sexual fidelity? How do you and your husband feel about that?" Isa's tone was challenging.

"I suppose like a lot of people who came of age during the sexual revolution. At first, we agreed to sexual freedom in principle, but that was when we were first falling in love and we wouldn't have been interested in anyone else. Then after we'd been together a while and a little fling might have looked tempting, we were honest enough to admit we'd be devastated if the other one had an affair. Not to mention the way AIDS has changed the whole equation."

"Why do you think it's any different for lesbians? It's like that line from Shakespeare: 'If you prick us, do we not bleed?' Susana and I felt about fidelity the same way you and your husband do. Sure, I get attracted to other people on occasion. I'm sure you do, too. Sometimes you meet someone and there's that electricity. So what do *you* do, Margo, when you get turned on like that? You fantasize like wild, right, the next time you're making love with your husband?" She stopped the van outside a gaily painted building from which children were emerging. "Hang on, I'll be out with Mickey in a jiff."

Back home, Isa got Mickey settled for a nap, then joined Margo in the living room.

"Turn on your tape recorder," she said. "I'm making a confession."

Holy shit. Isa didn't look like someone about to confess to a murder. Unless about-to-confess murderers generally looked calm and sad.

"You and the police and the *National Enquirer* all want to know about Susana and me," Isa said. "There's only one important thing to know. We loved each other. We shared our lives. I knew what things Susana liked to eat and her favorite movies. She knew where I was really ticklish. If she was away traveling for a week and I went to the airport to pick her up, we'd take one look at each other and we'd both get these big, silly grins spreading all over our faces. Let me show you something."

Isa got a black art portfolio from a shelf and handed it to Margo. She then excused herself to go outside and do yoga. She was visible through the window, laying down a mat in the garden and sliding off her skirt, leaving her clad in white tights and a cornflower-blue tank top.

Margo opened the portfolio. It contained drawings of Susana, dozens of them: Susana working, Susana playing with Mickey, sitting with a coffee cup, taking a bath. Perhaps a third of the drawings were nudes, in which Susana's thin, angular body appeared not that of a neurotic woman who never ate, but the delicate form of a dryad. The artist of the portraits seemed drenched with the knowledge of every aspect of her subject's face and body. The drawn figures almost breathed.

Outside, Isa raised herself into a headstand, her body perfectly straight. Tears flowed upside down from her closed eyes into her hair.

18 / Art Appreciation

"These drawings are lovely," said Margo when Isa came back in.

"Thanks. Not at all cutting edge—in order to be cutting edge you have to create from your head. I have this stubborn habit of creating from my heart. That's why I wanted you to see these. I only draw like this when it's someone I love."

"Have you ever tried showing them in a gallery?"

"I found out long ago that what I do isn't the kind of thing the art world gets excited about."

"But you used to be serious about art, didn't you? You were Louise O'Quinn's assistant . . ."

"Until she took one look at Susana's work and gave Susana the job instead. Who raked up that old story? Louise, I bet. And she said I didn't mind because I was unambitious."

"Not true?"

"Hell, I don't know. Louise gets a lot of mileage out of bragging about the artists she's 'made.' But she can break an artist, too. Say someone displeases her and she doesn't make the little phone call that would land them that first New York show. Or she breaks your spirit. I don't blame her at all for latching onto Susana. Everyone could see Susana was a genius. What I hated was the way Louise fired me. She could have just been honest and said, 'I've found this incredible, brilliant young artist and even though you've got some talent, Isa, this woman is extraordinary and I have to have her working for me.' Instead, she fed me a lot of crap about how I lacked ambition and vision, as if she was dropping me because of my own deficiencies and not because of *her* ambition to link her career to Susana's. I was only in my twenties then and I'd been so thrilled to get the job with Louise. I hung on every word she said."

"Did you ever resent Susana for taking your chance away?"

"Susana didn't take anything from me! Sometimes I walk into Susana's studio and look at the sheer volume of creativity, and it breaks my heart that that isn't happening for me. But that wasn't Susana's fault. If I've felt mad, it's at myself for internalizing the asinine things Louise old me. And at Louise. Of course, when you consider Louise's former assistants, I'm sure I'm not the only one who . . . let's say, might feel like slashing her Rolls."

"Did you . . . ?" Had Isa even been at the Capelli that day?

Isa shook her head. "My bet's on Peter. Peter Vance, you met him, he was helping Tom. Peter is another Louise O'Quinn alum. Word has it he actually kept track of the hours he worked for Louise and expected to be paid for all of them. In retaliation, Louise made sure *Artweek* assigned a cutthroat critic to cover his first important show. Peter's career has never really recovered. I think he's had a bit of success locally, but success in San Diego barely pays for materials at the art store."

"But if his work is good—"

Isa snorted. "You're not that naive, are you?"

Margo had noticed before that when stung deeply, Isa stung back. Isa's abandoned art career must be a deep wound.

"What people say about the art world is true," Isa said. "It's incestuous, it's highly competitive, and it's ruled by marketing. Which reminds me, I asked Barbara Scholl to put together some information for you. Susana's sales records. People keep saying how much I'm personally going to benefit from Susana's death. But I'm not the only one. A lot of people have a major investment in Susana, and you can bet her prices will go up now."

"How much?"

"Barbara should be able to give you an idea. She said you should drop by late this afternoon. Her gallery's in Santa Monica," Isa said, naming a community on the west side of L.A. noted for having the trendiest of everything.

"The art market is in a slump, *bien entendu*." Barbara Scholl made an imperceptible adjustment to the silver and malachite brooch fastening the apricot-colored woven shawl she wore over a pale cream suit. Then she cast her gaze around the Scholl Gallery, everywhere but at Margo.

In spite of the art dealer's air of having far more valuable things to do, only one customer, an older man wearing a polo shirt and casual slacks, browsed among the paintings. He was attended by a well-dressed balding man, whose murmurs seemed to be stimulating the potential buyer to look closely at each painting, then step back and regard it from ten or fifteen feet away.

"Alan, for instance, had his own gallery on Melrose until a year ago." Barbara nodded toward the balding man, with an expression Margo could have sworn was a gloat. "Of course, we haven't felt the slump here. In fact, the end of the boom has actually been advantageous for the best-established dealers. Prior to the inflated prices of the eighties, if a collector had a piece to sell, we dealers were often called on to broker the sale. When prices became so out of line, *tout le monde* went to the auction houses. More money passed through

Sotheby's during the eighties than the gross national product of a dozen small countries. That situation had to cease and it finally did.

"The point is, *bien entendu*, that although Isa may want to believe that one of Susana's collectors could have murdered her in anticipation of her prices doubling or trebling, I don't expect her work to experience that kind of jump. It will rise somewhat. But Susana won't be another Basquiat." After pausing just long enough to assure herself that Margo didn't immediately place the reference, Barbara smiled—a point scored?—and leaned closer to Margo's microphone to explain. "Jean-Michel Basquiat was a graffiti artist whose prices went through the roof after he died several years ago. His paintings were selling in about the thirties at the time of his death from a drug overdose. A year later, they were going for two and three hundred thousand. Basquiat was overrated to begin with, but my point is, those times are over. I wanted to make sure you knew that before I gave you Susana's sales records, so you understand I'm only doing this as a favor to *la pauvre* Isa and not because the records have the slightest relevance."

Margo marveled (and felt slightly sick) at the way the art dealer had pooh-poohed the idea that one of Susana's collectors had killed her to make a killing on her art—*not* because Barbara found the notion preposterous but because, given the current market, Susana's prices wouldn't increase sufficiently.

"Of course, the records are Isa's property now, aren't they?" Margo said. "Susana must have had access to them?"

"Susana concerned herself with creating great art. That, *chérie*, is why artists need people to manage their marketing. You'll see that the records Susana kept on her own, before we began handling her eight years ago. *Impossible!*" Giving the word a French pronunciation, Barbara threw up her hands in a sparkling display of rings and daggerlike coral fingernails. "If you'll come with me . . ."

Although Margo herself was slender and fairly graceful from years of dance, Barbara was the kind of petite woman who occasionally made her feel gawky; she suspected the art dealer cultivated the effect. Barbara inserted a plastic card that opened a door at the back of the gallery, and they passed into an office. Of four desks in the room, only one was occupied, by a young woman who stiffened to attention when Barbara walked by. That office looked posh, but going from it to Barbara's private domain was like leaving a modest country palace for Versailles, especially since the decor was pure Louis XIV; the paintings on Barbara's wall, however, looked absolutely contemporary.

"Pluralism and appropriation are key elements of postmodernism," said Barbara, noticing Margo's perusal of the room. "One isn't limited to any single historical period. That's what's so liberating about it."

Margo wondered what the art dealer enjoyed being liberated from. She tried to picture Barbara cavorting barefoot in a field, but the image wouldn't hold.

"*Naturellement*," said Barbara, before handing Margo a large manila envelope. "I assume that if you contact any of these people, you won't mention how you received their names. These are major clients and they place a high value on our discretion. Well, I won't keep you any more," said Barbara brightly. "*Au revoir*."

"I'd like to look this over before I go. In case I have any questions."

Barbara frowned, but directed Margo to one of the empty desks in the outer office.

• • •

The Scholl Gallery recorded its sales using a computer program that could sort the information in various ways, and the envelope held two different lists. The first, a meticulous chronology based on the date each sculpture was completed, noted when the piece was sold, for how much, and to whom. The list also included the date, price, buyer, and place of sale in the event of a resale. As Barbara had said, Susana's own record-keeping, prior to her association with the gallery, was sketchy: Some of the earliest buyers' names were unknown and question marks followed several prices. The two student works Margo had seen at Louise O'Quinn's didn't even appear on the list. Nevertheless, the list documented how Susana's career had taken off, her prices rising during the course of a decade from a few thousand dollars to recent figures of $50,000 or $60,000, and not just for new work but for resales of earlier pieces as well.

The second list was an alphabetical rundown of Susana's buyers, fifty-two individuals and institutions that had purchased the seventy or so sculptures she'd created in her lifetime. About a dozen museums in the U.S. and Europe owned her work, as did several film actors and a number of names Margo recognized as heavies in the business end of the entertainment industry. Of people she had met, she noticed that James Carmichael had bought two sculptures during the past two years for a total of $116,000. Bernard Capelli had a work by Susana in his personal collection, purchased six years ago for $30,000. The best deal had gone to Barbara Scholl herself, an $11,000 bargain bought early in Susana's career.

The young woman in the office with Margo had been making phone calls nonstop, and although Margo was only half listening, she gradually realized the calls were all alike: "Mrs. Pollard, this is Jean Moss at the Scholl. I know you wouldn't want to miss our show of Ver Hume. Yes, the German neoexpressionist. Caroline Brice came by last week and just loved it, and we had Joe and Georgia Temple here the other day. Did you see the review in the *Times*? Well, they raved, they just raved. Several paintings have already been spoken for, of course, one by a major film director, but there are still a number of outstanding works available. If you let us know when you'll be coming by, we'll make sure Barbara is here to meet with you in person." ... "Dr. Baines, this is Jean Moss at the Scholl. Yes, just calling to remind you about the Ver Hume show . . ."

Margo wondered if the young woman had learned her condescending tone from her employer or if it had been a requirement for getting the job. She also wondered how much the gallery needed to drum up business.

"Do you always do this for a show?" she asked when Jean Moss had finished the latest call.

"Informing our clients of our current exhibitions? Of course." Clipped words accompanied a sneer that seemed directed at Margo's black silk slacks and mustard blazer, an ensemble Margo had always fancied as clean-lined and even elegant. Jean Moss was wearing a tailored pink linen suit that made her look like a society candy striper, and an abundance of gold jewelry.

"How's the attendance been at this one, Jean?"

"Excellent. Are you familiar with Ver Hume's work?"

"Savage, don't you think? Full of energy." Margo didn't know whether to pat herself on the back for having read a review of the show or to kick herself for trying to one-up a cultural snob. "Are you usually here alone?" she added. In spite of Barbara Scholl's denial that problems in the art market had affected her gallery, the empty desks indicated she had had to reduce her staff.

Ignoring the question, Jean looked at her watch and pulled a makeup bag from her desk. She propped a mirror on her desk, applied a line of lip pencil, and filled it in with brown-ish lipstick. Next she gave her short, frosted hair a strafing of hairspray. Her whole person now shellacked, Jean Moss stood up.

Margo checked her own watch: five-thirty. "Quitting time?"

"Goodness, no. I work until nine. This is sherry hour." The face under its industrial strength makeup softened, and she said rather wistfully, "I developed a fondness for after-noon sherry when I went to Smith. Barbara's an alumna, too."

Margo, while at the University of Wisconsin, had devel-oped a taste for jug wine and Milwaukee beer. "Sherry sounds divine," she said.

Sherry hour at the Scholl must have been a popular event at one time; a dozen empty glasses stood ready on the table. But the drinkers today were limited to Barbara, her two employees, Margo, and a man from a gallery down the street, who announced that things there were "dead, dead, dead."

Margo poured herself a glass. "Thanks for the informa-tion," she said, joining Barbara in front of a painting of two grappling, semiabstract figures. "By the way, you said Susana's prices will go up, even though it won't be a dra-matic rise. Can you give me some kind of dollar estimate?"

"A rough one, *bien entendu*. I sold a piece of hers two months ago for $58,000. I'd expect to get at least $80,000 for it today."

"Are current owners of her work likely to put it up for sale now? And if they do, would you know about it?"

"Certainly someone might put a work on the market, especially in L.A., where so many people depend on soft money. An actor goes half a year without a project and suddenly he needs some cash, so he puts some of his collection up for sale. And that might very likely go through us. As I said, the slump has brought a number of collectors back to galleries when they want to sell."

The sherry seemed to make Barbara friendlier. She sipped steadily but with great delicacy, and Margo observed that no matter how often she brought the glass to her mouth, none of her lipstick smudged. Had young Jean Moss learned that trick yet?

"Even if the sale is handled by someone else, I'd be informed of it," said Barbara. "As you may know, there's been a great deal of discussion in recent years about artists deserving remuneration in the case of resales. In the past, someone might buy a young artist's work for a few hundred dollars, then the artist became known and the collector could sell the same work for $50,000, while the artist got nothing. These days most artists, certainly any who have clout, are insisting on a resale agreement when they make a sale, guaranteeing a percentage of future sales. I'm Susana's fiscal agent, so I'd know of any resales because her percentage comes through me."

"What about the sculpture you own? Have you thought of selling it?"

"I hadn't thought. It's in such a perfect place at my beach house. But of course I could put the Italian piece there. . . ."

Before Barbara became lost in financial reverie, Margo got in, "How did you like the Tropico? It's charming, but I understand the room service leaves a lot to be desired."

"*Affreux*! Awful."

"Why did you stay there?"

"Pure *bêtise*. Stupidity."

Margo groaned inwardly. Having done nothing but stimulate a certain Gallic terseness in Barbara Scholl, she dropped the attempt to be cleverly devious.

"Barbara, who were you meeting at the hotel on Saturday?"

Like a character in a movie, Barbara dropped her glass. Amber sherry spilled over the beige carpet.

"Was it Isa?" pursued Margo—Isa had been concealing something; was it this?

"Isa!" A sound not unlike a hoot issued from Barbara's perfectly painted lips.

For a moment Margo could almost imagine Barbara Scholl dancing barefoot in a field.

19 / The Nun's Story

Barbara recovered quickly from her burst of hilarity. "Alan!" she commanded softly. She stepped aside and scarcely nodded acknowledgment as her employee scurried over and knelt to blot up the spilled sherry with several napkins.

Grasping Margo's arm, Barbara led her to a corner of the gallery.

"It's quite tawdry to speculate about others' private lives," she said, tightlipped. "And perhaps just as tawdry to honor such speculations with an answer. But to set your filthy mind at rest, if I did meet anyone in San Diego, it wasn't Isa. Or Susana, in case that little twist occurred to you. The fact is, *chérie*, I can't believe either Susana or Isa would have an affair. Susana cared more for her art than for anything else. And Isa has always struck me as a one-woman woman. Or at any rate, a one-person woman. I hadn't really given it any thought, but I suppose Isa's bisexual." She kept her grip on Margo's arm, digging in her nails, as she escorted Margo to the door.

Barbara hadn't quite hidden a smirk, and as Margo drove toward the freeway, she speculated that the tawdry subject of her artists' sexuality interested Barbara Scholl very much indeed, as did any information that might increase her ability to manipulate them. Prior to the women's movement, Barbara might have been downing her sherry with other ex-Smithies, ripping apart absent friends at the country club. As it was, she had profited from the way feminism had expanded women's career horizons, without absorbing any of the movement's deeper message about transforming consciousness. Becoming a power in the art world had simply enlarged the scope for her cattiness.

In fact, Barbara Scholl seemed a far more likely candidate for murder than did Susana. Alan, the former gallery owner now reduced to mopping up his boss's spills, had shot her a look of hatred. And Margo would bet Alan had plenty of company among others Barbara had bested, dominated, and humiliated, talents for which she seemed to have an appetite as well as a gift. Barbara hadn't denied having an assignation when she was in San Diego. Margo wondered what kind of person would attract or be attracted to the art dealer. Perhaps a young artist willing to sleep his or her way to the top?

Crawling through rush-hour traffic, Margo became aware that she was exhausted. She forced herself to stop thinking about Susana's murder and instead sampled the L.A. radio fare. There were several National Public Radio stations in Los Angeles, a situation she considered a luxury, and not just because of her choices as a listener—if San Diego had more than one NPR station, she might be able to do the work she loved without having to kowtow to Alex. That fantasy shortened the hour it took to get back to Isa's.

As Margo approached the house, she glimpsed Isa talking inside with someone clad in a strange black cape. Walking up to the house, she realized the visitor was a nun.

Margo's one personal relationship with a member of the clergy had consisted of sometimes excruciating encounters with a friend's father, a rabbi with a truly Godlike voice. Rabbi Hirshman had once approached her six-year-old self, booming, "How do you do?" Puzzled by this unfamiliar question, Margo had tried to get by with just smiling, a ploy the rabbi had demolished instantly. "HOW DO YOU DO?" he'd repeated several times, advancing until he loomed over her. Resigned to having to say something, she'd squeaked out, "I do fine."

Margo didn't know why a nun was here with Isa, but Margo beat her to the punch. "How do you do?" she said, entering the living room, where she noticed a half-empty wine bottle and two glasses.

"Yo," said the nun, then laughed. "I mean hello. I spend all day with kids in the barrio and I start to talk like them." A plump woman of about thirty, she stood and extended her hand.

"This is Sister Benjamina," introduced Isa.

"Isa, this is family! I'm Angie here. Angie Soto, Susana's cousin." At the mention of Susana's name, a look of sorrow crossed Angie's round, olive-complected face, but it didn't find a home there.

"Angie is the only member of Susana's family who accepted Susana and me," said Isa.

"They were coming around, Isa. You should have heard Graciela this Easter, saying how beautifully Susana used to decorate the eggs when we were little. By next Christmas they would have invited her, and in another year or two, both of you. And of course the children."

"You never believe anything but the best of people."

"Not true. Look where I work—a barrio youth program and a shelter for homeless women downtown," she explained to Margo. "Anyone who lacks cynicism gets chewed up and eaten for breakfast. But you're right, Isa, I really do perceive the Christ in everyone . . . even in you."

Isa threw a pillow at her, and Margo, shocked, tried to

imagine engaging Rabbi Hirshman in a pillow fight.

"Ai, Margo is going to think we're nuts," said Angie. "Really, Margo, we're just slightly tipsy and really very sad. Isa tells me you've come all the way from San Diego to help her and that I might be able to help you. The shelter I work at, Casa de Mujeres, is where Susana met Dawn. I'll take you there after dinner."

"Also, Angie is the one person Susana always confided in, from the time they were kids," said Isa. "They grew up next door to each other. She told Angie things she'd never tell me."

Isa sounded wistful and Angie took her hand. "You know Susana and I were like sisters," she said. "And once I became a nun—in spite of how much Susana tried to talk me out of it—she said talking to me was a little like being in confession. She would never go back to the Church, but she still loved the Catholic ritual."

Margo thought of the sacred feeling Susana had created in her installation, the sense of mystery and beauty.

"We haven't even given you a glass of wine!" Angie exclaimed.

Over wine Angie filled Margo in on Susana's family, a big Mexican-American clan consisting of Susana's mother and father, a grandfather who lived with them, and eight siblings, most of them grown and with their own places near their parents in East Los Angeles. That was the immediate family. In the house next door resided Angie's mother—who was Susana's father's sister—and her three youngest children, who were still at home; the older three, including Angie, lived nearby. A close family, its harmony had been disrupted when Susana had come home on college breaks spouting new ideas, criticizing her father and brothers for machismo, and announcing—not diplomatically—that she was a lesbian. A major rift had occurred when Susana received a scholarship to graduate school in San Diego. Her father had forbidden her to go. Susana had defied his authority. Susana's relationship with Isa had precipitated the final break. Susana had brought her lover home and an hour later stormed out, she and her father mutually vowing she would never enter the house again.

"But that was years ago," said Margo. "Didn't they have some kind of reconciliation since then?"

"Never," declared Isa, but Angie said, "Actually, her mother called her on the phone sometimes, when no one else was home."

"See?" said Isa. "Didn't I say Susana told Angie things she didn't tell me?"

"Family stuff, Isa," soothed Angie. "No big secret. Hey, I'm hungry and great smells are coming from the kitchen. Where are the kids?"

"I've already fed Mickey and put him to bed," said Isa. "I think Orion wants to watch television in his room."

"No way! I'll get him." Angie winked and hurried out of the room.

"Angie is everyone's favorite aunt," said Isa as she and Margo put a fragrant casserole, salad, and bread on the table. "Even Orion's."

Nevertheless, although Angie led Orion to the dinner table, she couldn't make him eat; he picked at his food. Nor did he respond to attempts to converse. Angie asked about the T-shirt he was wearing, and Orion mumbled and looked slightly sick. (The shirt advertised another rock group Margo hadn't heard of, Dead Can Dance. Orion mustn't have considered the name's current implication when he'd put on the shirt.)

Isa changed the subject. "Orion, remember how nice Barbara was the other night? Margo went to see her this afternoon."

"Mom?" He had turned so pale Margo thought he was going to faint. He whispered something in Isa's ear, she said, "Okay," and Orion left the table and went back to his room. He didn't take any dinner with him.

"Were Orion and Susana close?" Margo asked Angie after dinner. Angie was driving her to the women's shelter.

"I know they cared for each other. I think Orion's feeling bad because he didn't try harder to be friends with Susana. But Susana wasn't an easy person. And face it, it's tough enough for a kid to accept mom's new husband. Think how much tougher it is, especially for a boy, to accept mom's new 'wife.' "

At the Casa de Mujeres—the House of Women—on Los Angeles' Skid Row, Angie made introductions and then sat back while Margo spoke with the director of the shelter and two homeless women who had known Dawn; as much, they agreed, as anyone could know a person who never talked.

"So you never heard her speak?"

"Uh-uh," said Sharon, a heavy black woman.

"Not even when she cut herself bad once and needed help," added Olivia, a small woman with dark curly hair and a livid scar on one cheek.

"We have a doctor here one night a week and I got Dawn to see her," said the shelter director. "She couldn't find any obvious organic cause for Dawn's muteness. But even if it's psychosomatic, that doesn't mean Dawn can turn it on and off whenever she wants."

Dawn hadn't responded well to other attempts to communicate—asking her questions where she could nod yes or no, or giving her paper and a pencil to write. So what the women knew of her came from observation, rather than from things she had shared. Dawn had begun hanging out on Skid

Row about two years earlier. Before meeting Susana, she'd had several other "protectors" at one time or another—other homeless people, at one time a social worker. That seemed to be Dawn's main resource, the ability to inspire protectiveness in others. Sharon and Olivia, as well as the shelter director, felt that if Dawn found someone in San Diego who would look out for her, she was likely to stay there, rather than return to Los Angeles.

"She takes things," put in Sharon.

"You mean she steals?" asked Margo.

"It's more like a crow seeing something shiny and grabbing it. Dawn sees a pretty candy wrapper or a comb or stone in the road, and she puts it in her bag. Some lady at the Casa gave Dawn shit once because she took something of hers—something little, maybe a hair ribbon—and Dawn gave it right back. You know how you look when you're caught stealing, or you even think you're going to be caught?" asked Sharon. Olivia nodded. "Well, Dawn didn't look like that. She just looked confused."

"What about violence? Do you think she could have attacked Susana? Maybe had a fight with her?"

"She was a scared rabbit. She'd run before she'd fight."

"You weren't here the time some lady tried to take her shoes," said Olivia. "Those boots with fringe she always wears. She fought like a tiger."

"With her knife?" asked Margo.

"Nah, Dawn just jumped on the lady."

"She wouldn'ta pulled the knife on Susana," Sharon said.

"What about pushing her or hitting her?"

"She'd never hurt Susana," said Sharon. "She'd never go after Susana with that knife."

Throughout the discussion at the shelter, Margo sensed that Angie, sitting silently, was measuring or judging her in some way. She asked about it when they returned to Angie's car.

The nun laughed. "Was I that obvious? All right, I wanted to see how you were with the women. If you treated them with respect. You did."

Angie didn't speak again, however, or invite speech, until they had left the freeway. Then she pulled over on a hilly residential street.

"I told you that after I became a nun, Susana regarded talking to me a little like going to confession. I thought of it that way, too. Sure, Susana told me things because we'd always talked to each other, but she also told me because she trusted me to hold her confidences sacred. Like keeping secrets for each other when we were kids, but bigger than that, because this time God was involved. You're not Catholic, are you? So this probably doesn't make sense to you. But I had to know what kind of person you were, because what I'm going to tell you represents, to me, breaking a sacred trust."

Angie paused. Margo became aware of the chill in the car. Deceptive Southern California doesn't look like a desert, and no matter how long she had lived there, she forgot that the day's warmth rarely lasted past sunset. She pulled her jacket tight around her, for all the good the lightweight fabric would do.

"Susana came and talked to me a few months ago," Angie said. "She had just gotten back from a trip through the Southwest—Colorado, New Mexico, Arizona. Something happened on the trip, something she found out about, that upset her. How can I say this? She felt that possibly an injustice was being done and that she might be in a position to correct it. But for one thing, she wasn't sure if it was a real injustice or just a misunderstanding. She was worried that she could do more harm than good by getting involved. And if she did decide to get involved, she wasn't sure of the best way to do it. We talked for about an hour. She didn't make any decisions right then, so I don't know if she did any of the things she discussed with me. And I don't know if this has anything to do with her death."

Margo waited for her to continue. But apparently the nun had finished.

"Angie." Margo reached for her hand and came into contact with a string of beads—Angie was fingering a rosary. "You have to tell me more. Give me a name. Or some details about the injustice Susana wanted to correct."

"No names. I won't be responsible for casting guilt on someone who most likely had nothing to do with Susana's death." Angie started the car.

"Was it a man? A woman?"

As Angie drove silently, Margo felt a flood of resentment toward all religions and the blind obedience they demanded— taking someone as smart and funny as Angie and implanting a control box in her brain. Had Susana been as stubborn as her cousin? Had it so exasperated someone that they had pushed her into her sculpture?

Margo tried one more time. "What about Susana's trip? Who did she see? Did she mention a specific place where she found out about this thing?"

"Margo, she didn't tell me that. Honestly."

"Angie, don't you think Susana would want you to tell me the whole story? In case it leads to the person who killed her?"

"She might," agreed Angie. "But like I said, this isn't just between Susana and me. It's between Susana and me and God."

20 / Altered State

Jill had heard that if an event occurs when you're in a particular physical state, for instance, drunkenness or extreme fatigue, your best chance of retrieving the memory of the event is to be in the same state again. She would have liked to trash the new marijuana she'd used the day of Susana's murder, but she was getting desperate. The cops had found out about the fight she'd had with Susana, and they kept coming around and asking about it. Hell, they even knew about Jill trapping Dawn in Tom's installation—had she gabbed her head off that night, when the cops questioned her while she was stoned? Even Lyman had gone from smiling in a reassuring fashion to pushing for hypnosis, and Jill really didn't go for the idea of some hypnotist rummaging around in her head.

She rolled the joint and smoked it fast, not just inviting the memory but begging for it. And it came.

Saturday, shortly after Jill had done the grass, Susana had come to her performance space. Susana had guessed Jill had locked Dawn into Tom's installation, and Jill admitted it. They argued. That much Jill had remembered before. Now more of the scene returned.

"Come on, Susana," Jill said. "Dawn wasn't seriously traumatized. And I was giving her a little back for what she's done to everyone here."

"What are you talking about?" demanded Susana.

"Your little angel takes things. My Black and Decker drill, that snowball of Carola's, who knows what else?"

"I don't believe it. And even if it were true, that's no reason to do what you did to her. That was like torturing a kitten."

"You think that was worse than what you've done to her? Finding a homeless, emotionally ill woman who can't say a word for herself and keeping her around as virtual slave labor?"

"Fuck you, Jill!" Susana pushed her and Jill stumbled backward.

What a thrilling development! Jill would have loved to shove back, but she needed to psych herself up for her performance. Her tone was conciliatory, even though she couldn't go so far as to offer an apology she didn't mean.

"I didn't know Dawn would get so freaked out," Jill said. "Or that it would be so long before anyone found her. She's all right now, isn't she?"

"It's hard to tell with her." Susana spoke calmly, as if her small act of violence toward Jill had exhausted her anger. "Are you sure about her taking things?"

"I saw her with Carola's snowball. I tried to get a look inside her bag—I want that drill back—but she ran away."

"I'll talk to her. But stay away from her, Jill, okay? If you want to play practical jokes, play them on me. But leave Dawn alone."

Susana left then. Visually, Jill had focused on Susana's sharp shoulder blades showing through the black jumpsuit she always worked in, as she went through the door. Emotionally, the memory held no anger, either felt by her or coming from Susana. Jill was certain she and Susana had parted on good terms.

So why did she have one final image, of Susana coming back and standing in the doorway—just standing there, not saying anything? And looking horrible?

21 / Job Security

For possibly the first time since Alex had become station manager, Margo was looking forward to the Wednesday afternoon staff meeting. Driving back to San Diego from Isa's that morning, she anticipated Alex asking how the Susana Contreras story was going . . . and herself saying, "I've got an exclusive with Susana's lover, Isa Reid." Maybe she had a chance at the full-time reporting job after all!

She arrived at the station at eleven and kicked Dennis Zachary Powell out of an editing room—Alex had given her priority on editing facilities. It didn't exactly increase her popularity with the rest of the staff, but she needed that room. She spent the three hours before the meeting editing the Isa interview and recording her own introduction and segues so the piece could air during *All Things Considered* late that afternoon. No time for lunch—on the way into the meeting, she grabbed one of the yogurts she periodically stocked in the station refrigerator; the yogurt was two weeks past the expiration date on the carton, but it smelled fine.

Margo was putting the first spoonful of yogurt in her mouth when Alex opened the meeting by turning to her. Top story of the week! The disturbing thing was, Alex didn't sound as if he were about to launch into encomiums. Margo put down her spoon.

"*Where* did you go to journalism school?" said Alex. It was generally bad news when he asked a question to which he already knew the answer.

"Here. San Diego State."

"Oh. Right." Alex had never made any attempt to hide his disdain for SDSU, the alma mater of most of the staff. "Did they teach you anything about doing interviews there? About how to approach touchy subjects?"

"Of course. Alex, what's the problem?" Margo spoke firmly, but her limbs felt like jelly. Just as Alex believed in public praise, he believed in public flogging.

"You may recall that this radio station happens to be publicly supported. That means we depend on the goodwill of this city. I got a call from one of our strong friends in the community who was outraged over the way you're investigating the Susana Contreras story."

"Who was it? Someone I interviewed?"

"That doesn't matter."

"Maybe I was getting too close to something."

"It's possible. But a seasoned reporter handles things with a little finesse. If I hear one more complaint, I'm going to have to give this story to someone else."

"I want to know who called!" Margo protested, although she knew defensiveness really brought out the bully in her boss.

"I expect my reporters to conduct themselves professionally. That includes taking criticism like professionals."

She was sure she heard a snicker. Dennis? Ray? It could be any of the half dozen full- and part-time reporters, virtually all of them threatened by Margo's presumed rise in Alex's estimation; they needn't have worried.

As Alex continued the meeting, Margo stirred her yogurt without eating it; the little blueberries resembled rabbit turds.

All of those public radio stations in Los Angeles. If she could find a job at one of them, she could get a little apartment in L.A. to stay in during the week and see Barry every weekend. Or she and Barry could move to north San Diego County and cut her commute by half an hour. It would still be a hellish drive.

Calming down a little, she realized Alex wouldn't have raked her over the coals unless he'd been badly raked himself. As precarious as her own job was, Alex's position as station manager required keeping happy a board of some dozen powerful San Diego citizens; and after only five months on the job, he hadn't built the kind of alliances that would allow him to step on a few toes. Did anyone Margo had interviewed sit on the board of KSDR or contribute heavily? Louise O'Quinn was the obvious person who came to mind. Louise wasn't a member of the board, but surely she sent the occasional thousand dollar check to public radio; and she wouldn't be shy about raising a little hell.

"Alex? Excuse me, Alex?" Standing in the doorway, the receptionist, Lisa, spoke tentatively; nothing except breaking news was supposed to interrupt the staff meeting. "There's a policeman here and he insists on talking to Margo."

Great! She could just see her job chances plummeting another few notches.

Lieutenant Donny Obayashi was waiting at the reception desk. Margo took him into her office.

"Play this, okay?" Obayashi handed her a cassette tape

The tape was from the Mexican restaurant the Friday before, and he had cued it to the last thing she'd recorded, when Jill went into her fake convulsions. There was a cry—Jill's—and exclamations of "Jill!" "What is it?" before Margo had turned off the tape recorder and tried to help.

"What happened there?" said Obayashi.

Margo explained.

"You mean there was nothing wrong with her? She was just doing it as a joke?" he said.

"Not a joke. Jill called it an art-life experiment—playing with the boundary between art and life. The idea is, is a stage the only place where Jill can do one of her performances?"

"You don't say." Obayashi's intelligent brown eyes showed great interest, but Margo didn't think it was because he found the concept aesthetically intriguing. "Did she pull stunts like that a lot?"

"What she did in the restaurant is the only incident I know about. Do you know about something else?" she said, responding to Obayashi's bemused look.

"You did interviews with the artists in this show, right?" he said, ignoring her question. "All three of them—Susana Contreras, Tom Fall, Jill Iverson?"

Margo nodded.

"Did you know any of them before?"

"No."

"Not Jill Iverson, for instance?"

"No."

"But you got to like her. She's a likable gal. The kind of person I'd call a kook, but—"

"What's the point, Lieutenant?" said Margo. She had fished for enough information herself to know when someone had cast a line in her direction.

"Why didn't you give me the tape of your interview with Iverson?"

"I did!" Margo had stopped at KSDR before leaving for Los Angeles the day before and handed all of her Capelli tapes to a student assistant to dub and then deliver to the police department.

Obayashi shook his head. "It wasn't there."

"Well, it wasn't intentional. I'll make a dub for you now," she said, opening her tape drawer, to which the assistant had returned her originals. The tape drawer was the one part of her desk she consistently kept in order; there was too much at stake if she misplaced a tape.

The Capelli tapes were in a neat stack, fastened with a rubber band. She checked the labels: "Tom Fall," "Susana Contreras," "Susana Contreras followup," "Friday lunch/Opening." The interview with Jill was missing, nor was it among the other tapes in the drawer.

Obayashi had watched silently while she went through the tape drawer.

"You might think you're helping your friend by withholding that tape," he said.

"I thought I *was* giving it to you." She hadn't inventoried the tapes the day before.

"You have zilch security here," mused Obayashi. "While that receptionist was away, getting you out of your meeting, I could have taken anything."

"But you'd have to know where to take it from."

"True." Obayashi sounded as if he thought Margo might have tipped Jill off as to where the tape could be found.

Margo promised to look for the cassette. For now, she'd make the police a copy of the version she'd transferred to reel-to-reel. That tape was already edited, but it still contained Jill's statement: "*I'll do anything to get a reaction.*" What would Obayashi make of that?

Margo was running late after dubbing the tape for Obayashi. As she grabbed her tape recorder and a blank cassette, Ray Fernandez came into the office and shut the door. For the first time all week, he looked friendly. Damn! This was not the time for the heart-to-heart she and Ray needed to have.

"Alex was rough on you," said Ray. No wonder he was smiling, having witnessed her humiliation.

"Yeah," she said, moving to leave.

He caught her arm. "I know who called this morning and complained. I was by the reception desk and I heard Lisa transfer the call. It was Bernard Capelli."

Margo hadn't even talked to Bernard Capelli! Someone must have called Bernard and asked him to intervene, which widened the field considerably. Even one of the artists or Isa might have had Capelli's ear, although Margo was more inclined to suspect someone from the money end of the art business—Louise, Barbara Scholl, or the man she was on her way to see, James Carmichael.

22 / The Collector

Charlotte Meyers was occupying her usual Wednesday afternoon post at the Capelli's information desk. The septuagenarian volunteer laid down her current reading matter—a Stephen King novel with a bloodcurdling cover—and greeted Margo enthusiastically.

"Didn't they give you the day off, since the foundation is closed all week?" Margo asked her.

"Do you think I'd miss all the excitement? Seriously, this is a tragedy. I came because who knows, they might need me. My official job is just to sit here at the desk, but I've had a lifetime of office experience, so sometimes I help out with other things, too."

A light bulb went on above Margo's head. Hadn't James's secretary said that whenever she had to do bookkeeping, she got help from one of the volunteers? And hadn't Charlotte done her husband's books for years?

"Charlotte, when do you get off work today?"

"I was about to leave, but it's years since anyone's asked me that. What have you got in mind?" she said roguishly.

"I'm seeing James but I should be done in half an hour. Could I take you out for a drink?"

"It's years since anyone asked me that, either. Wait till I tell Al! But let's make it coffee, there's nothing I love more than coffee. At the Caff Fiend," she added, naming a particularly hip hangout nearby. "Besides," she added, "if you don't mind my saying so, you look like you could use some coffee, dear."

Coffee? What Margo really wanted was a new body, preferably one ten years younger. She rarely slept well in a strange place, and at Isa's, her usual travel insomnia had been exacerbated by too much to think about. What kind of injustice had Susana uncovered that Angie refused to reveal? She had asked Isa, but it was as Isa'd said before—there were things Susana used to tell Angie that she told no one else.

Margo blamed her exhaustion for what happened next with James Carmichael. If she'd been just a little more alert, she might have realized the danger she was walking into.

The Capelli's upstairs administrative offices were reached by a stairway just beyond Susana's installation. Climbing the stairs, Margo heard an odd sound that made her think of baseball or tennis—the smack of wood hitting against something? In the outer office she found James Carmichael, boy wonder of the art world, juggling. In front of him—in mid-air—floated a stick that looked rather like a small baseball bat, except both ends were equally thick and tapered to a thinner middle. James was rhythmically hitting the stick back and forth between two thin wooden rods, keeping the stick directly in front of him, its center at about waist height.

Margo applauded.

"Hi!" called out James. "Just working off a little tension."

The Capelli Foundation was an extremely tight ship, Margo had been told. James, his secretary, and a part-time membership coordinator were the only regular employees. Services such as public relations and security were contracted out. James was the only person in the office this late in the afternoon.

"These are called devil sticks," he said, making the middle stick do a flip, then catching it. "Do you want to try?"

"Sure. What do I do?"

"Hold one of the hand sticks in each hand," he said, giving her the two thin rods. "That's it. Then you place the center stick on the floor in front of you, it's got to be standing vertically. You get it going with the two hand sticks. You want to be hitting the center stick about halfway between the middle and the top."

Tests of coordination had never been Margo's forte, and she handed the sticks back to James after several fumbling attempts. Gleefully he got the center stick into the air again.

"The trick is to establish a rhythm and maintain equal force on both sides," he said, the stick dancing magically before him. As if in a single fluid motion he caught the three sticks in one hand and gestured for her to follow him into his office. He tossed the hand sticks into a red plastic box that held other juggling paraphernalia; she saw several balls and brightly colored plastic clubs.

"I'm generally limiting my contacts with the media to news conferences," said James, sitting at his desk. He hadn't put away the center stick but bounced it against his knee with a nervous energy that made Margo feel edgy. "But I know you're interested in the artistic side of all this. That's why I'm happy to give you an interview. I'm concerned that with everything else happening, the artists' work won't get the notice it deserves."

The director of the Capelli Foundation proceeded to deliver an insightful, refreshingly jargon-free critique of the artistic significance of Tom's and Susana's installations and how they fit into the Capelli's mission of promoting postmodern art. He concluded by announcing that the show would reopen the next week—Susana's installation, as well as Tom's—

and Jill's performance was going to be rescheduled. The Capelli board had decided it would be unfair to the artists and the public to keep the show closed.

"Wasn't Susana's piece dismantled by the police?"

"That's right. It will have to be partly reassembled. The police have finished whatever tests they had to conduct, so it's just a matter of our staff reconstructing it." He rapped the devil stick sharply against the desk, scowling like a thwarted child.

"Is something wrong?"

"Not really. One of our part-timers, someone we could have used to put Susana's piece back together, quit this week without giving any notice. He just left a message on the answering machine that he'd gotten a grant and was going to Rome. I think he actually called from the airport."

"Who was it?"

"I don't pay much attention to the part-time staff. Peter something?"

"Peter Vance?"

"That's it."

That was strange. If Peter had received a grant, surely he'd known about it for some time, at least long enough to make a plane reservation. Had he kept his good luck a secret just so he could quit his job precipitously, a way to thumb his nose at a boss who barely knew his name—the same kind of resentful act as vandalizing Louise's car? Peter had stood up Tom at the opening. But had he really not come to the Capelli that night? Or had he gone first to see the installation by Susana, the acclaimed darling of the same art critic who'd thwarted his own career? Had he killed Susana and fled, the grant nothing but a fiction to get him on a plane out of the country? Nevertheless, it was James Carmichael, not Peter, who was noted for going into rages, Margo reminded herself, hearing the *whap! whap!* of the juggling stick against the Capelli director's leg.

"I understand the price of Susana's work will go up now," she said.

"Most likely." *Whap!* "Her lifetime body of work will be evaluated, and I think the ultimate critical judgment will come out in her favor."

"What about the pieces of Susana's that you own? Those are in your personal collection, aren't they, not in the Capelli's? Will you sell them?"

The juggling stick thwacked against the desk.

"Unlike the stereotypical collector of the past decade, I don't buy art as an investment," said James Carmichael. "I buy things I love and want to have around me. Susana's work is even more valuable to me since there will be no more. No matter what kind of price they might bring."

Margo didn't feel ready to ask him about the Capelli finances, not unless she had something concrete on which to base her questions; and not just after she'd been threatened with having the assignment taken away. James, in any event, got up and walked her to the door. As they stood in the outer office murmuring polite goodbyes, the telephone rang; it was picked up by the answering machine.

"James," came an angry voice over the speaker. "It's Sophie. I gave you a week, goddammit . . ."

James ran into his office to grab the phone. He closed the door, but he'd neglected to turn off the answering machine.

"Soph, I sent you half," Margo heard James say.

"Fuck half." Margo remembered that Sophie was the name of James's former wife. James tried to break in, but Sophie pounded away, "You want me to give the kids half dinners, half an education, only left shoes? Or maybe you'd prefer right shoes? I told you, James, I'm not going to let you play this game. You'll be hearing from my lawyer." She slammed down the receiver.

Inside James's office, something smashed. Then something else.

"James, are you all right?" Margo called.

It wasn't that she felt no fear. It was that she couldn't keep herself from opening James's office door. In one look she took in the shattered glass frame of a photograph on the wall and James himself, who seemed unaware that he was waving the wooden juggling stick above his head. He was advancing toward her faster than she would have thought possible.

She stepped backward, running into the secretary's desk.

Cursing—at Sophie, at all women—James seemed beyond rational speech.

"I'm sorry, I'll go now," Margo said, trying to edge around the desk toward the door.

James blocked the way. As if in a trance, he came at her, the stick swishing through the air.

"James! Cut it out!" she yelled.

He pulled back the stick like a home run hitter about to send one out of the park.

Margo thrust her leg into a kick, aimed for his groin, and connected. James howled and stepped back, giving her just enough room to flee.

23 / Gotta Dance

"What's wrong?" Charlotte Meyers regarded Margo intently over the black table.

A lot of things at the Caff Fiend were black—the furniture, the dyed hair of many of the patrons, and the regulation garb of tight-fitting slacks, vests, and leather jackets. Unlike the beach areas of town, where everyone looked like a blond surfer, San Diego's downtown style was decidedly bohemian; natural blonds who hung out here dyed their hair jet black. It was a look with which Margo fit in marginally, in her dark skirt and red blouse. Charlotte, however, resembled a strange bird, her vast body plumaged in a turquoise dress.

"Just tired. The coffee will help."

"Decaf? Hah!" exclaimed Charlotte. They had agreed to share a carafe of decaffeinated brew, Margo because she was shaking after the incident with James and didn't figure her system needed more stimulation; and Charlotte grumbling about doctor's orders.

"You came running out of there pretty fast," said Charlotte.

"Um." All it would take was one motherly cluck of concern, and Margo would fall weeping onto Charlotte's massive breast, sobbing out her terror.

"Decaf Viennese?" The ultra-hip young waiter set a carafe and cups on the table as if performing a large favor.

"Can we get something to eat, too?" Charlotte asked him. "What do you think, Margo? A hamburger for protein?"

"Charlotte, this place is vegetarian," said Margo. The waiter looked murderous, and Margo might have enjoyed watching Charlotte take him on, but at the moment she was too close to hysteria. "Let's get a cheese and fruit plate."

"And a brownie," Charlotte called after the waiter, who gave no sign he'd heard. "You look like you need the energy. Cheese and fruit!" she fumed, emptying two packets of artificial sweetener into her coffee and stirring noisily. "First they tell you no sugar, then you have to drink ersatz coffee, now it's no meat. There's only one thing missing. Taste. You take your coffee black? No wonder you're thin. Your last name is Simon, isn't it? Are you Jewish, dear?"

Margo's mouth dropped open before she uttered, "Yes." Charlotte's was the kind of question she would have expected from an old yenta back in Connecticut where she'd grown up. California Jews tended to be more assimilated. The few yenta types she had met in San Diego were less likely to ask her religion than to quiz her on her astrological sign (Aquarius).

"Married?"

Margo nodded. Being around the garrulous Charlotte made Margo feel as if she were visiting her Aunt Rose, an irritating person, but one who was oddly comforting.

"*Mazel tov.* And what does Mr. Simon do?"

"Actually, Mr. Dawes. He's an oceanographer at the Torrey Institution at UCSD."

Charlotte's eyebrows went up, and Margo could hear her thinking, *Dawes doesn't sound Jewish.* Barry, in fact, was a Welsh lapsed Catholic. All Charlotte said, however, was, "One of my son's wives does that. Uses her maiden name. It's progressive, they tell me. But a little hard on the children. Do you have children, dear?"

"Two, from my husband's first marriage." To forestall queries about her own (ambivalent) intentions in the reproduction department, Margo said quickly, "You help with the books at the Capelli sometimes, don't you?" She realized she felt much calmer after Charlotte's dithering.

"I help out a little," answered Charlotte. "That Carola's a nice girl, but I don't think she knows how to add two and two."

"I'm not sure how to ask this, I'm not familiar with bookkeeping. Does everything seem all right to you?"

"I don't do much, just some bank reconciliations, things like that." Charlotte removed her lavender-tinted glasses, breathed on the lenses, and wiped them with a napkin. Margo recognized the gesture; she did the same thing when she was wearing her glasses and wanted to avoid someone's eyes. "A lot of the financial information is on computer and I've never understood computers," said Charlotte. " 'User friendly'— what do I know from 'user friendly'? Give me a ledger book any day, that's friendly enough for me."

The waiter came back with their food. At Charlotte's insistence, Margo ate some cheese and apple slices.

"Have you noticed any irregularities in the books?" she tried again. "Money not accounted for? Maybe money in the wrong account?"

"Mind if I have a taste of that brownie?"

"Charlotte!"

"You're right, my doctor would kill me. If the brownie didn't kill me first."

"A little brownie is good for you, help yourself. What about the books?"

Charlotte slowly chewed a mouthful of brownie and washed it down with coffee. "You know, when I was young I never had to look for things to care about. They were just there.

My family didn't have much, and all of us had to work hard to keep food on the table and a roof over our heads. I married Al and we were poor, too. Then, after a while, we weren't so poor, but there were always the children to think about. And I helped in the business, too. So three years ago we move here, retirement in the sunshine, a nice change from Pittsburgh, right? Al has his golf, but what do I have? Gossiping with the other ladies in the condominium complex? That gets old—why not, all of us *are* old. But how many times can you hear about Ann Halloran's gall bladder surgery before you want to go after Ann with a knife yourself? Then someone tells me about this art museum. I always liked art. I never had the time for it, but when I was a girl I used to draw. My first job was in a fish market and they had me do the signs. I wouldn't just put up the prices, I'd make a picture of the fish and it was a good picture. If we had cod, my picture looked like a cod, not a trout." She reached across the table and forked another piece of brownie.

"Like I said," she continued, "someone tells me this Capelli museum needs volunteers. And it's another world. I see things I never would have believed were art, but I meet the artists and they're all very nice about explaining. I welcome people to the museum and hear them say how glad they are that a museum like this exists in San Diego. There's nowhere I'd enjoy volunteering my time so much. And it's just a short drive from the condo. So . . ." She paused.

"So?"

"So who gives a damn if they're not the world's greatest bookkeepers?" Charlotte tossed her head, disturbing not a hair of her short apricot-dyed coif. But for an instant Margo saw the image of a young woman—a girl who took pride in her drawings—who must have had flowing hair.

"Charlotte, have you talked to anyone about it? Just giving them the benefit of the doubt and assuming that any mistakes were made innocently, if there are discrepancies they should be told."

"Like I said, I don't know from computers. How am I supposed to know if I'm reading the whatchamacallit, the printout, right? Besides, I promised Carola I wouldn't tell James I was helping her." She pulled the brownie over to her side of the table and dug in. "I heard you on the radio when I was driving over here from the Capelli. Talking to Susana's girlfriend, poor thing. Are you investigating Susana's murder? Tell me about it." Charlotte spoke firmly, a clear message to back off on the question of Capelli finances. "You're not eating," she added.

Margo spread some Brie on a piece of French bread. Charlotte coaxed information out of her skillfully, even getting her to relate how James had nearly attacked her, a story to which Charlotte listened with consternation.

"You don't think there's a connection between all this and the bookkeeping, um, problem?" said Charlotte.

"I don't know. Susana's cousin said Susana had discovered an injustice—I suppose that might be it."

"Her cousin the nun?" Charlotte sounded dubious of the entire Catholic hierarchy, from the Pope on down. "James really came at you with a baseball bat?"

"A thing like a baseball bat."

"Here's what I'll do. If you want to go to Mr. Capelli and say there *might* be a bookkeeping problem, you can tell him he's welcome to call me. Here's my number." Charlotte wrote it on a napkin. "I'll talk to him. But not to anyone else. And if you try to report this on the radio, I'll . . . I'll deny I ever said anything," she concluded, emphasizing each word as if she were remembering them from one of the steamy novels she liked to read.

Lingering after Charlotte had left, Margo poured the last of the coffee from the carafe into her cup and stared into its depths. So James *was* fiddling with the Capelli finances; that was the clear implication of what Charlotte had said. Was that the injustice Susana had discovered? And had Susana confronted James with it, provoking the same kind of blind rage he'd gone into after the phone call from his ex-wife? In her mind Margo again saw him advancing on her, so transformed by anger he didn't even seem to realize who she was. Telling the story to the soothing Charlotte, Margo had been able to chuckle over the spectacle of the director of the Capelli menacing her with a juggling stick. Now she felt shaky again. She got out her datebook to copy Charlotte's phone number from the scrap of napkin . . . and realized it was Wednesday, which meant that her dance class started in half an hour, only a few blocks away.

If it were anything else, she would have canceled and gone home for a hot bath. But dance hath amazing powers to heal the spirit. She phoned Barry to let him know she had returned from Los Angeles and would be home later. Jenny answered—Jenny in a mood, handing the phone to her father with a grunt.

"What's the problem?" Margo asked him. "If you can say."

"We're making pizza from scratch," said Barry brightly.

"Is Jenny off pizza this week?" It was comforting to discuss the domestic details.

"That's right." A woeful note crept into his voice. His daughter's unpredictable dietary rules bothered him more than they did Margo, who had gone on a few weird diets herself at Jenny's age.

"And your pizza's so fantastic!"

"You're talking about me!" accused Jenny in the background.

"Jen, you're such a dickhead," came the latest favorite cuss word among David's sixth-grade set. "Yow! Da-ad!" he exclaimed; Jenny must have retaliated physically.

"Save some pizza for me," said Margo. "Especially if you're doing one with eggplant and Greek olives on it. And good luck."

Only five blocks separated the coffeehouse from the dance studio. But where the Caff Fiend sat amid a lively cluster of galleries and retail spaces, the studio was located deeper in San Diego's old warehouse district, a lonely area even in the daytime. Margo scanned the dark street carefully before leaving her car; she saw no one but a man pushing a shopping cart on the next block. She always kept a leotard and tights in the car (taking them out to wash when they smelled disgusting), and she changed into them in the dressing room of the studio.

The weekly improvisation class she attended would look bizarre, she knew, to anyone whose idea of dance was a disciplined ballet class. Margo had loved the beauty and discipline of ballet herself, when she'd studied it as a girl. But at thirty-eight she was less interested in perfecting her arabesque than in using dance for some of the same reasons primitive people danced originally: to express emotion, confront the mysteries of life, and build a sense of community. Often the class of six women began by sitting in a circle and talking about what was happening in their lives; it was information that Fay, the teacher, used as a springboard for improvisation exercises.

Margo had thought she'd want to discuss Susana's murder. Once in the studio, however, she didn't want to talk at all. Bypassing the usual chat that preceded class, she went to the far end of the room and began stretching. The others, responding to her mood, stopped visiting with each other and came out on the floor as well.

"Stretch whatever needs stretching and pay attention to your breath," instructed Fay quietly.

Margo had the feeling of breathing—really breathing—for the first time since the confrontation in James's office; maybe for the first time since Saturday night, when Isa had called out for a doctor.

After the warmup, Fay suggested that they each "dance their week," not so much acting things out but finding qualities and moods. Fay beat a drum and Margo took herself back to the moment when she was standing next to Susana's metal bed, the doctors bending over the artist's body and getting no response. Reactions she had made herself suppress at the time, she played out now: shock that took her careening around the studio; sadness that brought her to her knees.

She moved next into the flurry of activity that had happened since the murder and her confusion about the people she had talked to. What was important and what irrelevant? Who was lying? Throwing herself into flailing movements, she tried to avoid thinking in words but instead focused on images: Tom and Vicki Fall, at odds in their perfect suburban house. Louise O'Quinn's face etched with grief, against the opulent background of her estate. Jill Iverson stoned and evasive. Isa Reid sobbing and the exquisite drawings she'd done. Barbara Scholl denying that her gallery was in financial trouble. The women at the shelter convinced of Dawn's innocence because Dawn wouldn't have come at Susana with her knife . . . but the women didn't know how Susana had actually died. Angie saying that something had happened on Susana's Southwest trip—"some injustice" Susana had found out about—but refusing to give any details. Finally Margo went back to the scene with James Carmichael, alternating between taking the fierce posture of a warrior and expressing the shakiness she'd felt inside. At last she gave into the shaking, exaggerating it, until it was gone.

As she flopped, spent, onto the studio floor, she became aware that nearby, Tess, who had two toddlers, was miming pushing a swing. And Laurie was running in place, as she often said she did in her fast-track job.

Margo walked out of the studio feeling exhausted, but it was a clean physical exhaustion that she knew would lead to sleep, instead of the jangly, raw-nerves-exposed tiredness she had felt before. She was standing on the street saying good night to the other class members when two street people came toward them. One of the transients was huge, but as they came into the light outside the studio, Margo saw that both were women. She reached into her pocket. She no longer gave anything to male panhandlers, having been hassled once too often, but she always tried to carry pocket change in case a woman asked.

The women approached them, the big one making the request. The other woman, her face partly obscured by the slouchy brim of a stylish burgundy-colored hat, was Susana Contreras.

Margo nearly screamed. A closer look revealed her error. On the thin woman's feet were fringed boots and on her narrow face an absence of expression that could denote a lack of intelligence or could simply be the numbness produced by years of living on the street. The woman was not Susana, but Dawn, wearing one of Susana's black jumpsuits. As in the picture Isa had sketched, the hat, partially covering Dawn's forehead, had eliminated the difference between the two women's hairstyles.

Pretending to reach out with money, Margo grasped Dawn's wrist. "Please, can I talk to you?"

Dawn jerked away and the big woman whomped Margo's arm so hard she fell to the ground. The two took off running, Tess and Fay in pursuit. Margo picked herself up and chased after them.

"They disappeared," Tess panted, when Margo caught up with her and Fay two blocks later. "How's your arm?"

"Hurts like hell."

"Should we take you to the emergency room?"

"Nah." Margo wiggled her fingers, wincing. "Everything moves."

"Who was that?" said Fay.

Margo briefly explained as they walked back to the studio.

"Look at this." Tess stooped beside a building and came up holding a burgundy hat. "It's the one Dawn was wearing. Boy, the Salvation Army is carrying great stuff these days. Yours, for bravery," she said, giving it to Margo. "As long as I get to borrow it sometimes."

24 / An Assertive Woman

Black-robed and imperious, the legendary Martha Graham danced center stage, her eyes emphasized dramatically with thick wings of black liner, her elbows crooked sharply above her crouching form. A mythic figure, pitiless as a Sphinx, she seemed indifferent to the hushed audience . . . and to the one sorry dancer who, alone among the chorus, kept muffing the steps. The young woman, auburn hair flopping across her face, stumbled and faltered until finally, even Graham noticed her. "Stop!" she commanded. "You!" Everyone in the huge concert hall followed her pointing finger as the hapless dancer looked up. Margo, in the audience, saw that it was Vicki Fall. "You haven't got the movement," said Graham severely. "Watch." She demonstrated a demi-plié with a deep pelvic contraction. "Now do it right." Vicki pliéd and contracted until sweat dripped from her body and tears coursed down her cheeks. But Graham wasn't satisfied. "That's not it!" she snapped. "Off the stage!" Vicki raced, sobbing, into the wings, while the chorus, doing perfect contractions, shrieked, "Off with her head! Off with her head!"

Margo woke up feeling as if she'd done several dozen pelvic contractions herself. She must have danced harder than she had realized the night before. And she had slept in, until after eight. Barry and the kids must have slipped away quietly over half an hour ago. She reached for her glasses . . . and yelped in pain. Her arm, where Dawn's Amazon friend had struck it, had turned purple.

While she cooked oatmeal in the microwave, she kept seeing the scene her unconscious had served up during the night. She could understand dreaming of Martha Graham, right after her dance class. But what was Vicki Fall doing in the dream, as inept and humiliated onstage as she generally seemed in life? Margo cringed, thinking of her visit to the Falls' on Sunday, especially remembering Tom petting the cat and then complaining about it when Vicki came home. Not to mention his transparent attempt to play the attentive husband, unpacking the groceries and urging Vicki to recount how they'd spent the day before.

Awkward with her left hand—naturally she had reached for Dawn with her dominant right—Margo stirred raisins and honey into her oatmeal. And stopped. Every bit as phony as Tom's solicitousness that day, she realized, was the way Vicki had produced a detailed account of how she and Tom had spent the afternoon of Susana's murder. Vicki, who seemed unable to recite a grocery list without going off on five tangents, must have been rehearsed to tell such a coherent story.

Margo called the Falls' home, but hung up when Tom answered the phone. She wanted to see Vicki without her drama coach knowing about it. Besides, Vicki was probably at work already. What had she said she did? Margo tried the Capelli and was in luck. Carola happened to know Vicki sold shoes at the Nordstrom in the Fashion Valley shopping mall.

"The upstairs department with the funky shoes," said Carola. "Not the one on the first floor with the boring, conservative little pumps. I was there last week and bought some turquoise basketball shoes."

There was one more call to make, to arrange an appointment with Bernard Capelli. Reaching Bernard's real estate development company, she was blocked by his secretary, a man with a *Masterpiece Theater* accent who insisted that all media contacts related to the Capelli Foundation be directed to the foundation's public relations agency.

"Please tell him," she tried, grasping at straws, "that if truth is beauty, then I've found something really beautiful."

The secretary made no comment as he repeated the message, but there was a smirk in his voice. He could no doubt recite the entire *Ode on a Grecian Urn* from memory.

Margo's sister the Yuppie would have approved, which was why she felt sheepish about her first stop after leaving the house—the dry cleaner, where she dropped off the hat she had inherited from Dawn. "Who knows where it might have been?" Audrey Simon Siegel would have asked. Then again, Margo had an excellent idea where the burgundy hat had spent the past few days: lying low in various places not noted for their cleanliness. Both Dawn and her ham-fisted friend had smelled rank.

Audrey would have relished Margo's next destination as well. A marketing executive who pulled in more in two months than Margo earned in a year (a fact she had "accidentally" let slip at a family reunion), Audrey was a connoisseur of major department stores.

Customers in Nordstrom's shoe department were scarce on a Thursday morning, and Margo had to fend off two eager salespeople before Vicki Fall emerged from a back room. Vicki briefly looking panicked when she spotted Margo, but then approached her, smiling professionally.

"Hi. What kind of shoes are you looking for?"

"Actually, I came to talk. Can you take a break?"

"Uh-uh." The panicky look again.

"Okay, I'll try these. These. These. And these." Margo pointed to the four nearest pairs of shoes, barely seeing them. She asked Vicki to bring two different sizes of each. That ought to take time.

She took a seat at the edge of the shoe department, where a monitor blaring music videos would keep their conversation private, and considered what strategy might induce Vicki to part with information. But, once resigned to it, Vicki actually seemed to want to talk.

"You must think I'm a fool," she said, slipping Margo's foot into a pink espadrille. "Putting up with Tom, I mean. But you have to understand, I was really young when he and I got together, I didn't know anything about standing up for myself. And we got into a bad pattern, you know, the kind of thing that's no one's fault. We just established a negative dynamic where he puts me down all the time, and I figure I deserve it." She said the words as if they were newly minted. "At least I used to figure I deserved it, until I started an assertiveness class. Did you ever take assertiveness training? You don't seem like you'd need it. Get up and walk around in the shoes, okay? So it looks like I'm really waiting on you. The mirror's right over there," she said loudly.

Margo paraded obligingly. "They're comfortable, but I don't know about pink," she announced, before sitting back down and saying quietly, "I didn't take assertiveness training, but I sure could have used it in the first relationship I had." She'd certainly had a number of occasions lately to recall her years in Santa Fe.

"Did you let him get away with criticizing you?" asked Vicki happily, then blushed. It reminded Margo of her own thrill of recognition when other women in her consciousness-raising group had complained about their men; and then her dismay at being glad to hear anyone else was experiencing that kind of pain.

"God, yes," she said. "And making decisions on his own that should have been *our* decisions, like where we'd live. And deciding how our money would be spent."

Vicki laced Margo into a pair of buttery brown ankle boots. "How did you change it finally?"

"I didn't. I left him and I did better the next time around. Of course, that's not the best solution for everyone."

"Oh, I know. That's one reason I'm doing the assertiveness training, so I can make it work with Tom. Mostly I'm challenging him on small things, you know, they say to start small." Whatever she had thought of made her smile—a big thing on which she'd challenged Tom and won?

"My boyfriend even got me to lie for him," ventured Margo. Actually, that was one transgression Rick hadn't committed, but the memory of their relationship was sufficiently soiled that a little more dirt wouldn't do any harm.

Vicki froze.

"Are you okay?"

"Yes. Here, give this a try." Vicki held out a purple suede loafer. Margo took it from her and slipped into it herself; Vicki's hands were trembling. "You know, don't you?" she whispered.

"That you were lying on Sunday?"

Vicki gave a deep sigh. "The thing is, I didn't realize how much I was lying. Would you walk around in the shoes? The manager's looking. What I mean is, I thought I was covering up one thing, but it turned out Tom lied to *me*, so I wasn't even telling the lie I thought I was telling. Well, I told you things were changing. Because of my assertiveness class."

This sounded like Vicki's true conversational style—rambling, unfocused, infuriating—in contrast to the smooth story she had told the day after the murder. Margo made herself listen calmly as Vicki went on,

"I figured out he was lying to me and I put my foot down. I said he'd better tell me the truth, or I was going to go to the police and say I'd lied before. It's one thing to make a choice to lie when you know the truth yourself, don't you think, but it wasn't right of him to ask me to do that without giving me all the information."

"What was the real story?"

"It's so easy to misunderstand, but see, I know how hard Tom worked for the chance to show at the Capelli. This was such an important opening for him. He's been showing at little galleries for several years, of course, but this—"

Margo couldn't stand it anymore. "Are you saying you weren't actually together the whole time from five to six?"

"Right. I had to put on my dress, so I went into the control room, you know, where Tom had the computer. When I came out he was gone. Walk around again, okay?"

"Let me try the ankle boots again. What time was this?"

"Quarter to six. I know that because I didn't want to put on the dress till the very last minute, since I planned to return it to the store the next day. I feel kind of bad about doing that, but I'm always really careful never to spill on a dress, I wouldn't bring it back if I messed it up. That's okay, don't you think?"

"Sure." Margo suppressed an urge to scream. "What happened with Tom?"

"He came back a few minutes later. He told me he'd gone to take a look at Susana's installation, but he couldn't get in because the door was locked. And then, after Susana was killed, he asked me to tell everyone we'd been together the whole time, he said it just might complicate things to say he'd gone there."

"But that wasn't the truth, either?" And that definitely wasn't the right question. Vicki hung her head and Margo checked the ankle boots in the mirror. They really were comfortable. "How did you find out he was lying to you?" she said and hit the jackpot.

Vicki smiled and said defiantly, "How dumb did he think I was? He said he couldn't get into Susana's room because of the lock on the door, but I started thinking about it, and I remembered there was no lock on Susana's door. I told him that and I made him tell me what really happened. It's going to sound awful, but this show meant so much to him. See, he did go into Susana's room and he saw that she was dead. Not lying on the floor in a pool of blood or anything like that. She was already on the bed and had something over her, a shawl or something. He wouldn't have even known she was dead, except he went over and tried to talk to her. Anyway, he said there were a few things that needed to be cleaned up before the opening started, just small things."

"Such as?"

"The candles weren't lit, so he did that. And there was some junk on the floor, and he pushed it under the bed. It was a terrible thing to do and I told him so. But you had to understand how much he wanted this show. You should have seen him when Peter didn't show up—I thought he was going to cry. It was so important to him to have everything perfect."

"Vicki. Are you sure Tom was telling the truth the second time?"

"Oh, yes," she said.

Margo believed it as well—not because she trusted Tom, but because he couldn't possibly have had enough time to argue with Susana, kill her, move the body, and then take care of the final preparations in Susana's installation.

"But, please, you can't tell him I told you!" cried Vicki, suddenly reverting to the browbeaten young wife.

What the hell was she going to do with Vicki's story? thought Margo, striding into work in her new ankle boots. Before she could use the information, she would have to approach Tom and ask him to confirm it. And even though she'd say an anonymous "someone" had seen him enter Susana's installation, he might guess she had heard the story from Vicki; at the very least, he would take it out on Vicki. Which was an outcome Margo Simon, barracuda-journalist, shouldn't care a fig about. Nevertheless, she did.

Beyond the personal dilemma it posed, the interesting thing about Vicki's story was what it said about the killer: that although extremely calculating, he or she hadn't been one hundred percent in control. There *had* been mistakes— not lighting the candles, not cleaning everything up. Without Tom's finishing touches, the murder probably would have been discovered earlier.

Picking up her mail, Margo found something that drew her attention completely from Tom Fall. Isa had faxed her Susana's itinerary for her Southwest trip, with notes of any-one Susana might have seen. The list of towns appeared in small, tidy printing that must have been Susana's. To one side, Isa had scrawled several comments, including one she had underlined twice: *Greg Miscik, another of Louise's ex-protégés.* Margo looked to see where Greg Miscik lived . . . and stared, with a sense of inevitability, at the neatly printed *Santa Fe.*

25 / The Santa Fe Trail

"Sure," Alex had said.

Cruising through the bright sky somewhere above Arizona the next morning, Margo still felt stunned at having gotten such easy agreement to her request to go to Santa Fe. She had marshaled her arguments carefully before knocking on Alex's door: the likelihood that Susana had discovered some kind of wrongdoing while on her trip through the Southwest, the calls Margo had made that afternoon to track down Greg Miscik, the artist's phone message that he was working on a painting series and wouldn't return any calls until next month—if, he added, he returned them at all. (A dog barking in the background on his message tape sounded mean, but the impression of meanness might have come from Miscik's surly tone.) Margo had barely begun presenting her case, however, when Alex acquiesced.

Maybe Alex had felt guilty for the dressing-down he'd given her the day before. More likely, KSDR had some kind of restricted grant that applied only to staff travel, or free miles donated by the airline that had to be used by a certain date. Margo had never been deeply involved in station fundraising, other than the inevitable on-air pledge drives, but anyone who worked in public radio became familiar with the oddities of grants—the funding limited to local history programming, the endowment for 1930s jazz. Margo wondered if going to

Rome had been a condition of the grant that allowed Peter Vance to quit his job at the Capelli. Or had he just gotten a big check and decided he'd be more productive in Europe than at home?

Joni Mitchell, on Margo's Walkman, sang about the last time she saw Richard. Margo thought of the last time she'd seen her own Richard. She supposed having purely professional motives ought to have been a condition of her going to New Mexico. Not that she didn't think Greg Miscik might turn out to be an important lead. But Santa Fe had been calling her for days.

The plane landed in Albuquerque, and she rented a car and headed northeast on I-25. She had thought she could use the hour and a half drive to reacclimate to the look and feel of the landscape, that the highway would carry none of the emotional whammy that was sure to hit her when she entered Santa Fe itself. But God, the land and the sky! Vaster and wilder and more glorious in the dazzling midday light than she could ever have remembered. Over the years Margo had convinced herself that she had only come to New Mexico because Rick had pushed it; she'd seen her lack of choice about where they lived as yet another symbol of their doomed relationship. She had fooled herself. The initial impulse may have been Rick's, but she had responded to this land viscerally, profoundly herself. Mother Earth and Father Sky, devotions she had come to dismiss as fuzzy-headed dabbling with Native American religion. Driving down the highway, the Sandia Mountains beyond the horizon to her right and the Sangre de Cristos coming up, she felt again the awe that earth and sky had evoked in her. By the time she got to Santa Fe, the lump in her throat had swelled so huge it was impossible not to cry.

She followed the directions Eileen had given her, parked, and sat in the car waiting for the tears to stop.

Eileen Johnson was the one friend she'd stayed in touch with from the old days. When Margo's pottery sales had faltered, she had often waitressed with Eileen at Lloyd's Santa Fe Café, a homey place where Lloyd had let Eileen set up her baby's playpen in a corner of the dining room. Lloyd would have let Eileen turn half the restaurant into a nursery if she'd wanted, because when the mood took her, Eileen drifted into the kitchen and created delectable concoctions of meat, vegetables, and the ubiquitous fire-in-the-mouth New Mexico chiles—the same ingredients from which Lloyd produced nothing but greasy burgers and burritos. Word would spread that Eileen was cooking, and the customers lined up outside. In those days Lloyd kept trying to persuade Eileen to cook full-time. But it wouldn't be as good, she'd insisted, if she didn't feel inspired. (Eileen took the same attitude toward love, avoiding getting trapped by any one man.) Finally, however, Lloyd had won her over. *Looks like a career*, she'd written to Margo, in one of the sporadic but warm letters they'd exchanged for years. *What a fate for a flower child!* Eileen had been such a sensation, she had opened her own place a few years ago. She'd had her third child by then and decided she'd better adopt the establishment's financial values, since she had no intention of buying the rest of the package: monogamy, marriage, white picket fence. *I may have become a capitalist*, she wrote, *but my sex life remains my own.*

Eileen had found a career indeed, thought Margo, sitting in her rented car outside Eileen's on Guadalupe Street. Even at one-thirty, people kept entering the bright blue-painted door. Dry-eyed at last, Margo glanced in the car mirror and considered touching up her face—did women in Santa Fe wear makeup now or had they remained true to the natural look of earlier decades? She settled for a couple of swipes of blusher and fresh coral lipstick before opening the car door, placing her feet in her new boots firmly on the ground, and walking into Eileen's.

She had half feared the kind of fashionable Southwest establishment that has spread beyond New Mexico and Arizona—the salmon and turquoise tones, painted wooden cacti, and a pricey air that wafts around like whiffs of cilantro and chile from the kitchen. Eileen's place did smell like chile and cilantro, in fact it smelled fantastic. But it looked as funky as Lloyd's Santa Fe Café, although it was twice the size. Compounding Margo's sense of *déjà vu*, in one corner a child was constructing something out of Lego blocks, with the help of an enthusiastic diner. Then Lloyd himself came over and enfolded her in a bear hug. "Didn't Eileen tell you?" he said. "She made me manager so she could concentrate on the food."

Lloyd took her into the kitchen, she and Eileen hugged, Eileen opened two beers from a small local brewery, and they sat at one of the restaurant tables.

"This will be the best meal of your life." Eileen was talking fast, a little nervous. "Are you hungry?"

"You're looking at a woman who's had nothing but airplane food today," said Margo, nervous, too. She wished she could stop staring at Eileen's hair. At a time when everyone, men and women, had had long hair, Eileen's had been the longest, a brown silk waterfall to her butt. Now she wore it boy-short and slicked back, chic as any urbanite's. Ten years was a long time.

"Better for cooking, reassures the customers they won't find anything disgusting in the soup," said Eileen, noticing Margo's gaze. "Know what I did with the hair they cut off? Hung it on my bedroom wall. When I really like a lover, he gets a souvenir." She displayed the same gap-toothed grin—

and the same tendency to omit the subjects of sentences—as when she'd regaled Margo with her romantic exploits during slow hours at Lloyd's Café.

"Eileen!"

They both laughed, recognizing Margo's tone—mildly shocked but amused—from the long afternoons when they used to lackadaisically refill salts, catsups, and hot sauces, and discuss everything under the New Mexico sun. It was a discussion they resumed, as Eileen's employees served them a feast: vegetable tamales and a chicken dish flavorful with green chiles, fresh herbs, and sun-dried tomatoes. Everything was accompanied by hot homemade blue corn tortillas. Eileen hadn't exaggerated, the food was divine. Margo ate happily while Eileen filled her in on old friends, local politics, and her own life as a culinary trendsetter.

"Did you find anything out about Greg Miscik?" asked Margo over an incredible pear tart and velvety-smooth coffee.

"Represented by the Macefield Gallery. They carry the most non-traditional art in town. Philip Macefield just moved here a few years ago. Cornish or Irish or something, you'll like him. . . ." The dreamy look suggested that Eileen had gotten to know the art dealer intimately. "Anyway, Miscik's supposed to be good. So of course, doesn't sell as well as the tourist-pleasers who paint insipid scenes of peaceful Indians. He'd do better in New York, but out here he can keep his expenses to just about nothing. Has a place out toward Chimayo. A mountain man survivalist, you know the type—beard, pickup truck, probably doesn't care too much for us wimmenfolk. Doesn't like visitors, maybe."

"What do you mean, maybe?"

"Patty Rios, remember her? Said she was trying to get all the artists to donate work for a benefit. Went out to Greg's place and he wouldn't even talk to her. Chased her off . . . she said with a rifle. But Patty embellishes. Plus, she could probably get Gandhi mad enough to chase her off with a rifle. Doesn't know when to give up."

"I'm not surprised you didn't have much luck phoning Greg," said Philip Macefield, owner of the Macefield Gallery. "I must say, I doubt that going out there will do you any good, either. When Greg's got a big project going, he's fiercely protective of his space." The New Age term sounded odd delivered in Macefield's British accent. "But I'll draw you a map if you still want to try. And since you're here, let me show you some of his work." Macefield, a graying man in a multicultural mix of tweeds and turquoise jewelry, drew her attention to three paintings displayed prominently. "These are triptychs, where a single painting occupies three distinct canvases or panels. I don't know how conversant you are with art. Do forgive me if I'm telling you things you already know."

The paintings juxtaposed serene nature scenes, on two of the panels, with powerful images of dismembered animals. Margo had a sense of having seen much the same thing before, but in a less disturbing form.

"There are three more in the series, but they've been sold," said Macefield.

"How are sales going in general?" she asked, genuinely curious and also wanting to distract herself from Miscik's unsettling paintings. "Has the slump in the art market affected you?"

Macefield laughed. "I'm hardly in the same league with the galleries on the coasts that carry the best-known artists. You have to be rather higher up than I am to start with before you can slump significantly. It's an educational process here, with the tourist trade. Most of the people who come into the gallery haven't been exposed to contemporary art. One of my artists, a ceramicist, sells most of his work through a more traditional dealer. But some of the pieces he cares most about, his risk-taking works, are here." He indicated two abstract sculptures that looked so delicate she had to touch them to be sure they were made of clay. "They make you want to touch them, don't they?" said Macefield. "Everyone responds that way. I expect to sell a number of those when the summer season gets into gear. Well, I'll do you a map for Greg and call him to say you're coming. But as I said, he may not talk to you. By the by, don't worry about his dog. He looks like a monster, but he's perfectly harmless."

Driving away, Margo reflected that it was restrained of Macefield not to capitalize on the ceramic artist's being blind. Because naturally, the wondrous sculptures were the work of her former love, Rick Dunham. Margo would be staying with Eileen for two days, until Sunday, and she'd planned to look Rick up and say hello. It had seemed a good idea when she was a thousand miles away, an adult thing to do. But now that she was actually here, she found herself worrying that she and Rick would still have the knack of making each other furious. Or perhaps worse, that after all they'd shared, they would have nothing to say to each other. Distressing thoughts, but she preferred them to worrying about canine monsters.

She had lingered at Eileen's restaurant and the gallery, and had forgotten that driving thirty miles of mountain highway took significantly longer than zipping the same distance down the San Diego Freeway. It was close to five o'clock when she turned down the dirt road, shortly before Chimayo, on Philip Macefield's map. Later than she'd planned. But there should be no problem. She would talk to Greg Miscik—or not talk to him, if he refused—and either way she'd be heading back to town before the sun set.

Miscik lived only a mile off the highway, but Margo's rented Chevy Nova jounced for what seemed forever as she steered carefully around the potholes and rocks in the road. Away from New Mexico too long, she hadn't even thought to ask the rental agency for something with four-wheel-drive. At last she saw the house, a rough adobe with a truck parked in front of it and junk littering in the yard. Wild barking started. Fight or flee, telegraphed her adrenaline, upping her heartbeat and drenching her palms with sweat.

WHERE'S THE DOG?

Running toward the car, an enormous animal, Macefield's monster, its great teeth exposed in its yapping mouth.

Miscik would come out after it and see that she was here. It would just be a minute, she reassured herself. She turned off the motor and tried to breathe deeply, closing her eyes to the leaping animal beside the car. Margo had never been able to figure out if a dog had terrified her when she was a child or perhaps she'd seen a frightening movie; a psychic once told her she was killed by a dog pack in a past life. Whatever the reason, her fear of large barking dogs was every bit as intense as it was irrational.

At last she heard a door open. Thank goodness, the slavering beast's owner would call it off. She rolled down the window a few inches.

"Hi! Philip Macefield gave me—"

The bearded man held a rifle.

"It's all right," she shouted over the dog's yelps. "Philip Macefield called and asked you to talk to me." She restarted the car, nevertheless. Miscik didn't look welcoming.

Greg Miscik didn't yell at her to leave. He just fired. It looked as if he was pointing the rifle into the air above the car, but she didn't stick around to check his aim. She gunned the motor and turned, trying not to drive any closer to him. He was still shooting. The dog gave chase as she took off down the road. At least he wouldn't fire straight at her—he might hit the hound of hell.

She had made it about halfway down Miscik's mile-long road back to the highway when one of the tires blew out. The car careened toward the right. She fought to steer, squeezing the brakes, and brought the car to a bumpy stop in a bush.

With joyous tongue, the dog caught up with her.

26 / The Misogynist and His Dog

Half an hour later Margo was sure of two things. First, she couldn't drive the car on three good tires and one flat. Each time she had tried, she'd stopped after five seconds of the grinding noise the rim made as she lurched down the road. Second, the dog wasn't going away. The behemoth paced alongside the Chevy, its head nearly window-high. Wouldn't Greg Miscik eventually call his best buddy home? Miscik, at any rate, hadn't come after her with the rifle. He probably figured the dog would do the job for him. The beast had stopped its incessant barking, saving its energy for an occasional hungry-sounding *woof woof.*

At five-thirty the April sun remained bright on the mountaintops, but dusk was settling in their shadows. Even in the car the air carried a chill. Nervously clammy in her wool turtleneck, Margo began to wish for her heavy jacket, inaccessible in the trunk. Rule number one of mountain driving: Always carry blankets in the car. The rental place mustn't have heard that one. The Chevy was pristine. There were no blankets, nor any discarded bits of chocolate bars to keep up her blood sugar, and definitely no potential weapons. In her own car she would have found half a dozen things— one of the kids' baseball bats, her tape recorder (which was with her other luggage in the Chevy's trunk), several books she could have thrown. Even one of the canvas sacks she and Barry used for grocery shopping might have served as a shield.

She thought of the dismembered animals in Miscik's paintings. Did the dog supply the models?

Philip Macefield had said the dog was harmless, she reminded herself. She reached for the door handle, but lost her nerve. She started the car—the dog yawping at the sound—and tried to drive again, crawling on the crippled tire. It was no good. She wouldn't mind destroying the rim to get back to the highway, but she was afraid the rutted dirt road would not just wear down the rim but bend it, and then she wouldn't be able to drive at all.

There was no escaping the next bit of her destiny. She had to change the tire.

"Nice puppy," she muttered as she scanned the ground outside and formulated her plan of attack.

Fiddling under the dashboard, she found the lever that popped the trunk open and pulled it. That diversion took the dog to the back of the car. Instantly Margo opened her door, sprang out, and grabbed two rocks she had spotted. The dog came at her, barking ferociously.

"Get out of here!" she yelled, hurling the rocks. One of them hit and the dog took off. She raced to the trunk and got her hands on the tire iron.

The dog skulked fifty yards down the road.

"Go away!" she shouted again, waving the tire iron.

The monster ran.

"Do you really know how to change a tire?" asked Ben, Eileen's oldest son, at breakfast the next morning.

"Sure. Your mom and I changed one together once."

"Nah, she can't do anything on cars," said the twelve-year-old. "One time we got a flat driving up to Taos, and she just sat there and let this truck driver change it."

"I bet he was a good-looking truck driver," said Margo after Ben had left for baseball practice. The two other kids were playing in the yard.

"Gorgeous." Eileen laughed. "A Navajo. Say, I've been thinking about your problem with Greg Miscik. Know who's friends with every artist in this part of the state, who could probably get Miscik to talk to you?"

"I don't think I want to hear this."

"You were going to call Rick anyway."

"But not to ask him a favor!"

"Margo, why not let him help you?"

"Eileen, why not change your own goddamn tires? See, just thinking about Rick makes me argumentative."

Eileen handed her the phone.

"You look the same," said Rick Dunham, "seeing" her by running his fingers lightly over her face.

"Older."

"More character. Same broad cheekbones. Still furrow-browed"—he tapped her forehead—"from too much thinking."

Margo sat back, out of his reach. She was determined not to replay *that* particular fight. Rick had aged, too, his features smoothing out across a broader, happier face—for which she gave credit to Rick's wife, a small woman with a generous smile who had met Margo at the door and then, with no sign of jealousy, left them to catch up. Another change was in Rick's hands, thickened and stained by years of working with clay. When he'd touched her face, she had felt tough calluses.

"You have worker's hands," she said. "And your work is beautiful. I saw some pieces at the Macefield Gallery."

"Right, you went there on the trail of Greg Miscik." A sour tone, with no acknowledgment of the compliment. "Which is why you called."

"I was going to call you anyway. And I did love your work. I was drawn to it even before I knew it was yours. God, let's not do this all over again."

"My distrust of your motives and your convoluted explanations?"

Margo lifted his hand to her jaw, to show him she was openmouthed with surprise. Neither of them had been given to self-analysis in the old days. Why do all that work when a good fight could clear the air?

"An unexamined life is not worth living?" she said.

"Two years of therapy. How about you?"

"About the same." To get over Rick and, even more, to change the kinds of behaviors and beliefs that had led her into such a destructive relationship in the first place. "Truly, Rick, I loved your work, apart from anything else."

"Thanks. And, apart from anything else, you want me to help you get to Greg Miscik. Okay. Let's pick up a couple of six-packs on our way out of town—Miscik's a Coors man. You don't still drive like it's the Indianapolis 500, do you?" he said as she led him to the car.

"That wasn't me, it was that Volkswagen Beetle, the steering was defective."

"Margo, you just never wanted to buy a German car, so you kept complaining about the way the car drove."

"Well, you never drove it, did you? So how come we bought the car you wanted?"

This time Rick broke the momentum. "Tell me about yourself. You're married, right? Any kids?"

They politely chatted about their current lives. Margo told him why she wanted to see Greg Miscik. For the last ten miles they listened to the radio without talking. She had always liked being quiet with Rick; no wonder, she realized now, when the alternative was so often a fight.

The barking started as they walked toward the house, the hellhound bounding out of the woods toward them.

"Hey, Goldie," said Rick; the beast came to him and he fondled its head. "Greg!" he called.

"Oh, it's you, Rick." Greg Miscik lowered his rifle. For someone Rick considered a friend, Greg didn't sound real happy to have a visitor. But he let them into his house—a neater place than Margo would have expected, with canvases on every wall and more stacked in a corner—and accepted the six-packs, breaking out cans for the three of them. Goldie padded over, tail wagging now that his master had given Margo the okay. The dog seemed to hold no grudge over the rocks she had thrown at it the day before.

Miscik sat silently, guzzling his beer, while Rick explained that Margo was an old friend who wanted to talk about Susana Contreras.

"What for?" He was asking her, but he looked at Rick. "If you want to know something about Susana, why not ask Susana?"

Margo glanced around the house. The room where they sat contained the bed and work area. There was a small kitchen to one side and that was it. She didn't see a television or radio, didn't even know if the house had electricity. There were no newspapers around, either; Greg probably wasn't pretending that he hadn't heard what had happened to Susana.

"Susana's dead," she said.

"Come on. How?"

She told him.

If Greg Miscik felt any sense of loss, he did his macho best not to show it. "I always think lesbians are a little twisted, y'know. Susana and that girlfriend of hers, what's her name—Isa—they used to have some real knock-down-drag-outs, worse than I've seen men do to each other. One time Susana pulled out a chunk of Isa's hair. So the next day Isa shaves her head and calls it a performance. Have they arrested her yet?"

Margo was surprised she could dislike someone as much on short acquaintance as she disliked Greg Miscik. She kept her voice level, saying, "Susana was upset by something she found out when she was traveling out here. Isa thought she might have visited you. Did she?"

"She called when she was in town and we had a couple beers."

"I'd like to ask you what you and she talked about. Mind if I . . ." She took the tape recorder from her bag.

"Uh-uh. No recording." He stood up and remained standing even though Margo put the recorder away. "Rick, are you sure she's okay?"

"Hey, Greg, she used to be my lady." Margo forced herself to smile, wondering if Rick had used that particular term because he remembered she loathed it.

"No shit," said Miscik. He eyed Margo for the first time, as if she were a heifer he'd just heard had won a ribbon at the rodeo, even though the heifer didn't look like much. Then he got himself another beer and took his time coaxing off the pop-top.

Margo recalled a chronic argument she and Rick used to have, about Rick's fondness for redneck behavior. The infuriating thing about Miscik was that, while a native redneck might be unaware of what he was doing, Miscik knew perfectly well that he was stringing her along. He probably considered cussedness an art form. He sat down slowly, scratched his side, and pulled at the sandy hair that straggled to his shoulders from a plate-sized bald spot.

"Look," said Miscik. "All that happened is Susana and I got together for a few beers and I told her about this hassle I was having."

"I heard she found out about some kind of injustice."

"Shit, she might have gone around calling it an injustice, but that was Susana, she turned everything into a political cause. It was more like a misunderstanding. And it's settled now." He found a new place to scratch. Margo wondered if he had picked up the habit from the dog or if he'd just caught its fleas.

"What was it?" asked Rick.

"See, Susana and I both worked for this art critic when we were in grad school—I was a year after her. When I finished school, I was going to do some traveling and I wasn't sure where I'd end up. So, at least the way I remembered it, this lady, the critic, said she'd keep some of my paintings for me, like storing them, y'know. It seemed like a good idea. In fact, I didn't think about the stuff for years. Then around six months ago I did some paintings similar to the ones I'd left with her—triptychs—and some of them sold pretty fast. That doesn't happen to me real often, and I started thinking maybe my old triptychs would sell, too. So I wrote to this critic and asked for them back. I said I'd pay shipping costs and all that. But she said I'd given her the paintings as gifts. I wrote back saying that wasn't my recollection. But the fact is, I didn't have anything in writing saying I'd just loaned her the paintings. And she's one powerful lady, I'd just as soon have her on my side. Hell, the old paintings probably wouldn't sell like the new ones anyway, they're less mature work."

The phrase *less mature work* certainly had a Louise O'Quinn ring to it. Margo had realized why Miscik's paintings at the Macefield Gallery looked familiar. She'd seen one of the early triptychs, with that same juxtaposition of tranquil and violent images, hanging in Louise's guest room.

"What did Susana say when she heard your story?" she asked.

"She got kind of worked up—I was worked up at the time, this was before things got settled, see—and she said maybe the same thing had happened to her. She left some sculptures with this lady, the same way I did, where she pretty much forgot about them. They were student works, anyway, they weren't going to bring anything like the kind of prices Susana was getting later on. But when I told her what happened to me, she said maybe she'd ask for her work back, too. For the principle of the thing." He shook his head, as if the concept of acting on principle boggled his understanding.

"Do you know if she ever approached Louise about it?"

"I . . . Hey, I never said any names." He looked alarmed. Clearly, when he had tossed out various trappings of civilization, career aspirations had survived the trash. "I don't know if Susana did anything."

"Did she say what was she going to do if the critic wouldn't give her work back?"

"She was talking about hiring a lawyer, or maybe contacting one of the big art magazines and badmouthing this lady— and I didn't say any names, okay? Anyway, like I said, we were both drinking and we got kind of worked up. Hell, we were ready to go to this lady's place and just destroy our work. No sane artist is ever going to do that." Miscik reached under his collar and engaged in a vigorous bout of scratching that must have left nail marks. Margo was feeling itchy, too.

Fleas from the damn dog probably infested the dusty couch she was sitting on.

"You worked for this lady," she said on impulse. "Did you like her?"

"Did I *like* her? Didja hear that, Rick, did I like her?" Miscik crushed his empty beer can in one hand, an apparent gesture of male solidarity. "This lady wasn't like that. Women always think they have to like everyone and everyone has to like them. It's fucking irrelevant. You think the President and the Russians worry about whether they like each other? That's not the point, the point is being able to work together. That's what women don't get, and it's why men run the world. But this lady, she's like a man. She doesn't *like* people, she has business relationships with them, power relationships. You scratch my back, I'll scratch yours." An unfortunate metaphor, thought Margo, whose fingernail had strayed discreetly to her leg; she was afraid if she really got going, the two of them, she and Miscik, would keep it up like gorillas in a zoo.

"This lady gave me a job and I *liked* that fine," said Miscik. "She helped my career and I *liked* that. She taught me to shoot and I *liked* that, too. Matter of fact, if she was going to kill anyone, she'd just shoot 'em clean. She grew up on a ranch and handled firearms her whole life. Not that she'd ever have to shoot anybody. This is the kind of person, if she has trouble, she calls her lawyer. Hell, she calls ten lawyers."

"Is that what she did to you? Called her lawyer? Is that why you stopped trying to get your work back?"

Miscik gave her a bleary look. "Gotta pee," he said. He stumbled out the door. And didn't come back.

"Do you think that's what she did? Sicced her lawyer on him?" said Rick as they drove back to Santa Fe. After waiting ten minutes for Greg Miscik to return, Margo had gone to look for the outhouse. She hadn't seen one, nor any sign of the painter.

"Makes sense. He didn't want to admit he was scared off by a city slicker lawyer, so he's hiding out in the woods now."

"Margo, I think he was lying."

"How come?"

"Tone of voice. The way he hesitated sometimes. I've had a lot of experience reading people's voices, and something felt off."

"Come on, Rick," she said. He'd struck a nerve and she found herself unable to not react. "You used to say that when you accused me of being insincere, that you could read voices and you could tell if I was sincere or not."

"How about you? Aren't you a good judge of voices now, from working in radio?"

"Probably better than most. And other than thinking Greg Miscik was a total jerk, I didn't hear anything that made me distrust his story."

"Maybe he wasn't lying, then. But he wasn't telling the whole truth. Let me listen to the tape you made of him, and I'll tell you where I picked up on it."

"I didn't tape him. Didn't you hear me ask if I could and he said absolutely not?"

"Yeah, but you had some kind of small recorder, didn't you? Hidden in your bra or something?"

"Hidden in my bra! No wonder you think people lie to you. It's how you operate!"

"Margo, you should talk."

"Hey, who had an affair first?"

"I don't know. Who did? Margo, watch the way you're taking these curves!"

• • •

"Did you find out what you wanted?" asked Eileen over late-night brandies. She had just gotten home from a busy Saturday evening at the restaurant.

Margo, who was massaging Eileen's feet, groaned. "All that therapy, and it was like old times. Except we used to have a little passion along with the stupid fights. This time all we had was the stupid fight."

"Actually, what I meant was, what did you find out from Greg Miscik?"

"That's the point. There wasn't much." Margo summarized the talk with the redneck artist, concluding, "I think he was trying a bit of a scam himself, and Louise called his bluff." That was pretty much what Rick had suggested, and what she had, with such knee-jerk opposition, denied. "What I really learned about was myself. And I'm not crazy about what I found."

"Because you and Rick went at it again? Situational regression, that's all. You don't fight like that with Barry, do you?"

"Of course not. Barry's a rational human being."

"So are you."

"Mommy." Eileen's youngest, three-year-old Sam, padded into the kitchen, rubbing his eyes. "Wanna drink of water."

"I'll get it." Margo went over to the sink and turned on the tap.

"No. Me," demanded Sam. "Lift me up."

Margo hoisted him up so he could fill his cup himself.

"Earth to Margo," said Eileen a minute later.

"Sorry." The plastic cup was overflowing, and Margo put the child down.

For a moment she had been holding not Sam, but Isa's son, Mickey, at the Capelli opening. Mickey was saying Isa had gotten mad because Orion was supposed to be baby-sitting him, but Orion hadn't been there. That was on the Saturday Susana was murdered; when, according to Isa, all three of them—Isa, Orion, and Mickey—had spent the entire afternoon together at the Tropico Hotel.

27 / Fashion Statement

Margo hadn't planned it, but when she stopped at the dry cleaner on her way to work on Monday morning, she realized the flowered challis skirt and navy jacket she was wearing went perfectly with the wide-brimmed burgundy hat she'd snagged from Dawn. In the car mirror she adjusted the hat at a jaunty angle. She felt not at all jaunty herself. She genuinely liked Isa, and she dreaded having to ask her why she'd lied and said she and her two sons were together on the afternoon of Susana's murder.

Was Isa protecting Orion, who was supposed to be baby-sitting Mickey but was absent? Orion didn't get along with Susana—Isa had even said that once Dawn thought Orion was threatening Susana and Dawn had come at him with her knife. Or was Isa protecting herself? Because if she had asked Orion to watch Mickey, that meant Isa hadn't been there, either.

Margo had already tried calling Isa from Santa Fe and again when she'd returned to San Diego. She tried a third time from her office, again got the answering machine, and left another request for Isa to call her.

She turned next to her mail and phone messages. At the top of the pile was a note from the student assistant who had duplicated her cassettes for the police, insisting he had only gotten four cassettes from her and couldn't have been responsible for losing the interview with Jill. A minor mystery. It wasn't as if tapes never disappeared; Margo had probably left the cassette sitting in the machine when she'd initially transferred the interview to reel-to-reel. Of course, every reporter initialed his or her cassettes, so why hadn't the tape made its way back to her mail slot or desk? It could be on her desk, she realized, scanning the disaster area in front of her. She wasted ten minutes searching for the tape, before she made herself give up and go back to her mail.

A phone message directed her to call Bernard Capelli's office, resulting in the satisfaction of hearing the "Masterpiece Theatre" secretary tell her Bernard would be delighted to see her; she made an appointment for two-thirty that afternoon.

Margo called Isa again, left another message. She got Tom Fall's answering machine as well; she wanted to find out exactly what Tom had seen when he'd gone into Susana's installation and found her dead. The one person she managed to reach was Louise O'Quinn's assistant, Ed. Margo questioned the motives as well as veracity of the story Greg Miscik had told her. However, if Susana *had* requested the return of her student sculptures, she hadn't gotten them back; Louise had proudly pointed out the sculptures a week ago. It seemed worth a visit to Louise's current assistant-protégé.

"My father's a carpenter, Chicago union man and all that," said Ed Milewski over the sound of rock music from the student with whom he shared studio space at the University of California-San Diego. "I never thought I'd follow in the old man's footsteps, but look at this." He showed Margo his current work, carefully fitted wooden boxes with glass doors, in which he was arranging a variety of objects to suggest a narrative. "I'm the first generation of my family to go to college and they're all pissed I didn't go into something that will support them in their old age. Medicine or engineering or something."

"My family felt the same way," Margo said encouragingly. She was glad that, despite Ed's abstracted air, he was one of those people who open up when facing a microphone. "I was supposed to become a doctor or a lawyer. Or, even better, marry one."

"Of course, some artists make fantastic money," said Ed excitedly, pushing up his glasses with a grimy hand. "I'm getting ready for my first big one-man show, next month at the Trask Gallery downtown. Leave your address and I'll make sure you get an invitation."

"Thanks." She felt touched by Ed's naïveté. Had she ever been so young that she, too, thought she'd be plucked swiftly from the crowd, recognized for her superior merit without paying years of dues? She thought of Greg Miscik in his rude cabin with no plumbing. Surely that was a more common fate for a serious artist than Susana's stardom.

"I've been talking to everyone I met at the Capelli the week before Susana was killed," she said. "I was wondering if you noticed anything when you were there that might have been connected with Susana's death. Or maybe you knew about some kind of tension in her life, or a problem she was having with someone."

"No, but I hardly knew her."

"She used to work for Louise, didn't she, in the job you have now?"

"Years ago."

"Didn't Louise and Susana stay in touch? They looked like they were good friends, when Louise dropped by that day."

"Did they? I don't notice things very much, my girlfriend's always telling me that. She'll be wearing a new dress, for instance, some intense color like magenta, and I won't even see it. She says how can I be an artist if I never look at things? But all the time I really am looking, it's just that I'm looking inside. That's what the boxes represent, interior realities."

"I'm surprised Louise took you shopping with her the weekend before last, if you don't notice clothes." Certainly his own garb—torn jeans and a T-shirt—showed little sartorial flair.

"Weekend before last." He crinkled his forehead. "Oh, right, the day Susana got killed. We weren't just shopping. We parked in the lot at Horton Plaza and then went to some of the downtown galleries nearby. Then Louise had some things to pick up at Horton, and I tagged along. My dad and all his union buddies would squawk that it's not in my contract, but Louise has a bad back, so if she buys anything heavy, she needs me to carry it for her."

"Did she? Buy anything heavy?"

"Oh, man. Sorry, as I said, you're asking the wrong guy. Let's see, I did carry something, took something to the car for her. So she must have."

"Were you together the whole time? I suppose she might have tried on clothes or something and you agreed to meet back in an hour?"

"No, we stayed together. That's something I do remember because the police asked about it. We were there from before three till around six, long enough that we had to pay for parking—you know how they charge for parking at Horton if you're there over three hours? Then Louise dropped me off at home and I got back downtown for the opening around seven.

"By the way," he added, "if you want to talk to the students who were helping Susana set up her installation, their studio is just three or four doors down."

The studios were in a row of old Quonset huts, reminders of UCSD's initial incarnation as a World War II military base. Margo peeked into the huts she walked by, but didn't see the people who had been putting pepper on Susana's wall. She did, however, spot a familiar head of prickly blond hair.

"Jill, how're you doing?"

Jill Iverson looked up. And turned white.

"Jill, are you okay?"

"Go out and do that again." Color was returning to the artist's face. "What you just did. Come to the door and stick your head in like you did."

"Okay." Although puzzled, Margo complied. Maybe she was participating in an art-life performance.

"Stay there!" commanded Jill. "I'm having the most incredible flashback!" She sat silently for a moment, staring at Margo, then jumped up and pulled her into the room, demanding, "Where did you get that hat?"

Margo explained about seeing Dawn wearing it and retrieving it after Dawn ran away.

"Dawn? It was Dawn!" Jill hugged Margo and danced around the room. "Rather stylish for Dawn, don't you think?" She giggled. "Can I have a look at it?"

"Not until you tell me what this is all about."

"Fair enough." Although Jill motioned for Margo to sit down, she herself kept moving—dancing around, lighting a cigarette. "At about the time Susana must have been killed, I was a little stoned. Well, okay, a lot stoned. A woman wearing that hat, the exact hat you've got on, came and looked in the door of my room. She looked really upset, but she didn't say anything. I figured it was Susana. The awful thing was, I couldn't remember what happened next. Zip. The memory was gone. I've had some intense experiences with mind-altering substances, but I'd never completely blacked out before. It was driving me nuts. I didn't think I had killed anybody, but what was Susana doing there? Why didn't she talk? If I couldn't remember, was it because whatever happened next was so terrible that I had to repress it? But when I saw you in the hat and you said how you got it, I realized it wasn't Susana I saw. It was Dawn, with the hat covering her hair."

"I made the same mistake."

"See? No wonder I couldn't remember what happened next. Because nothing happened! Dawn looked at me, she didn't say anything of course, because she never says anything, and then she just went away. Let me see it now." Jill snagged the hat. "It's beautifully made, isn't it? You don't happen to know what this is? This white design printed inside, like a seashell?"

"Some kind of manufacturer's mark?"

"Must be." Jill put the hat on. "Tell me again how you got it." She lit a fresh cigarette, although half of the previous cigarette still smoldered in a saucer. After Margo repeated the story, Jill returned the hat, chattering, "It looks better on you. Hats look best on tall women, don't you think? A shorty like me can wear a little beret or something like that, but to really carry a hat you've got to be tall." For someone flooded with relief, Jill was awfully jumpy.

"Is that why you got the lawyer?" asked Margo. "Because you thought Susana came to your door and you couldn't remember what happened next?"

"Yeah. Hey, I better call Lyman right away." She was scrabbling through things on a piled table, knocking papers to the floor.

• • •

As soon as she got rid of Margo, Jill picked up the phone and made a call. She bounced in her seat with excitement as she heard the phone ring on the other end. She hadn't felt so good in ages, hadn't enjoyed an art-life experiment as much as she was enjoying this one—setting things into motion, not knowing what would happen next.

28 / The Jitters

It was nearly noon when Margo left Jill, intending to return to KSDR and pick up a sandwich on the way for a working lunch. Once in the car, however, she didn't drive to the freeway. Instead, feeling giddily as if she were playing hooky, she crossed the UCSD campus toward Barry's office at the university's Torrey Institution of Oceanography. He had just finished teaching a class. And he was hungry.

At one of their favorite Italian restaurants, north of the campus in Del Mar, she and Barry spent a leisurely hour savoring a superb pasta with roasted vegetables and plenty of garlic, a salad bursting with crab and exotic bitterish greens, crusty bread, and a lovely white wine. Sitting on a terrace with an ocean view on a paradisiacally sunny day, Margo let herself simply enjoy her husband's company—his generous humor, the way he occasionally pushed back the thick, sandy hair that flopped over one blue eye, a gesture she'd always found impossibly sexy.

Relaxing took some effort, however. Not specific thoughts but a feeling, an edginess, would come over her, and she had to force herself to push it away. Over dessert she stopped resisting the urge to talk about Susana's murder.

"Louise O'Quinn has an alibi," she said. "She was shopping at Horton Plaza with her assistant at the time Susana was killed." She recounted her conversation with Ed Milewski.

"It was hard to imagine Louise getting physical, anyway. She wouldn't have taken it well if Susana really did threaten to sue her or to make a stink in the art press about the student sculptures. But as Greg Miscik said, Louise could have fought back with her own lawyers. Or she could have settled things by just paying Susana for the sculptures. She could afford it, even if she had to pay Susana's current prices."

"Are you sure she could afford it?" Barry was spooning up the last of their shared dessert, a poached pear with dark chocolate sauce. "Just because she's got that incredible house and drives a Rolls doesn't mean she's doing all right."

"I haven't gotten any sign Louise is hurting financially. But speaking of financial problems, there's James Carmichael. I'm not suggesting he killed Susana to profit from her work increasing in value, that's too convoluted. But James was under a lot of pressure and he could go into rages." Margo suppressed the shiver in her voice. Barry rarely objected to anything she did in her job, but she'd figured he might make an exception if she ever told him about James nearly attacking her. "And he'd be capable of doing the cover-up. He springs into action in a crisis." She described the way James had taken charge when Dawn was stuck in Tom's installation.

"What about Dawn? Is she in the clear?"

"Everyone I've talked to is convinced Dawn would never harm Susana. But Dawn was at the Capelli at about the time Susana was killed—that was when Jill saw her in the hat." Margo summarized her conversation with Jill that morning. "The thing is, I still can't see Dawn covering up up the murder."

"Sounds like James is your favorite suspect," said Barry.

"I don't know. I think he's capable of committing the murder and covering it up. I also think he's been taking money from the Capelli. But how would Susana have known about that? Actually, there's one other person who's having financial trouble and that person was connected financially to Susana. Barbara Scholl handled all of Susana's sales, even resales that Susana might not have been aware of. Wouldn't it have been easy for Barbara to falsify the figures she gave Susana? And then what if Susana found out? Barbara denies her gallery has been affected by the slump in the art market, but she's had to cut back on her staff. And she lied about the afternoon of the murder, saying she got to San Diego two or three hours later than she really did."

"Margo, the police have the authority to look into Barbara's records and also into the Capelli Foundation's books. And Barbara isn't the only one who lied about the afternoon of the murder. Aren't you forgetting Isa?"

Margo closed her eyes. Maybe Greg Miscik was right, that "liking" people was a female handicap.

"Isa's a more sympathetic character than Barbara Scholl or James Carmichael," Barry went on. "But she did lie about that afternoon. Maybe she's protecting her son, maybe he killed Susana . . . but do you really think a kid just a year older than Jenny could have pulled off the cover-up? And even if Susana's family is contesting the will, it may take a little longer, but eventually Isa will inherit."

"Greg Miscik said Susana and Isa used to have violent fights." Margo made herself continue the argument. "There was no reason for him to lie about that."

Margo's edginess, rather than abating as she'd talked things out, had intensified. She and Barry had taken separate cars so she could go on to her appointment with Bernard Capelli's office nearby. She kissed Barry goodbye, found a telephone, and tried Isa again.

"Isa, it's Margo. Please call me," she said into the answering machine, which recorded her urgency as impassively as it would have registered a computerized sales call.

Feeling really jittery now, she considered hopping in her car and not stopping until she reached Isa's house in Los Angeles. But she ought to at least keep her appointment with Bernard Capelli. And when she phoned the radio station for messages, she discovered Isa had returned her earlier call. Isa was on the way to San Diego herself, there was business of Susana's she had to attend to. Could Margo meet her for a drink later on?

Half an hour later Margo sat in her Toyota amid the Mercedeses and Porsches in the parking lot of the Capelli Company, feeling too shaky to drive. What on earth was wrong with her? Overwork? The wine at lunch? Certainly there'd been nothing upsetting about the conversation she had just had with Bernard Capelli.

Bernard had reacted predictably when Margo shared her suspicions that James Carmichael was embezzling from the Capelli Foundation. Clearly aware that he was speaking to a reporter, the chairman of the foundation voiced complete confidence in his executive director and gave no sign that anything about the foundation finances might be unknown to him. Thanks for the tip, he said, he'd look into it. But he had no doubt it was nothing but a misunderstanding on the part of the volunteer who helped with the bookkeeping; an older woman, after all, she was probably unused to the latest accounting practices. Then Bernard showed Margo the Important Art adorning his designer office and patted her hand a few times. *Had Bernard approached Susana? Had she fought him off?* Just fifteen minutes after their meeting started, Margo had returned to her car . . . and sat unable to put the key in the ignition.

A BMW pulled into the parking space next to her and a man got out. He glanced at her indifferently. People probably had nervous breakdowns outside the Capelli Company daily, especially people driving six-year-old economy cars. If Margo had eaten or drunk anything with Jill that morning, she would have suspected Jill of having drugged her, "just to get a reaction."

Jill! Margo realized it was seeing Jill that morning that had triggered her nervousness. Something about Jill's mood . . . that made Margo run back into the Capelli Company to phone Jill at her UCSD studio. No answer. She tried Jill at home. The phone rang repeatedly rather than triggering a machine, as if Jill had Call Waiting and she wasn't picking up the other line. Margo's anxiety having focused at last, she raced back to the car and drove as fast as she could up the Pacific Coast Highway to Jill's house in Encinitas.

The cat was yowling when Margo approached.

"Jill, are you home?" she called, pounding on the door. "Jill!"

She was reminded of her last visit, when she'd found Jill passed out in the living room. But this time the front door was locked.

"Jill!" she called again.

No answer.

She went and peered in the front window. All she could see was the kitchen, with no one there. She could hear the squawk of the telephone left off the hook. She stood on her toes to peer through the side windows, into the empty bedroom. God, she was going to feel stupid if Jill was just out at the grocery store.

Around the back of the house, the windows looked into the living room. Jill Iverson was sprawled on a chair.

"Jill!" screamed Margo, pounding on the window . . . although she knew Jill wouldn't answer.

There were red-and-white splatters on the wall behind the artist. The splatters, not only blood but bone and brains, came from Jill's head. Margo could see the handgun lying on the floor at Jill's side.

29 / True Confessions

"It's exactly like Jill not to leave a suicide note. Even to file the registration off the gun. Just to make it harder on everyone. I know that sounds rotten and it must have been horrible for you to find her, Margo, but you can't expect me to have sympathy for the person who killed the woman I love." Isa paused for breath. "I suppose you knew about the big fight she and Susana had, the one the police lieutenant mentioned?"

"No," mumbled Margo. Some crime reporter she had turned out to be. She'd had no idea that one of the caterers had heard Susana yelling at Jill, or that it had been Jill who had enticed Dawn into Tom's installation and trapped her there; the caterer had stood in the hall long enough to catch a good bit of the argument.

"Why don't I make some tea?" said Isa. "Just tell me where you keep it. Unless you want something stronger."

"Tea's fine. In the cupboard on the right."

Margo had asked Isa to her house, rather than meeting her somewhere, because Margo felt barely capable of moving. After finding Jill dead six hours earlier, she had called the police, using a phone at a neighbor's. She'd survived the detectives' questions, asked some of her own, and forced herself to return to the station to do the story. When she'd finally gotten home, she had taken a shower that violated every principle of water conservation—pelting and very long. She'd started crying in the shower and continued for an hour in Barry's arms. Barry had made her eat something; she hadn't noticed what. After that, she was tempted to put on her nightgown and crawl under the covers, receiving Isa while she lay in bed. But she was glad she'd managed the formality of sweats, since Susana's lover had arrived with Susana's art dealer in tow.

"We both had business of Susana's to take care of in San Diego," Isa said, explaining Barbara Scholl's presence. "And there's something I want Barbara to tell you."

Whatever that might be, Barbara hadn't yet revealed it. Instead, they had discussed Jill's suicide and the news that the police had been on the verge of charging Jill with Susana's murder.

"I can't get over the irony of Susana being killed because she was speaking up for that psychotic she picked up at a women's shelter," said Barbara when Isa left the room to make tea. She had barely spoken until then. Margo's veil of shock lifted enough for her to notice that Barbara looked ill. The art dealer was as impeccably attired as ever, in a silk blouse and tailored slacks, accessorized with striking jewelry. But her eyes were glassy and her hair lusterless, like an expensive racehorse off its feed.

"Tea for three. Earl Grey." Isa brought in the pot and cups on a tray and poured. Handing Margo a cup, she said abruptly, "I lied to you about the afternoon Susana was killed."

Margo recalled dully that she'd been itching to ask Isa about this very thing. Curious the way Isa was volunteering the information, now that it no longer mattered.

"Barbara and I came here to tell you the truth," continued Isa.

Barbara? Had Barbara and Isa been having an affair after all?

"I wasn't with my kids that afternoon, the way I said I was," Isa confessed. "I was hanging out in the hotel room—doing yoga, taking a nap. I left Mickey with Orion by the pool around one o'clock. I came out later, around three, and Orion was gone. He didn't show up until after six, and he wouldn't say a word about where he'd been. I was furious, both because he'd left Mickey alone by a swimming pool and because we were going to be late for Susana's opening—I figured he'd done it accidentally on purpose to get at Susana. Later, after we found out Susana was murdered, I was terrified Orion might have done it. What if he took the car, went over to the Capelli, and had a fight with Susana? It didn't make any sense—why go over there voluntarily, when he was only coming to the opening because I was dragging him? But nothing made much sense right then. Orion kept refusing to tell me where he'd been, and I kept imagining the worst. So, I told you and the police and everyone else we were together all afternoon. I told Orion to say exactly the same thing. Finally, the other day, I got him to tell me what was going on. And I felt that I—that we—owed it to you."

Isa turned to Barbara, who gripped her teacup but seemed unable to force any liquid through her lips. The truth had been growing on Margo, but she was still astonished when Barbara Scholl said,

"He was with me."

"Orion?" gasped Margo, even though the clues to Barbara's mysterious assignation were falling into place—the Coca-Cola ordered from room service along with the champagne, Barbara's distress when Margo asked whom she had been seeing. And no wonder Orion had gone white when Barbara's name came up at dinner the week before. Margo would have burst out laughing, except for the genuine look of unhappiness on Barbara's face.

"Yes, Orion. In my bed. Making love." Barbara bit out the words. "Why not? Would you think it so bizarre if our sexes were reversed? If it were an adult man and a young girl? The French—"

"Frankly, Barbara," interrupted Isa, "if a forty-year-old man seduced my sixteen-year-old daughter, I'd want to file charges. But there you are, the double standard still reigns. Since Orion's a boy, I almost feel proud of the kid. Not that I want him to keep seeing you. I don't want him exposed to such materialistic values at an impressionable age. Besides, he might catch something. Well, Margo, you seem beat. Why don't we leave and let you get to bed?"

Two weeks later James Carmichael resigned as director of the Capelli Foundation. The official word was that James had decided to become a private art consultant, based in New York. Margo could get no one to confirm that James had been asked to resign after being caught embezzling—not Bernard Capelli, nor Charlotte Meyers, and especially not the accountant on the foundation board. Even gossipy Carola parried Margo's questions about her ex-boss by griping about Peter Vance, who had called from Rome but refused to say where he had gotten his grant. Carola wanted to apply, too. She saw no reason for Peter to be stingy with information about a grant that financed his work and study in Europe for two years!

30 / A Rising Star

"Margo, what do you wear to an art opening?"

"Almost anything, Jen. Let's see what you've got."

"Just a minute! Just a minute! . . . Okay."

Permitted entry to Jenny's bedroom, Margo decided not to challenge her stepdaughter's fiction that the opened windows and sprayed cologne disguised the smell of cigarettes. At the moment Jenny's humor was too vile.

"Sorry about the Padre game," said Margo as Jenny gathered an armful of clothes from the closet and laid them on the bed.

The girl's scowl stated balefully that Margo had said the wrong thing; although there'd been no right thing to say, ever since Barry and David had left for a baseball game an hour ago and then, too late, Jenny had cried that *of course* she'd wanted to go with them, hadn't everyone known? Attending Ed Milewski's art opening was a lousy consolation prize, she was making that clear . . . especially since it was an outing with her stepmom instead of her dad.

"How about this?" Margo held up a print miniskirt and knit top that she'd helped Jenny pick on a recent shopping trip.

"Yecch! I don't even know why I bought that, that color's horrid on me."

Margo blinked hard, feeling tears stinging her eyes. She'd been ridiculously vulnerable to Jenny's moods lately, because she was ridiculously moody herself—depressed, irritable, and seized often with the kind of jumpiness that had afflicted her the day of Jill's death, a month ago.

She knew her jitters came partly from the brouhaha that had erupted at KSDR. Dennis Zachary Powell, caught ripping a page from another reporter's notebook, confessed to sabotaging several of his colleagues' stories. Spurred by the fear of losing his job under Alex's regime, Dennis had committed minor acts of mischief that hadn't ever compromised the station's on-air product, but had made others' work more difficult; filching Margo's cassette of her interview with Jill, for example, was one of Dennis's misdemeanors. Dennis deserved another chance, pleaded his attorney, especially since he was now seeing a psychiatrist. Alex the Merciless fired him all the same and promoted Claire De Jong, his handpicked Washington colleague, to the news director job, a move many believed Alex had planned all along. That opened Claire's reporter slot, and Alex was taking his time filling it. (The other full-time job, rumored for months, seemed to dissolve; Margo suspected Alex had started the rumor just to get more work out of everyone.) Thus, Dennis's fall, which might have led everyone to valuable discussions of ethics, had instead intensified the competitiveness and tension among KSDR's part-time staff.

"Get it off my clothes!" howled Jenny. Margo shooed the cat—Jill's gray cat, which she had brought home the night of Jill's death. She'd planned to keep the poor, scared animal just temporarily, but somehow it had stayed. It was a neat little puss she'd named Grimalkin, not knowing what Jill had called it; a cat that sometimes hid trembling under the bed when a car backfired. What had it seen?

That was the deeper root of Margo's malaise: she couldn't believe Grimalkin had witnessed its mistress shooting herself.

In spite of Jill's fingerprints being on the gun, Margo remembered Jill's wild relief at seeing Margo in Dawn's hat—relief that she hadn't killed Susana. Barry theorized, quite sensibly, that the hat might have told Jill conclusively she *was* a murderer and her relief came not from innocence but from having her uncertainty resolved. She might have misled Margo, just as she'd left no note, simply to muddy the waters; perversely conducting art-life experiments to the last.

"I think I'll wear this." Jenny stood in front of the mirror in a sheer purple skirt and a short, off-white cotton cardigan that fit closely at her waist. She looked lovely, but Margo wisely forbore to say so. "Can I borrow one of your hats?" She wandered into Margo and Barry's room and reached the burgundy hat off a hook on the wall—Dawn's hat, that Margo had worn the day she'd discovered Jill; that she could hardly bear to look at now. But Jenny didn't know that, did she?

"Here, Jen, the brim goes down over your forehead like this."

Jenny stubbornly readjusted it. "I want it this way."

Again, Margo felt close to tears. *Get a grip,* she told herself.

"You aren't wearing that?" said Jenny.

"A lot of artists dress this way."

Margo experienced a moment of purely adolescent vengefulness herself, imagining Jenny's chagrin at accompanying a woman clad in a yellow sweatshirt and droopy gray leggings, both stained with clay because she had thrown some pots that afternoon. Nevertheless, she shed the sweats and threw on a rose silk dress—a forties-style thrift store find—and the ankle boots she'd bought from Vicki Fall. If she had to stand for two hours, she intended to do it in comfort. Besides, her teenage fashion arbiter surprisingly declared the combination "cool."

She was about to transfer keys, wallet, and lipstick from her usual Guatemalan carryall to a smaller handbag, when she noticed the delicate ceramic sculpture sitting reproachfully on her dresser. The sculpture was about ten inches tall, and she managed to stuff it inside her carryall.

"Shouldn't you wrap it up or something?" said Jenny. "I mean, won't it break if you carry it like that?"

"Umm."

Rick Dunham had called two weeks ago and exacted a promise to show his work to some local art dealers in return for information he had to offer her. She had regretted the promise immediately. Schlepping the sculpture to the opening would discharge her obligation, no matter what condition the piece arrived in. Besides, all Rick had told her was something she could have deduced herself, had she given it a moment's thought. Greg Miscik had stopped trying to retrieve his student paintings because Louise had offered him something better: an entry to the L.A. art market. Rick had learned that Miscik was now being represented in Los Angeles by Barbara Scholl. "I told you he wasn't giving us the whole story," said Rick triumphantly.

Just thinking of that made Margo grit her teeth. One of the most important lessons of adulthood ought to be never to say *I told you so*. She tossed her bag into the back seat of the car.

"You'll break it!" remonstrated Jenny.

"Fasten your seatbelt."

"Can you believe this?" said Tom Fall, the first person Margo recognized at the bustling opening. "A one-man show at the hottest gallery in San Diego? It's one thing for Louise to have Ed work for her. But to get him a show at the Trask *and* get critics here from the major art journals? This guy is no Susana. Believe me, Louise has lost her touch."

Margo plucked a glass of champagne from a passing tray. She would have dismissed Tom's criticism as sour grapes, but she was hearing a number of similar comments, expressed with varying degrees of charity. "He has promise, but is he really ready for this kind of show?" . . . "Not bad for student work." . . . "I can't believe I made the trip from L.A. to see this." In fact, hadn't Louise herself said she was less than thrilled with this year's protégé?

"What's a . . . a Broly?" asked Jenny. She had drifted off while Margo was talking to Tom and now reappeared.

"No idea."

"I'm hot."

"Me, too." Margo consciously ignored the girl's sulky I-don't-like-it-here tone. "They're bringing around cold drinks, Jen."

"I'm going to go outside. Just for a few minutes."

"Stay near the gallery, okay? This isn't a good part of town." The Trask was two blocks from the Capelli Foundation.

"Ma-argo!"

"Jenny, I mean it."

"Yeah, all right."

As Jenny retreated, the hat bobbing through the crowd atop her long dark curls, Margo sank into a familiar preoccupation. If the burgundy hat had told Jill she *wasn't* a murderer, could it have also told her that someone else *was*? Someone she had seen wearing the hat earlier?

"Glad you could make it!" exclaimed Ed Milewski. The ripples of the crowd had brought Margo face to face with the young artist.

For all his guileless, gee-whiz manner, Ed must have allowed someone to take him shopping for the grand event. He was wearing artfully loose fawn trousers, a print dress shirt with a Western bolo tie, and a stylish red jacket that struck the perfect note of offbeat chic. And he was keenly aware of the art world nobs in attendance: Barbara Scholl and several other major dealers and collectors were down from L.A.! he exulted. And Barbara, as well as Bernard Capelli, had accepted Louise's invitation to a post-opening dinner party!

"Gotta go, I think those are the Hansons," said Ed, noticing Louise O'Quinn beckoning him toward an elderly couple.

Louise smiled vaguely at Margo, as if she couldn't quite place her. Louise seemed unaware of the negative remarks about Ed's art . . . or about her own judgment in promoting him. Arrayed in a hand-painted silk dress in blues and purples, its classic lines accenting her strong-boned face and gray hair, she had the air of a monarch overseeing a favored courtier's debut.

"Champagne, ma'am?"

"Thanks." Margo placed her empty glass on the waiter's tray, took a fresh one, and nearly collided with the brim of a peacock-blue sombrero with a black band, worn by Barbara Scholl.

"*Chérie, comment ça va?*" exclaimed Barbara, kissing the air next to Margo's cheeks. "Not really up to Louise's standard," she murmured. "But perhaps the young man has other talents, *n'est-ce pas?*" Margo had thought Barbara might prefer to avoid her, given her embarrassment at their last meeting. But apparently the art dealer had decided to play her affair with Orion as a sophisticated romp. Barbara was elegantly turned out in a black coatdress and the eye-catching blue hat.

Margo chatted with Barbara for a moment before, groaning inwardly, she made herself take out Rick's sculpture. It had survived the ill treatment in her bag, worse luck. "A friend of mine in Santa Fe does fantastic ceramic art," she said, her words coming rapidly as Barbara's eyes glazed.

"Barbara, you look dashing." A woman came up and exchanged air kisses with the dealer. "That's a Broly, isn't it? Do you know, it's the third I've seen tonight. Another month and I'll be at the top of the list."

Margo caught Barbara's arm. "What's a Broly?" She felt a small chill of alarm.

Barbara sneered as if Margo had just confessed she'd never heard of Michelangelo. "Patsy Broly designs hats. Custom hats, no two alike. If you want her to do one for you, you have to get on a waiting list for up to two months, because she really works with you—measuring your head precisely, trying different sample forms, trying colors. Color is absolutely crucial in a hat, *bien entendu*, since you're not just complementing an outfit, you're wearing the hat directly on your head so it has to work with your hair and your eyes. Interested, *chérie*? A little toque would look nice on you, especially if you did something with your hair. I could get you to the top of the list. I've not only bought ten or twelve hats from Patsy myself, I've introduced her to people all over Southern California who are in the market for art-to-wear. Everyone in the art world knows her. And I helped her choose her logo."

"Her logo?" Margo felt slightly dizzy, her mouth dry.

Barbara removed the hat and pointed to a design printed inside—a white seashell. "No words, just a distinctive graphic."

"Do you . . . do you have any of her hats in a sort of purply red, a burgundy?"

"A hideous color with naturally auburn hair like mine," Barbara said with a straight face. "And, *entre nous*, Patsy saves her best purples for Louise."

"Louise."

"Louise O'Quinn. Purple is fabulous on her. Louise buys more hats from Patsy than I do. If you want a Broly, give me a call. As I said, I can get you to the top of the list."

Louise O'Quinn wore burgundy Broly hats. And Dawn took things, a crow attracted to pretties and shinies. Louise must have worn the hat on the day she'd visited Susana. Margo pictured Louise sweeping into Susana's installation in her orange cloak. She couldn't remember a hat, but Louise had probably been carrying it and had put it down someplace where Dawn snatched it. A burgundy hat, with the orange cloak? The combination was too garish, even for a woman who didn't follow fashion trends but set them.

Margo glanced over to where she'd last seen Louise. Ed was still there, treating another prosperous-looking couple to some boyish charm.

She scanned the room. Louise O'Quinn was nowhere in sight.

Neither was Jenny.

31 / Carpe Diem

"May I have one?" said the woman.

"What? Oh, sure." Jenny reached out her pack of cigarettes. She had assumed, when the woman started to speak to her, that yet another adult she'd never even met was about to chide her for smoking. Who did they all think they were, her parents? She already had *four* of those. After the first reproach, she'd slunk into the far corner of the gallery's back patio, hiding behind a post.

The woman took a cigarette, placed it between her lips, and leaned forward, holding her springy gray hair back out of her face. Responding to a cue she'd only seen before in movies, Jenny lit the cigarette, pleased she only had to strike the match once and that she managed to keep it from going out by sheltering it from the breeze with her cupped hand.

"I used to smoke Gitanes when I was young," said the woman in a voice that sounded as if she'd roped cattle and done who-knew-what-else. "French cigarettes with no filters. Nowadays I suppose no one even wants you to smoke these low tar things. Low tar, low taste, low risk. There's only one problem. Risk keeps us alive. *Carpe diem.* It means 'Seize the day'—take your enjoyment now and don't worry about tomorrow. They teach it to you in school, don't they, when you study John Donne, but then they tell you never, ever to do it yourself."

Jenny nodded fervently. The woman looked as if she'd taken plenty of risks—gone skydiving, shot lions in Africa, had grand passions. Jenny intended to have numerous grand passions.

"You're probably never supposed to drink, either," the woman said conspiratorially. "Would you like some champagne? Take my glass, I've already had some."

"Thank you." Jenny tried to remember what you said about the taste of champagne. Were you supposed to like it sweet, or sort of acerbic on the tongue, like the stuff she was drinking now? She decided not to make a fool of herself by saying the wrong thing. Besides, the woman seemed content to do the talking.

"Do you like art?" said the woman. "Or did you just come because you know Ed?"

"I came with . . . I love art. I think I'd like to be an artist. This is excellent champagne," she added, emboldened by the woman's interest.

"It's wonderful to find someone at an art opening who actually appreciates the art." The woman began to stroll down the alley. Jenny could have no more refrained from following her than a child could have resisted the Pied Piper. "I can see by looking at you, by the way you're dressed, that you have a fine sense of color," the woman said.

"Thanks. I like paintings." Was that what was in the gallery tonight? Jenny hadn't looked, there'd been too many people in the way. "I went once to see a Monet exhibit. It was wonderful."

"Ah, Monet. Some day you'll have to go to his garden at Giverny. It's not far from Paris."

"I'd love to go to Paris. Um, maybe we should turn around." They had walked half a block from the gallery, and she noticed a huddled form in a doorway, a homeless person sleeping there. "I promised . . . Well, this is supposed to be a bad part of town."

The woman laughed. "Not for me. Look." She opened her purse and showed Jenny the gun inside. "I always bring it when I go downtown. I'll carry it in my hand while we walk, just in case."

Where was Jenny? Not on the patio, and no one there remembered seeing her. Back inside the gallery, Margo scanned the crowd frantically for the hat or for Jenny's dark hair; Jenny might have actually decided comfort outweighed fashion and taken the hat off to be cooler.

"I'm looking for a fifteen-year-old girl . . . Have you seen a . . ."

How even to sound the alarm? *I think Louise killed Susana and now Jenny is wearing the Broly hat Louise left at the murder scene and I'm terrified Louise is going to hurt her?* Who would even follow that line of reasoning, much less believe it? Did Margo believe it herself? As she checked the women's room and every inch of the gallery, she thought it through. Say Susana had asked for her sculptures back, Louise refused, and Susana threatened to get a lawyer or tell the story to an art magazine. Up to that point, the story made sense. At the very least, Louise and Susana had reasons to be angry at each other.

"Have you seen Louise O'Quinn?"

What if Louise went to talk the whole thing out with Susana late Saturday afternoon, before the opening? Maybe she'd hoped to make peace, but instead they had an argument and Louise pushed Susana into the spiky bedpost, killing her. To cover up the murder, Louise lifted Susana onto the bed—didn't she have a bad back two days later? The hat could have fallen off when she and Susana were struggling, or in Louise's panic afterward as she tried to disguise the death. However, the scenario of Louise as Susana's murderer contained some major logical flaws. First, Louise went to the Capelli Foundation often; she could have worn the hat some other time. Further, she'd been with Ed Milewski at the time of the murder. Both she and Ed had said so.

"Have you seen a teenage girl? Long dark hair, burgundy hat?"

Unless, of course, Louise had induced Ed to lie. She had bought off Greg Miscik with an introduction to a major Los Angeles gallery. Had she purchased Ed's loyalty with this show? What if Louise had even financed Peter Vance's trip to Italy? thought Margo, forming connections instantaneously with a surreal, anxiety-driven clarity. Peter hadn't shown up at the Capelli on the night of the opening and he had left for Rome abruptly a few days later, with a mysterious, very generous grant. Had Peter seen something that night? Certainly the cups of Louise's protégés were overflowing. Except, of course, for Susana, the one person Louise couldn't buy.

But Susana wasn't the only artist who had no price! If Jill had identified the burgundy Broly hat—the hat she'd seen the night of Susana's murder—as belonging to Louise, she wouldn't give a hoot how much Louise could help her career. Neither would she have notified the police; that would have been too predictable and boring. If Jill suspected Louise of murdering Susana, she would probably have confronted her . . . "to get a reaction." And then? Oklahoma-bred Louise had handled firearms her entire life. Surely she knew enough about guns to make Jill's death look like suicide—to be aware that she had to file off the registration number and that, after shooting Jill, she had to get Jill's prints on the gun and powder burns on Jill's hand.

• • •

"That's a beautiful hat," said the woman.

"Thanks," said Jenny.

"Where did you get it?"

At that moment Jenny had no intention of admitting she had any parents, much less saying the hat belonged to one of them. "I just picked it up," she said airily. She offered another cigarette to the woman and lit one for herself. They walked along smoking companionably. Taking her courage from her new friend, Jenny felt a little thrill—fear and then the refusal to be scared—whenever they passed the occasional transient. *Carpe diem!*

"Salvation Army, I bet."

"Yeah."

"I'd like to buy it from you."

"That's all right, it's not for sale." What an idea! Jenny laughed. She felt as if she had never really laughed before.

"Do you have a lot of friends, dear? A boyfriend?"

"No real boyfriend. There's one guy I think is real cute, but he's older and he hasn't noticed me. I've got some close girlfriends, though."

"I suppose you feel like you'd do anything for each other. Like you all understand each other when no one else does."

"Oh, yeah. Definitely."

"Has a friend ever betrayed you?"

"Like telling something I told her, even though I asked her not to tell anyone else?"

"Something like that. Or she betrayed your faith in her. You thought she cared about you and then she did something that let you know she never cared at all."

The woman's voice filled with pain. Jenny was sure she had suffered intensely. Jenny was determined to live with complete intensity herself.

"I'll pay a hundred dollars for the hat," the woman said suddenly.

"A hundred dollars! It can't be worth *that* much. Anyway, I like it."

"Have you finished your champagne, dear? I bet you've never thrown a champagne glass. Throw it!"

"Against the building?"

"No champagne glass should be drunk from more than once!"

"I—"

"Throw it!"

Jenny let out a whoop and flung the glass against the wall. Giggling, she trotted over to see the breakage. She felt every bit as sparkling as the shards of glass.

"Now give me the hat," said the woman.

"Hey, what are you doing?" The woman had followed her to the edge of the alley and was sticking something into her side.

Margo had found a surprising ally in her search—Bernard Capelli. Bernard required no explanation. He'd simply responded to the urgency in her voice. Thank goodness! Ed Milewski might not have talked to Margo, but Bernard's presence got his attention immediately.

"I just got mixed up about where we were supposed to meet," Ed was saying. "Louise had me take some packages to the car for her and I thought I was supposed to meet her in this coffee place on the top level of Horton Plaza. But I screwed up. Turned out I was supposed to meet her at this bookstore. She was looking all over for me, and she was really steamed when she found me."

"And did Louise ask you to tell the police you'd been together the whole time?" said Bernard.

Ed hesitated a moment and Margo got the uncanny feeling he was calculating the relative influence of his employer and Bernard, and deciding with which art patron to cast his lot.

"It was essentially the truth. I just screwed up on the meeting place. And I know the car was in the parking structure, since I was taking things out to it, so how would she have gone anywhere?" He looked as earnest as a choirboy in front of a Christmas tree. But even a choirboy couldn't be so naive as to ignore the possibility that Louise could walk the six blocks to the Capelli Foundation from Horton Plaza.

In her mind Margo kept seeing Jenny going toward the patio. She and Bernard rushed outside and split up, she going left down the alley and he going right.

"This is a joke, isn't it?" said Jenny.

The woman said nothing.

"I'll give you the hat, okay? For free." Jenny hated the pleading tone that had crept into her voice. "I just didn't know you wanted it that much."

"And then you'll run and tell your mother all about the strange lady who forced you to give her your hat at gunpoint, won't you?"

"No. Oh, no, I promise I won't tell anyone."

"This way." The woman nudged her with the gun past a loading dock and into the shadows behind it.

"They'll catch you!"

"Darling, you should never have gone out walking by yourself in this part of town. But young people are so careless. Give me the hat."

Okay, thought Jenny. She would thrust the hat between herself and the gun, and then run like hell. But the woman had stepped back too far for that to work.

"Take off the hat and throw it over there." The woman gestured with the gun.

Jenny reached up, whimpering when her hands touched the soft felt.

Suddenly there was a swift, silent movement. A shabby figure flew at the woman, who cried out. The gun discharged. Jenny screamed.

When Margo ran up, Louise was on the ground, unmoving. Dawn crouched over her, driving the knife into her body.

"Stop it, Dawn!" yelled Margo, trying to pull the homeless woman away. Dawn slashed at Margo with the knife, then stabbed Louise again. "Stop it!" Margo reached into her bag and found Rick's sculpture. She smashed it as hard as she could over Dawn's head.

"Jenny! Jenny, are you okay?" cried Margo, stumbling into the shadow of the building.

"I'm fine, she missed me," came Jenny's shaky voice. "Did you get the gun?"

Margo went for Dawn's knife first, not trusting the strength of the blow she'd inflicted. She searched next for the gun, her feet crunching on the shattered sculpture as she stepped around the two unmoving women. She took the gun easily from Louise's limp hand.

Bernard Capelli came running, with at least fifty people from the opening. Margo gladly let a doctor take over.

"Is she . . ." mumbled Jenny, her face pressed into Margo's shoulder.

"I don't know, Jen." Not about either of them. She had worried she hadn't hit Dawn hard enough, but now Dawn lay so still. And Louise had been soaked with blood when Margo touched her; the blood was dripping down Margo's arm.

32 / "Art World Scandal Ends in Catfight"

"Contacted in Rome," said Margo into the microphone, "Peter Vance, a former Capelli Foundation employee, confirmed that he saw Louise O'Quinn leaving the foundation through the side door when he arrived on the evening of the murder." She signaled to Ray to stop recording. "Okay, now let's listen to the actuality and figure out what we want to use from it."

"Coming right up." Ray Fernandez had been finishing his shift when Margo arrived at the station at midnight. He had pitched in immediately, to Margo's enormous gratitude. She couldn't have made it to four A.M. without the spur of shared effort. And editing tape would have been nearly impossible. The blood on her arm hadn't been Louise's but her own, from Dawn's slash, the pain not even felt until her adrenaline rush had subsided. The wound was now stitched and her right arm in a sling.

Ray played back the telephone interview.

"It was about five-thirty and Louise was coming out the back door into the alley," came Peter's recorded voice, the connection to Rome crackling slightly.

"Did she look upset?" asked Margo.

"I don't know. I don't think so."

"What happened then?"

"She asked me to walk a few blocks with her. She said

she always felt she'd treated me unfairly and she'd like to make it up to me. I was all for that. An art patron she knew was looking for a young painter to support for a year in Rome. Because of some technicality of the funding, the painter had to be chosen the next day and would have to leave for Rome right away. Louise wanted to recommend me and said I should go straight to my studio and get my slides together . . . and not to tell anyone. In fact, this person wanted to remain anonymous and everything had to be done extremely discreetly. All the arrangements were being handled by Louise."

"Didn't that seem suspicious?"

"No struggling artist looks a gift horse in the mouth."

"Let's definitely use that," Ray remarked.

Margo on tape continued: *"When you heard later that Susana was murdered at about the time you saw Louise, didn't you wonder about Louise's presence at the Capelli?"*

"I was so caught up in my own plans at that point, I wasn't paying much attention to anything else."

"But you didn't tell anyone you'd seen her, did you? Are you saying it never occurred to you that Louise might have come up with this grant to influence you to cover for her?"

"Like I said, I was really caught up in my own plans."

"So nothing changed after you heard Susana was killed?"

There was a long pause and then Peter said, *"Off the record?"*

The tape recorder off, Peter had said he'd requested funding for three years instead of one, and he and Louise had compromised on two. He had also admitted vandalizing Louise's car.

While Ray edited the tape, Margo called the hospital for an update. Most of Louise's injuries had been superficial, but she had sustained one serious wound to a lung, requiring emergency surgery. She was now out of danger. Margo added that to her narration, along with the news that Dawn had suffered a mild concussion and would be fine.

"What I really find sleazy," said Ray as he and Margo sat at a pancake house at six A.M., "is how many people went along with Louise's cover-up to help their own lousy careers. First, Tom Fall found Susana dead, but instead of sounding the alarm, he made everything look nice so no one would cancel his precious opening. Then this guy Ed lied to support Louise's alibi, and he got a big show out of it. And Peter Vance virtually admitted blackmailing her. Do you think Ronald Reagan created this? Rampant careerism, to the exclusion of everything else?"

There was an awkward silence, as if they had both been reminded of the careerism currently rampant at KSDR. Margo broke the tension, saying, "It doesn't matter how long he's been out of office, I like to blame Reagan for everything, from the military buildup to my stepdaughter's moods."

"You're going to get the job." Ray was smiling. "After this story, you deserve it."

Margo wished victory tasted sweeter. It occurred to her that it wasn't true, as Greg Miscik believed, that Louise O'Quinn had only business relationships and didn't care if anyone liked her. Jenny had repeated the conversation she'd had with the critic. Margo wondered if it was the experience of feeling betrayed by Susana—more than any desire to keep the valuable sculptures—that had wounded Louise most deeply; that had goaded her to such anger that she had killed the protégé she most loved.

" 'Quick-Witted, Beautiful Teen Helps Catch Killer,' " read Barry out loud. "I'd give it a nine out of ten."

"A full ten!" said Margo. "Nine for the copy and another point for the picture."

Jenny, sitting at the kitchen table with them, giggled. She and David had spent the afternoon inventing tabloid-style headlines about her brush with death a week earlier. It seemed as therapeutic a way as any to deal with the trauma, better than anything Margo or Barry had devised for themselves. Barry was still experiencing guilt about not "protecting his women," primitive as he admitted that impulse was; and Margo kept flashing back in nightmares to the moment when she was running down the alley and heard the gunshot and Jenny's scream.

Next came ALL'S WELL THAT ENDS WELL.

"Not the most original," said Barry. "But apt. Louise has been charged with two murders and Jill's name is cleared. Dawn is back in L.A., with Susana's cousin, the nun, looking out for her. Even Rick Dunham got a happy ending. You broke one of his sculptures into a thousand pieces, but with all the publicity he'll sell another dozen."

"Not to mention the fact that Barbara Scholl decided to represent him after all. Hmm, I don't know about 'Art World Scandal Ends in Catfight.' Catchy, but a bit unfair to cats." Margo rubbed Grimalkin behind the ears, her thoughts turning sadly for a moment to Jill Iverson.

Margo was certain it was the designer hat she herself had worn that made Jill suspect Louise. Asking the art critic over to discuss it must have had all the crazy charm, for Jill, of driving down a mountain road blindfolded, and it had proved just as deadly.

"Look at this one," Jenny was urging.

"Did you do this, Jen? Is that me?"

Jenny nodded, grinning. Under the headline REPORTER THWARTS MURDERER, SAVES GIRL, she had drawn Margo charging up fiercely, a cross between Diane Sawyer and Wonder Woman in a chic miniskirted suit. It wasn't exactly the image Margo cultivated for herself . . . but not a bad way at all to be seen in Jenny's eyes.